A
ROYAL GUIDE
TO
MONSTER SLAYING

A
ROYAL GUIDE
TO
MONSTER
SLAYING

KELLEY ARMSTRONG

PUFFIN CANADA
an imprint of Penguin Random House Canada Young Readers,
a Penguin Random House Company

Published in hardcover by Puffin Canada, 2019

Published in this edition, 2020

1 2 3 4 5 6 7 8 9 10

Cover design: Kelly Hill
Cover art © Cory Godbey

Manufactured in Canada

Library and Archives Canada Cataloguing in Publication

Title: A royal guide to monster slaying / Kelley Armstrong ;
illustrated by Xavière Daumarie.
Names: Armstrong, Kelley, author. | Daumarie, Xavière, illustrator.
Description: Previously published: 2019.
Identifiers: Canadiana 20190232293 | ISBN 9780735265370 (softcover)
Classification: LCC PS8551.R7637 R69 2020 | DDC jC813/.6—dc23

Library of Congress Control Number: 2018946088

www.penguinrandomhouse.ca

Penguin
Random House
PUFFIN CANADA

For my nephew, Marshall Fields,
whose early enthusiasm convinced me
to keep writing Rowan's story.

CHAPTER ONE

"I know you love unicorns, Rowan, but please stop staring at mine. You're making him nervous."

I do not love unicorns, as my aunt Jannah knows. Jerks. All of them. I'm not staring *at* Courtois. I'm staring him *down*. Unfortunately, she's wrong about the third part, too. I can't make him nervous, no matter how hard I try.

We're in the castle courtyard, the high stone walls stealing the morning sun. Around us, the royal hunters prepare for their mission. A mission I *should* be joining. My twin brother, Rhydd, is and I belong at his side, keeping him safe.

As I scowl at Courtois, Rhydd's hand thumps on my shoulder. "Give it up, Ro."

"That beast stepped on my foot," I say. "On purpose."

"Yep, I'm sure he did. He *is* a unicorn."

I move away from Courtois only to stumble over my aunt's warg, Malric. The giant wolf lifts his head, upper

curling to reveal canines as long as my hand. The last person who tried to pet him lost two fingers. Even I know better. I quickstep out of his reach.

"Making friends with *all* the monsters this morning, aren't you?" Rhydd teases.

As I grumble, he leans in to whisper, "I know you're upset. You're worried about me going on the gryphon hunt."

"I'm not wor—"

"You're worried, and this is how you show it. By grumbling and scowling and staring down unicorns."

"It's not fair."

"I know," he says.

My scowl deepens, and I want to kick the dirt and growl and stomp. That would be childish, though, and I am not a child. I'm twelve. I'm a princess. One day, I'll be queen.

I don't want to be queen. I'll be horrible at it. Rhydd should get the throne. Even now, as scared as he is, he's trying to calm *me*. That's what a real leader does.

"Rhydd?" Jannah calls. "Saddle up."

As Jannah climbs onto Courtois, her sheathed sword swings by her side. I look at that sword, a gleaming ebony-wood center with a razor-sharp obsidian edge. I imagine it in my hands, and a lump rises in my throat.

This is who I want to be. This is who I *should* be. Not the queen, but the royal monster hunter. *Everyone* knows it. I hear the whispers, how my thoughtful brother should sit on the ivory throne, how his headstrong twin sister should wield the ebony sword.

We are Clan Dacre, the greatest hunters in the land, and

we united the clans with one promise: We will keep the monsters away. The oldest royal child always takes the ivory throne, and the next gets the ebony sword.

What if they're twins and one is a mere *two minutes* older? What if they're better suited for the opposite jobs? If they'd happily switch places? Too bad. This is how we do things.

I glance at Jannah again. She nods, her face impassive. Any other time, she'd be over here, teasing me and teaching me and telling me to saddle up, too. This hunt is different.

Today, my aunt and my brother go to kill a gryphon, the one monster we can't just drive back to the mountains. Once gryphons find our fat cattle and sheep, they're like starving travelers stumbling on a midwinter feast. They aren't leaving. Ever.

The last gryphon slaughtered a dozen people before my aunt slew it.

It also killed my father.

When I think of that, my fists ball up and my eyes fill with hot, angry tears. I want to run to my aunt and hug her and tell her I'm scared for her, beg her not to go. I want to grab my brother's leg and pull him off his horse and take his place, like I used to when we were little. I want to shout at my mother that this isn't fair, that if it's too dangerous for me, why is Rhydd going? I'm a better hunter. Let me go along to protect him.

My scowl swings to my mother. She stands at the gate, wearing a simple brown dress only a shade lighter than her skin. Her honey-brown curls are drawn up in a twist, secured with an ebony pin shaped like a sword. That pin reminds everyone that she's also a trained monster hunter, which means she knows exactly how dangerous this mission is.

When Mom glances at me, I look away. I should go to her. That's what Rhydd would do. He'd know she's thinking of our father, and he'd go over and tell her he understands she has no choice here. But I am not my brother.

The iron gates swing open. Beyond the courtyard, people line the streets to see the hunters pass. My aunt leads the procession on Courtois. The unicorn is what the children have come to see. He's as tall and sturdy as a draft horse, with a gleaming jet-black coat. His horn is iridescent, glittering pink and blue and silver in the morning sun. He's a wondrous sight, but I'd take a light-footed mountain mare any day. Or, better yet, a pegasus.

As the hunting party rides out, the children race to shower Courtois with rose petals. The older girls keep up with my brother, trying to get the young prince's attention. That almost makes me smile. But then I see the empty road behind them, littered with petals, and I remember the same scene from five years ago, when my father rode out to face a gryphon.

I turn away, my stomach knotting, and I notice a girl by the gate. About my age, she carries a basket of flowers. Her dress is coarse muslin, her sandals rough leather. Dirt smears one cheek. Her light brown hair blows in the wind, without even a band to keep it tamed.

I see her, and shame washes through me. I'm feeling sorry for myself because I'm going to be queen. How much would this girl give to change places with me?

"A rose, your highness?" she says, seeing me watching her.

I start toward her. My mother's maid hurries to press coins into my palm. I give them to the girl, and she hands me the whole basket. When her hair blows into her eyes, she shoves it back, nose wrinkling in annoyance.

I take out my hair clip. "This will help."

As I pass it over, her eyes glitter, blue as the clip's sapphires.

She curtsies, awkwardly, as if she's never done it before. Then she thanks me and takes off running along the cobbled road.

"That was very kind," my mother says as she walks up behind me.

I shrug. "I have others."

"That was your favorite."

I shrug again as I walk toward the castle.

"If you need me," I say, "I'll be in the rear courtyard."

Mom opens her mouth to protest. She doesn't want me to be alone today. Being alone means I could sneak off after Rhydd.

"I'm taking my sword lessons," I say. "And then archery."

She nods. "Excellent."

"Though I don't know why I bother," I call back. "Since I'll never be allowed to fight actual monsters."

Her sigh floats after me as I leave. Now I just need to keep busy until sundown . . . and then I can go after my brother.

As angry as I am with my mother for sending Rhydd, I know she didn't have a choice. I've read about kingdoms where the king's or queen's word is law. Tamarel is different. We used to be a nation of warring clans. When we weren't fighting each other, we were fighting the monsters that came from the mountains to the west. My ancestors—Clan Dacre—had a special talent for monster hunting, so we made a pact with the others. If we rid them of the monsters, the clans would unite under us. We did it, and we continue doing it, so we are the royal family.

Except it wasn't just my great-great-grandfather and his sister who cleared out the monsters. The entire clan helped. So while he got the ivory throne—and she took the ebony sword—the others understandably wanted their share of power. They get it through the royal council. The council's four members—all from Clan Dacre—vote on major decisions.

When news came that a gryphon had been sighted, one council member—my mother's cousin Heward—wanted Rhydd to join the hunt. Heward's children are next in line to the throne, and he'll jump at any chance to get rid of us. If either Rhydd or I die before we inherit our roles, they pass to the next pair of siblings.

When Heward insisted on Rhydd joining the hunt, the council had to vote. In the event of a tie, my mother would cast the deciding ballot. She didn't get that chance. Heward convinced two of the other members to back him, so Rhydd had to join the hunt.

Mom might be acting calm, as if sending Rhydd is her idea, but I know she's furious. I know she's plotting her revenge. And I know Jannah will keep Rhydd out of battle. I don't care. I still want to be there for him. And I will be.

I spend the day keeping busy, so no one will suspect a thing. Between lessons, though, I gather what I'll need for my trip.

I'm heading to the kitchen when a hulking figure steps from a side passage. I don't even jump. Some of my earliest memories are of seeing this shadow on a wall. Then Rhydd and I would run, screaming in delight, and wait for Berinon to scoop us up and swing us around, one under each arm.

Berinon is the captain of the guard. Growing up, he'd been my father's bodyguard and best friend, and a friend of my mother's, too, when she'd been a princess. Since Dad died, Berinon has kind of . . . I won't say he's taken over as our father—he'd never try to replace Dad—but he's edged into that empty space, accepting at least a sliver of it.

Berinon is the tallest man I know, and his shoulders are twice as wide as mine. His skin is as dark as Jannah's sword, and he has amber eyes and a wild mop of long sable hair never quite contained by its braid. Growing up, I heard my parents calling him "Ber" and thought his nickname was Bear. That's what he looked like to me—a huge, shaggy cave bear.

Today he swings out of that side passage and blocks my path.

"No, little one," he says.

I pull myself up to my full height.

He chuckles. "Even when you're grown, I'll be able to call you that. Now turn around, and we'll go riding before teatime."

"I'm hungry, and I want a snack."

"Tell me what you'd like, and I'll get it for you."

I glower up at him. He only crosses his arms and lifts an eyebrow.

"You want to sneak off and protect Rhydd," he says. "I understand. I'd even agree, if not for one thing: you are too much like your father, Rowan."

I glare. "You mean I'm no match for a gryphon. You

think I don't have the hunter's gift. I do. Dad wasn't Clan Dacre. I am."

"Yes, but it wasn't lack of natural talent that killed your father." He settles against a windowsill. "You've heard how I met him?"

"I know the song."

"Well, there's more to the story. Your father had been fostering with Heward's family, but like a certain princess, your father wasn't fond of the highborn life, and he'd sneak into the village. Once, when he was nine, he found boys taunting a younger child. He rushed to help, though the boys were years older."

"You heard the fight," I say. "You were apprenticed to the blacksmith, and my father confronted the boys right outside the smithy."

"Yes. Now, in the song, others tried to join the fight, and I held them off while your father defeated the three bullies. Which is . . ." He shifts on the sill. "That's not quite what happened. I found your father fighting like a cornered warg. He was a better warrior than any of those boys. Better than all three combined, though? No. I had to help him, or he might have been killed. In reward, I was made your father's bodyguard."

Berinon leans forward. "Your father was an incredible warrior. That's why he asked your mother to let him remain a monster hunter even after he became the royal consort. He was the bravest and kindest man I ever knew. But he could never look at a fight and realize he had no chance of winning. He rushed in when he should have hung back, as he did with that gryphon, too. You have his skill, and his bravery, and his heart. You also have his recklessness. Jannah will protect your brother."

He stands. "Now, are we riding, or are you going to stomp off in a temper?"

I scowl.

"Riding then?" he says. "Excellent. Let's go."

Later that day, I take tea with my mother and two visiting dignitaries, which pleases Mom enough that she doesn't insist I join the boring state dinner that follows. I tell the serving maid I'll take my meal in my room. Then I wolf down my fish and shove the bread and fruit into my travel pack, along with some dried meat.

My blade hangs sheathed at my side. It's a short sword, with an ebony-wood hilt and a silver blade. Only two people in the kingdom can carry an ebony-and-silver sword; Rhydd has the matching one. We got them for our twelfth birthday, replacing our dull steel training weapons. I keep mine razor-sharp and gleaming bright, mostly because I like the excuse to take it out and run my fingers over the etchings and feel the weight of the sword in my hand and dream of one made of ebony and obsidian.

I have a dagger, too, but I store that in my pack. I also carry rope, a needle and a bottle of sedative. Those are used to relocate beasts that can't be driven off easily. Finally, I pack my quill pens and my field journal. I'm very proud of my journal— it's full of notes and observations and sketches of every monster I've ever encountered. The book is nearly as beautiful as my sword, handcrafted paper with a soft leather cover dyed dark burgundy. On the first page there's an inscription:

To my favorite monster,

*May you find a way to fill each and every one of
these pages.*

*May you travel to the ends of our world and see every
monster ever discovered and discover a few more besides.*

*May you draw them all, and may you record every
fact that excites that wonderful brain of yours.*

*And may you never be too old to stop running to
your father and sharing all of it with him.*

Love, Dad

I read the inscription, blink back tears and tell myself that
he's watching from the other side, and he's there every time I
add a new page or a new fact or a new sketch.

I tuck the journal into its protective case and put it into my
bag. After I've packed everything and double-checked it all, I
fashion a figure in my bed—clothing bunched up under the
covers, with a brown fur wrap for my hair. Once Rhydd and I
turned twelve, our mother forbade anyone from entering our
bedchambers between dusk and dawn. As young adults, we
were entitled to our privacy. The most anyone will do tonight
is peek in with a candle, and the bed figure will pass for me.

Before I go, I leave my mother a note for morning.

I've gone to protect Rhydd. I will NOT
fight the gryphon myself. I'm only going
to watch over Rhydd and make sure he
doesn't fight either. I'll bring him home safe.
I promise.

Escaping the castle isn't easy. With the state dinner, staff and guards are everywhere. I know which halls are least used, though, and I've chosen a path with hidey-holes that I can duck into when I hear footsteps. I'm racing along one of those, my boots in hand, when I hear voices raised in argument.

It's one of the guards and a maid. Apparently, she caught him flirting with the maid of a visiting lady. She's upset, and he's trying to tell her it meant nothing, and I'm stuck in a window alcove, wishing they'd just kiss and make up. I have a castle to escape.

Then the guard and maid do make up. And they do kiss. They don't *stop* kissing. I don't watch them, of course. That's gross. But I can tell they're kissing by the noises, which are also gross. They kiss and whisper, and whisper and kiss.

I peek out, in case they're busy enough that I can sneak past them, but the corridor is too narrow for that.

I creep the other way. I'll have to take a different route. I can—

Footsteps sound. Heavy ones that I recognize.

Berinon.

He's heading straight for me. I look around. There's no place to go, no place to hide. I'm in a shallow window alcove, and the nearest room is too far away.

Maybe he'll turn into that room. It leads to a storage closet, so he's probably heading there to get something for my mother.

"Digory!" Berinon's voice echoes down the hallway.

I hear the maid squeak . . . because Digory is the guard she's kissing.

"Yes, sir!" Digory calls. "Coming, sir!"

I look from side to side. Digory is down the hall to my right . . . and Berinon is to my left. The clomp of their boots tells me they're both on the move. Both headed this way.

In a few heartbeats, one of them will be here. Even if I flee, Berinon will see my travel pack. He'll know exactly what I'm doing and order the guards to block my way.

I need to get rid of my pack.

I wheel to toss it out the window . . . and instead I find *myself* going out the window. Which isn't what I meant to do at all. I don't even really realize I'm climbing out until I'm hanging by my fingertips from the sill.

The footfalls stop.

Berinon or Digory must have spotted me. I should jump.

I look down . . . to the cobblestones thirty feet below.

No, I should *not* jump.

What was I thinking?

I wasn't thinking, as usual. It's like part of my brain works things through calmly and gives reasonable instructions like "Toss your pack out the window." Then the other part says, "Why just throw your pack out when you can jump out, too?"

Berinon is telling Digory to return to his post. Digory stammers apologies, but Berinon is already walking away. Digory scampers off in the other direction.

After a few moments, the hall goes silent.

I exhale a whooshing sigh of relief. Then I brace to heave myself up—

My body just dangles there, arms barely flexing. I don't have a good enough hold. When I try harder, my fingers slide.

I'm going to fall. I'm going to drop like a rock and crash onto the cobblestones below.

Or I can shout for help.

Those are my choices. Drop or shout for help. The first is madness. I could die. Even if I only twist my ankle, I won't be able to go after Rhydd.

Yet if I shout for help, the travel pack on my shoulder will tell everyone what I was doing. I won't be able to go after Rhydd then either.

What made me think I could do this anyway? It's not like when Rhydd and I would sneak away to a village festival. I'm about to set out into the countryside alone.

I'm *twelve*. And yes, if I lived in the village, I'd be done school and off to work like a grown-up, but I can't even imagine that. I don't feel grown-up. At all. I feel like a foolish child, hanging outside a window.

Is that it then? Am I giving up? Leaving Rhydd to face a gryphon alone?

I grit my teeth. Never. I can do this.

Or, at least, I can really, really try.

I close my eyes and ignore the pain shooting through my arms.

Relax and concentrate. That's what all my trainers tell me. Stop being in such a rush to do things and think about what you plan to do.

I shift my hands to find a better grip. At first, there's nothing, and I start panicking again. Then I find a divot where a stone has fallen out. I wedge my fingers into it. Once my right hand is secure, I move the left until I find the inside windowsill. I grab that and bring my right hand to join it.

My feet scrabble against the castle wall. One finds a shallow hole, and it gives me a foothold. I take a deep breath and then haul myself onto the window ledge and tumble through.

I leap up to look around. The hall is quiet. I stay crouched in the alcove, catching my breath and listening. When I'm sure the way is clear, I take off out the small rear door that leads to the stables.

Once I'm outside, the falling sun casts enough shadow for me to creep unnoticed to the stables. The grooms are gone—they're playing footmen for the dinner guests. I slip past my mare. She whinnies, and I back up to feed her an apple. That keeps her from noticing I'm saddling another horse tonight. I would love to take her, but if she's missing, the grooms will know I'm gone, so I choose a gelding instead.

A guard patrols the stables, but Rhydd and I have long known his route. I wait for him to pass before I hurry the gelding out, knowing it'll be ten minutes before the guard returns.

I make straight for the castle forest. I keep my lantern unlit and let the moonlight guide me down trails as familiar as the hallways of our castle.

A stone wall surrounds the castle forest. There's a gate at the back, which is guarded only when we're at war. Otherwise it's latched inside with a massive timber. Heaving that open takes as much effort as hauling myself through the window. I finally get it and lead the horse through. When the gate closes, the latch thuds back into place.

One last glance over my shoulder, and then I'm off.

CHAPTER TWO

'd eavesdropped on Jannah's plans, so I know where they're spending the night. If I ride straight through, I'll catch up to them before they break camp. The moon is bright, but when it slips behind clouds, I realize how dark and quiet it is, and how alone I am out here. I've never ventured beyond the village by myself, and as much as I'm trying to be brave, every crackle in the bushes sounds like a warg's paw crunching a dried twig, and every owl gliding overhead looks like a gryphon.

I remind myself I am *not* alone. I have the gelding. But this isn't *my* horse. He's new, and I am ashamed to admit that in my haste, I hadn't even checked his stall for his name. I apologize for that, and while he may not understand my words, my tone should be enough. People whisper that Clan Dacre hunters can talk to monsters. We can't. We understand animals' body language and their vocalizations: the noises they make. That isn't magic.

I talk to the gelding and rub his neck. He doesn't swivel his ears to catch my voice. He doesn't chuff in thanks at the petting. He is kind enough, but he isn't my mare and I am not comforted.

When the moon is high, I find a stream and tether the gelding for a brief rest. I'm crouching by the water, cupping some to my mouth, when I hear a weird chattering behind me. I squint into the darkness. I haven't bothered to light my lantern, but the moon has disappeared behind clouds, and all I see are shadows.

The chattering comes again.

The gelding stamps and whinnies. As I rise, my fingers reach for the lantern ring. Then a dark shape flies from the bushes and my hands sail up, knocking the lantern aside as the blur smacks into my chest.

A small horned beast hangs from my tunic. Its teeth clamp down as all four legs claw at me for a better hold.

I look down at the creature, no bigger than a small rabbit. And I laugh. I can't help it. My laugh only enrages the beast more. Its head shoots up to bite me . . . but that means releasing my tunic. It squeals in alarm as it starts to fall. I catch and then hold it at arm's length while it squirms and chatters and tries to head-butt me.

It's a baby jackalope. At this age, it looks like a rabbit with horns, but when it's grown, it'll be twice the size of a hare and sport a full rack of antlers. *Dangerous* antlers. Jackalopes use them for fighting, along with their jagged teeth and semi-retractable claws.

Before Clan Dacre took the throne, people used to catch

jackalopes and make them fight in pits. They nearly went extinct. We've outlawed all monster fights, but people still poach jackalopes for their antlers, which they think can be ground up as a cure for infertility.

Nonsense like that is all too common. When people see monsters, they see the work of magic and witchcraft. But monsters are as natural as any other creature. They're just rarer and more unique. A jackalope, for example, is a carnivorous rabbit, with a predator's claws and teeth and horns.

"You don't look very predatory," I say.

The jackalope gnashes its teeth at me, and I can't help laughing again. I give it a closer look. It's a male, a few months old, which means he should be eating solid food. Holding him at a safe distance, I rummage through my pack for dried meat. Then I put him down with a few scraps. He gulps those and snatches a second helping right from my fingers.

"You're hungry," I say. "Where's your mother?"

Because jackalopes are predators, they stay with their mothers longer than regular rabbits. This one is barely old enough to hunt, so his mother should still be around.

I give him more meat, and he lets me stroke his soft fur. Then he leans against my hand, and a weird grumbling vibrates through his flanks, like a cat's purr. I pat him some more. Then I rise to search for his mother.

I haven't had much experience with jackalopes. The only time monster hunters get involved with them is when they're poached. But for Clan Dacre children, monster studies are a daily lesson, like geography and history. From that, I know jackalopes live in dens.

While I search for the jackalope's home, he hops along behind me, squeaking. The squeaks are attention calls—*Hey, don't forget me, and by the way, do you have more food?*

As I walk, the jackalope's squeaks change to alert cries. The farther I go, the louder they get. When I change direction, he stops. That means he's warning me about something.

It must be his den. I continue, braced for his attack if I get too close to his home. I push past a shrub and then . . .

I see what he's warning me about.

I steel myself to walk closer. Then I crouch, sweep aside long grass and mutter a few words that I'm not supposed to know. My hand flies to my sword, but I don't pull it out. The person I want to fight is long gone.

The mother jackalope lies on the ground, her body riddled with arrow piercings. The killer took only her antlers. Somehow that makes it worse. I understand you might need to eat a jackalope if you're starving. You'd still harvest the antlers then. If we must slay a monster, we take everything. Even the meat goes to dogs if it's unfit for our table. We respect the life of a monster by making full use of it in death.

This isn't like that. It's poaching, and I vow to tell my mother and Jannah. They will send spies to nearby markets, searching for anyone selling jackalope antlers. Once I've made my promise, the outrage passes and I look at the dead mother, tears blurring my eyes.

When the young jackalope squeaks behind me, I back out of that grove. Then I sit on the stream bank and watch him drink.

I can't bring the jackalope with me. It's wrong to take a

wild monster from nature unless you can keep it as a companion. Jackalopes are untamable. All the field guides say so.

As I watch, the jackalope chases a toad. When he catches it, he squeals in shock and my laugh rings out, startling him again.

Obviously, he can hunt. He'll be fine. I'll leave him the rest of my meat. If I'm worried, I can stop by after the gryphon hunt and—

A voice drifts over on the breeze. Another one answers. It sounds like a boy and a girl. I squint up at the moon, now freed from cloud cover. It's past midnight. Kids shouldn't be out this late.

As the voices continue, the jackalope chitters and gnashes his teeth.

"You don't like the sounds of that either, huh?" I murmur to him.

He hops closer to me. The voices are coming this way.

"She must have had a den around here," the boy says.

I glance down at the jackalope. Then I scoop him up. He squeaks but doesn't protest. I hurry to a clump of tall grass and hide him in there and creep toward the stream—and my gelding—as I listen.

"It's spring, so she should have kits," the boy says. "Father says their antlers will be small, but he'll still give us three coppers each."

I'm nearly at the stream when the boy and the girl appear, two other kids following. They're all a year or two older than me.

When they see me, they stop. They eye me, and there's no sign they recognize me. I'm dressed in breeches and a tunic, the leather soft but unadorned, the sort of thing they'd expect from a landowner's daughter. I have my mother's honey-brown curls and heart-shaped face. From my father, I inherited my green eyes and my skin tone, a few shades darker than my hair. My snub nose and freckles are—unfortunately—all my own. Put it together, and no one sees me and says, "That must be the queen's daughter."

As the kids' gazes pass over me, my hand goes to my sword. They don't seem to notice. They look from me to my horse. Then the biggest boy smiles, flashing a gap between his front teeth.

"That's a fine horse you have, girl," he says.

"It's a fine sword I have, too," I reply.

They look down at my blade, still in its sheath, and the gap-toothed boy snickers.

"A fine *toy* sword," he says.

They chortle and elbow one another.

The gap-toothed boy says, "Give us your horse, my *lady*, and there'll be no need to draw your toy."

"I'll give you nothing but a stern warning. I found the jackalope you killed. That's poaching, and it's punishable by one year of hard labor."

"Jackalope? I've never even *seen* a—"

"Her body is lying over there, and I heard you say you were looking for her kits."

The gap-toothed boy steps forward. "Are you sure you heard that, my lady? I hope you didn't, or we'd have to make you forget it." He lifts his fists. "Knock it clean out of your head."

I pull my sword. He snorts. One of the other boys takes a slingshot from his pocket. The girl draws a knife.

I'm surrounded by four older kids, all bigger than me. I might be well trained in sword fighting, but I can't beat four of them. I've done exactly what my father did: started a fight I can't win.

I'm suddenly very aware of how quiet it is. How far we are from the nearest village. I could disappear, and my family would never know what happened to me.

I should lower my sword. Tell the poachers that I heard wrong. Let them take my horse, even. At least I'd escape with my life. But my hand won't move. My lips won't either. I see these four poachers, and all I can think about is that dead mother jackalope.

Rage swirls through me.

Put the sword down, Rowan. Berinon's voice echoes in my head. *Part of being a warrior is knowing when you can't win. When you must step aside. When you must run.*

I can't. I'm trying, but I can't.

A stone strikes my temple. I spin on the boy with the slingshot, and my sword spins, too. The tip of it catches his sleeve, and he yelps as if I've stabbed him.

The gap-toothed boy slams his fist into my jaw. I reel, pain ripping through me, and he charges, fists still clenched.

I lift my sword. I don't swing it. The gap-toothed boy isn't armed, so I cannot attack with my weapon. I only lift it to remind him that I have one. He leaps out of my way, but the girl charges. I smack my sword against her knife, the metal clanging. She gasps as her knife goes flying. Then all four of them charge me.

I back up, my sword raised. I don't want to use it. These aren't monsters. They're my subjects. They're kids, like me. If I accidentally kill one—

The gap-toothed boy yowls, and everyone freezes. He's dancing on one leg, the baby jackalope hanging off his trousers.

Another boy swings a club at the beast. I dive, hitting the ground in a slide, my sword still in one hand as I grab the jackalope. I manage to scramble up. Under my arm, the jackalope gnashes his teeth at the poachers.

"Stop that," I hiss to him. "You aren't helping."

The beast grumbles. Then he climbs onto my shoulder. He's too big to perch there, so he puts his forelegs on my head and chatters at the poachers.

The kids stare at me. I must look a little odd, with a jackalope on my head, and I'm waiting for them to laugh. But they only stare.

Then the girl whispers, "Her sword. I thought it was tin and blackened wood. But it's . . . it's silver and ebony. And the beast . . ."

"It obeys her," the smallest one says. "She speaks, and the monster obeys."

The third boy—the one with the slingshot—turns and runs.

The gap-toothed boy shouts, "Hey!" but the other one keeps going as fast as he can.

"It's the princess," the girl whispers. "Princess Rowan."

Oh no.

No, no, no.

I am going to be in so much trouble.

Which is, I guess, better than being dead. I could have told them who I was earlier, but Mom says we can't trust all our subjects. If someone finds me wandering about on my own, they might take me hostage. That's why Rhydd and I are never supposed to be alone, and if we are, we're supposed to hide the one thing that would identify us: our ebony-and-silver swords.

The gap-toothed boy stares at me. He looks at my sword. He looks at the jackalope. Then he runs.

"Wait!" I call. "Don't—!"

"I'm sorry, my lady," the girl says, as she falls to one knee, the youngest doing the same. "We didn't know it was you."

I want to deny it; insist they've made a mistake. Yet my sword—and the jackalope on my head—gives me away.

I should flee. Well, flee in the most dignified way. Sheath my sword and climb on my horse and be gone with a queenly nod and a "blessings upon thee."

But I keep thinking about that dead jackalope, and I can't leave.

"Yes." I straighten. "I am Princess Rowan, heir to the ivory throne. And you have poached on my royal lands."

The girl takes a step back, as if ready to bolt. I lift my sword and point the tip at her throat.

"Running from royalty is a capital offense," I lie, in what I hope is a convincing voice. "Stand firm and hear my message. I will not turn you in for your crime. You are young, and I will show mercy. I know that you may have been forced to commit this crime."

"Yes, yes, we were," the girl says, and she rushes on to tell a tale of woe, involving a sick mother, injured father, colicky baby brother and lame horse. Either she's an excellent storyteller or she's been born to the most unfortunate family ever. I'm sure it's the former, but it is a good tale, and I listen to the end. Then I take a money pouch from my pocket. I fish out two silvers—the largest coins I have—and I give them each one.

"This is your reward for not fleeing," I say. "And for the two who fled?" I give the girl two coppers. "That is my donation to their families, plus encouragement to cease their poaching. *Strong* encouragement. I have noted all your faces, and if you are ever found killing a jackalope again, you will lose *both* your hands."

The boy pales and teeters. I realize I may have overdone it, but it's too late to go back. At least it'll keep them from killing more jackalopes.

"Now take my royal blessing," I say. "Begone and poach no more."

They run, tripping over themselves as they disappear into the night.

CHAPTER THREE

Once the poachers are gone, I exhale and sink to the ground. I need to be more careful. If those had been adult poachers, I'd never have gotten away that easily. I shiver just thinking about it, and I pull my knees up, holding them tight until I stop shaking.

The jackalope wriggles onto my lap. Hoping for food, I guess. I give him some. Then I hunt for his den, and I find it, a hollow under a fallen tree lined with leaves and soft fur. I settle him into the nest and leave all my meat beside him before I return to my gelding.

I've barely set out when I catch soft thumps punctuating the thuds of the gelding's hooves. I look back to see the jackalope hopping after me.

I stop the horse and call "Away with you!" to the jackalope. He chatters at me and lopes up beside the gelding.

"You can't come along," I say.

He gives a great leap, as if to jump onto the saddle. He doesn't even make it halfway. He backs up to take a run at it. This time, he gets just high enough to scratch the gelding, who two-steps in alarm.

I sigh and climb off the horse. The jackalope squeaks and jumps, all his claws digging into my tunic as he clings to it, chattering up at me.

Another sigh. Then I dislodge his claws, set him down, turn him toward his den and tap his rump. "Go on. Your home is there."

He jumps on my leg and starts scaling it. I remove him— again—and set him down—again. Then I hurry to the horse and swing on. I consider making the gelding gallop away, but I can't bring myself to do that. So I only nudge him to a walk.

The jackalope follows.

"You're going to get tired," I call back. "And then you'll need to find your way home. Because I am *not* carrying you."

I ride for the rest of the night. Finally, the sun crests the horizon, staining the sky the color of a unicorn's horn, swirls of pink and blue. I'd enjoy the sight a lot more if I didn't have a jackalope sleeping on my head.

Yes, I'm carrying the jackalope, despite my threat. I'd meant to stick to it. I really had. But he started crying and falling behind. By then, we were miles from his den, and I didn't think he'd ever find his way back.

From the way he was crying, he might not even have *tried*

going back. I kept imagining us returning from the gryphon hunt to find a dead baby jackalope by the side of the path. I couldn't risk that. So I put him on my saddle, where he stayed for about half a mile before climbing onto my shoulder. Soon, he had his body draped over my head. Then he fell asleep.

He's snoring, too, each reverberation reminding me of how tired I am. I've never ridden this long at once, and I've never stayed up all night before. I'm ready to collapse in the saddle.

The sky is still pink when I spot smoke swirling over hide tents. I catch a whiff of breakfast meat, and my stomach growls. The jackalope wakes up. He sniffs the air and then *his* stomach grumbles.

"We're almost there," I say.

A familiar figure walks along the forest's edge. It's Rhydd. I prod the gelding to go faster, and a guard spots me, calling, "Halt!"

Rhydd turns as Jannah comes running, Malric at her side. Three hunters follow her. All five skid to a stop and stare.

"Yes, it's me," I say. "It's too late to send me back, so don't bother."

"Uh, Rowan?" Rhydd says. "There's a—*Why* is there a baby jackalope on your head?"

"Because he was too tired to run."

Jannah bursts out laughing, and everyone joins her.

"What?" I say.

She shakes her head. "Come, have breakfast, and you can tell us the whole story."

There are a half-dozen other monster hunters in Jannah's camp. While she's the royal monster hunter, she isn't the only person in Tamarel trained to hunt them. I've undergone the basic training, as has my mother. But Jannah also has her own troop. They can handle minor cases on their own. For larger ones, a couple might join Jannah. A gryphon hunt, though, requires all six.

Once we're in camp, I relax, something I haven't done since I jumped out that window and realized I might not get back in. From that point on, it's been one worry after another. That isn't normal for me.

Rhydd is the cautious one. If we swim in a new lake, he's wondering whether there's a monster beneath the waves. Maybe an undertow? Should we swim so far from shore? We should have told someone where we were going.

I always roll my eyes and tease him. To me, a new lake is a new adventure. I never understood his concerns. Now I do.

Coming here alone was like leaping from a cliff and having no idea if the lake beneath was deep enough. I've spent the whole night holding myself tight, anxious and afraid and trying so hard to pretend I was not. Now I can relax, and when I do, I'm exhausted.

There's no time to rest, though. And I certainly can't let anyone know how scared I'd been. I'm Princess Rowan. I don't get scared. So I regale everyone with my story; they laugh and slap me on the back. They tell me how brave I am, and I start to feel more like myself. But when I talk about the poachers, I skim over the details. I make the story funnier, less frightening, certainly less dangerous. Still, I feel Rhydd's gaze on me. He knows there's more to it.

As the hunters break camp, Rhydd and I sit off by ourselves on a giant boulder, feet dangling. The jackalope curls up on my lap, and I scratch the base of his antler prongs, which makes him purr, eyes closed as he pushes against my hand.

"You came all this way by yourself, at night." Rhydd shakes his head. "That must have been scary."

Not as scary as staying home and letting you face a gryphon alone. I don't say that, of course. I just shrug and keep my attention on the jackalope.

After a moment of silence, I say, "Are you mad at me?"

"If I say yes, will you promise to never do it again?"

I snort, and he laughs at that.

"Worth a try," he says. "You came for *me*. I can say that I didn't need it, that Jannah won't let me near that gryphon, but . . ." He glances over. "I'm glad you're here. And I hope, if it'd been the other way around, I'd have had the courage to come for you."

"Of course you'd have come. You'd have just done it differently." I kick the rock behind my feet. "You'd have handled it better."

He knocks his shoulder against mine. "Nah, not better. Just different."

"It was more dangerous than I realized. I'm lucky I made it here."

"And the fact you know that means I don't need to say it. Which is good, 'cause I hate playing the nagging big brother."

"Pretty sure I'm the older one."

"Not bigger, though."

I straighten, but even sitting, I'm a handbreadth shorter.

He grins. "Remember when you were taller than me? Dad told you to enjoy it while it lasted. Now I get to boss you around *forever*."

"Uh, no. Once I'm queen—"

"I'll still be bigger."

"That doesn't count. As queen, I can tell you what to do."

"You can *try*."

I'm about to retort when Jannah appears. "Time to head out, you two." She looks at the jackalope. "I suppose he's coming?"

"It's up to him." I hop off the rock and set the beast down. "This seems like a nice place. He could make a good life here. He—"

The jackalope jumps onto my leg and starts climbing. I sigh and scoop him onto my shoulder, whereupon he perches on my head. I sigh again, more deeply.

Rhydd snickers. "Nice try. Looks like you're stuck with him."

"Oh no. As future queen, I dub thee, Rhydd of Clan Dacre, keeper of the royal jackalope."

He walks away, calling back, "Like I said, you can try bossing me around. But I wouldn't recommend it. Time to admit you're the proud owner of a baby jackalope."

I grumble under my breath as I follow Jannah and Rhydd to our horses.

Like my brother, my aunt is dressed for battle, in knee-high boots, soft riding trousers and a heavy tunic. Today's tunic is crafted from the hide of a warakin—a cross between a boar and a wild dog, twice as savage as either. Others see our royal monster hunter's tunics as trophies, but to her they're failures. They're the beasts she *had* to kill.

Royal monster hunters used to slay every beast they encountered, like exterminating rats in a barn. But Jannah would say this *isn't* their barn—they don't actually live on our lands. If they've wandered here, they can be "encouraged" to wander out again. We can drive them back to the forests or the mountains. Or sedate and relocate them. Monsters have as much right to live as any other creature, and most of them happily stay in their own place.

If they get a taste for livestock—or endanger people—that's another story. Sometimes, rehabilitation is still possible. Like Malric, who'd been a pup when Jannah caught him raiding chickens. Other times, as with the warakin whose hide she wears, it's not.

A gryphon is an exception to the rule. It's one of the few monsters that *can't* be driven away. Which is why we're here.

As we ride, Jannah explains that the gryphon reports came from this region. Villagers have spotted the beast a half-dozen times, ravaging the local livestock. No one knows where to find it, though. That's our job.

We're riding along the foothills. Beyond them, fog-shrouded peaks rise, part of a mountain range infested with monsters and bandits. All the other kingdoms lie beyond that treacherous terrain. To cross it, you need an expert guide. Clan Bellamy is happy to help, for an outrageous price, but if you pay it, you're guaranteed not to be set upon by bandits . . . because they *are* the bandits. The other option is to join one of Jannah's convoys. This is a task Jannah added to her duties as royal monster hunter—she escorts trade caravans through those monster-infested mountains. Most people prefer Jannah, not surprisingly. The leader of Clan Bellamy doesn't appreciate the queen cutting into his profits. He'll be at the castle next week, hoping to negotiate a deal.

Jannah can cross the mountains because she trained for it. One of the ordeals all royal monster hunters face is the pilgrimage, where they must travel the mountain passage alone.

As we look for signs of the gryphon, Jannah tells us stories from her pilgrimage. She talks about the terrible beasts she fought—and the glorious ones she saw—and I hang on every word. I'm there with her, fighting a manticore. I'm there, seeing a phoenix nest. I'm there when she tumbles over a waterfall to escape a pack of warakins. I'm there when she wriggles through a cave tracking a basilisk. With the mountains close enough to *smell*, these old stories leap to life. My heart pounds and my very soul aches. I want to wheel the gelding around and gallop into those mountains and experience all that myself.

I want to . . . and I never will.

Beside me, Rhydd laughs when Jannah describes tumbling over that waterfall. He sighs at the story of the phoenixes. He grins at the thought of squeezing through that cave. But his heart doesn't race. His eyes don't shine. He's not *there* with her. And he doesn't want to be.

Jannah has tried to make Rhydd into a royal monster hunter. Yet some things can't be taught, as I've overheard her saying to our mother.

"He doesn't have the passion," she said. "He's like you."

"I always enjoyed a good hunt," Mom retorted. "I'm quite fond of monsters."

"So is Rhydd. He enjoys the hunt. He likes the beasts themselves. But he'd like both a lot more if he didn't know they were his future. That's the difference between you and him, Mari. You knew you'd never have to carry the ebony sword. He knows he must, and it means he can never relax and enjoy hunts or encounters. Rowan, on the other hand . . ."

"Unless you know a way to fix the situation, telling me this won't help. Make him a monster hunter, Jannah. Please."

She's tried. She's tried so hard. So has Rhydd. But it's not just our mother he takes after in this. Our father was the best warrior in the land, and Rhydd is truly his son. My brother has an instinct for swordplay that I envy. But, like our father, Rhydd does not have the Clan Dacre instinct for monsters. That can't be taught or I'd teach him myself.

"Can we talk about gryphons?" I ask. "Tips? Tricks? I know they have weaknesses, but I'm not sure I remember them all."

It would be hard *not* to remember them all, considering how few weaknesses gryphons have. This is for Rhydd—to reassure him they *can* be killed. I already know everything there is to know about the beasts.

When we were young, Jannah and my father used to play a game with us.

Which monster would you most like to see?
Which monster would you most like to touch?
Which monster would you most like to hear?
Which monster would you most like to meet?

At the time, we'd been deep into our monster lessons as our bestiary knowledge expanded. So the answers kept changing. Whenever Jannah introduced us to a new beast, we'd pay close attention. We'd imagine what it would sound like, look like, feel like, act like. Through the game, the monsters became real. They leapt off the pages, snorting and bucking and howling and slithering.

Once I learned about gryphons, my answer stopped changing.

I want to see a gryphon.

I want to touch its wondrous mane.

I want to hear its terrible screech.

I want to meet it, to stand before it and look up into those amber eyes and say hello.

The last one always made Jannah and my father laugh. *No, Rowan, you don't want to say hello to a gryphon . . . or it'll be the last thing you ever say.*

Five years ago, when villagers brought tales of a gryphon, my father snuck me out of a history lesson. We scurried into the courtyard, where he hoisted me onto the wall. Then he hopped up to sit beside me.

"Want to know what I'm off to see?" he asked.

"What?"

"A monster."

I rolled my eyes. "You're a monster hunter. You see them all the time."

"Not this one." He leaned over. "Guess what kind of monster?"

I looked at him, saw his eyes dancing, and my heart skipped. I could barely breathe the words. "A gryphon?"

He grinned. "A gryphon."

"Are you going to say hello to it?" I asked with a smile.

"I will. For you. From a distance. But do you know what else I'll do . . . ?" He leaned in again to whisper. "I'll touch its mane."

I giggled, my feet thumping against the wall.

"And I'll do better than that," he said. "I'll pluck out a tuft for your field journal."

When they brought my father's body home, my mother found a tuft of golden mane in his pocket. I threw it as hard as I could and spat on it. I never talked about gryphons after that. I swore I never wanted to see one. Now I'm about to, and I'm not sure how I feel about that.

When I ask Jannah for tips on gryphons, she launches into a lesson. A gryphon has the head and upper body of an eagle. Its forelegs are an eagle's, too, with talons the length of my forearm. The back half looks like a giant cat. It has cat ears and huge eagle wings.

Villagers say that a gryphon's gaze can paralyze a person. That's not true. It just has a razor-sharp beak, razor-sharp talons, razor-sharp claws on its hind legs . . .

Yes, a gryphon doesn't need a paralyzing gaze to kill. It does very well on its own. Very, very well, which makes it the most dangerous monster in our world.

As for weaknesses, well, it's not armored, which is good. Our swords can puncture its thick hide . . . as long as we can get close enough. Arrows won't do more than prick its skin. To kill a gryphon, one must ram a sword through its heart. That sounds easy enough, but it's not as if the gryphon is standing there waiting to die. It's dodging and attacking while the hunters are fighting for their lives, trying to get the right angle and leverage to drive their swords through the narrow gap between its ribs. It's like hitting a flying sparrow with a peashooter.

The trick to killing a gryphon is to weaken it first. Don't go straight for the heart, because if you miss, you'll lose your weapon in that thick hide. Weaken the beast with blade-slices and arrow-pierces. When it tires, strike the killing blow.

That's what Jannah explains. She also reminds us—well, *me*—that we are there as observers. For us, this is a lesson. Nothing more.

"Can you . . . ?" I clear my throat and sneak a glance at Rhydd. "I know that's how to kill a gryphon in theory, but how did *you* do it? With the one that . . ."

"Killed your father," Jannah says, her hands tightening on Courtois's reins.

"I'm sorry," I say. "I know you don't talk about it, and the bards . . ."

"The bards make up their own version, in absence of the truth. They tell the most heroic version." She glances at my brother. "You must get used to that, Rhydd. You must not argue, even when you wish to set the story straight. That was the hardest lesson for me to learn. The bards' tales of valor can be difficult to hear if that's not quite the way it happened. But those tales are for the people. So they may feel confident in the abilities of their monster hunters. What matters is not the way that the gryphon died, but the fact that it did."

Rhydd nods.

Jannah continues. "The bards say that your father and I attacked the gryphon side by side. When it grabbed him,

I made the killing blow, and it died. Unfortunately, it was too late for him, and he perished alongside the beast."

"And the truth?" I ask, my voice fainter than I'd like, my insides twisting.

"That is the truth, Rowan. With one omission. A small thing that is not small at all. As monster hunters, we sometimes make mistakes that will haunt us for the rest of our lives. The truth . . ." She inhales. "The truth is that the gryphon went for me. Your father leapt between us, and the beast grabbed him instead. And as it was distracted with him, I drove my sword through its heart. I chose . . ." Another deep breath. "I chose to focus on killing it rather than freeing him."

"But killing it *would* free him," Rhydd says. "That seems like the right decision."

"It was not. By the time the beast died, so had your father. Maybe if it happened again, I'd try to save him, and we'd both die. In the heat of battle, sometimes there is no way of knowing which choice is right. We can't foresee the future. We make a decision . . . and we live with the consequences."

Jannah reins Courtois to a halt. "And we've gone far enough. All the sightings were south of here, and I haven't seen any signs. Have you two?"

We shake our heads.

"Then let's pause to check our map."

She swings off Courtois. I try to do the same with my gelding but I'm too close to Courtois, and the beast nips my butt. I twist back onto the saddle, snarling at him . . . and the jackalope leaps from my head onto Courtois's neck and sinks his teeth in right below the unicorn's horn.

Courtois tosses his head. The jackalope doubles down, all his claws latching on for a better hold. I'm leaping from my horse when Courtois rears.

"Courtois, stop!" I shout, heart hammering. "Let me get him off!"

The unicorn ignores me. I rush in, and one flying hoof whips past my shoulder.

"Courtois!" Jannah barks.

Jannah grabs Courtois's reins and pulls him down. I'm lunging to seize the jackalope when the little beast snorts in satisfaction—as if he's subdued the terrible unicorn—and he jumps off by himself. Jumps and lands on Malric. The warg's head jerks up in surprise. The jackalope looks around and then settles onto the warg's broad back, as if thinking he makes a very fine fur rug.

"Bad idea," I say as I rush over. "Very bad." I scoop the jackalope up. "Sorry, Malric."

The warg eyes the jackalope. Then he sniffs it and slowly opens his massive jaws, one yellow eye on Jannah.

I yank the jackalope away. "Uh, no. Not a bunny dinner."

I hoist the jackalope by the scruff of the neck. "You are trouble, you know that?"

"He was defending his princess," Rhydd says. "Courtois nipped you, and he attacked. He's a jackalope bodyguard."

I glower at him as he tries to hide his laugh.

"Rhydd's right," Jannah says. "I always said I'd get a warg pup for you if I could. Now I don't need to. You have a killer jackalope."

"More like a *killed* jackalope," I say as I lift the beast, looking him square in the eye. "If he continues attacking monsters twenty times his size."

He licks his paw and grooms one ear.

"He needs a name," Rhydd says.

"How about BBR?" I say, looking the jackalope in the eye again. "Blasted Bunny Rabbit."

He bares his teeth and chatters at me.

"I don't think he likes that," Rhydd says.

"Good, because I'm not naming him. That would imply I'm keeping him." I glare at the jackalope. "And I am not."

"My lady!"

A shout rings across the open field. We turn to see a young man astride a pony, pushing it as fast as its short legs will go. The hunters—who have been keeping pace around us—drop their hands to their swords but leave them sheathed as the young man rides up. He's dressed like a farmer, with thick boots and coarse breeches.

"You are the royal monster hunter, yes?" he says, struggling for breath.

"Yes," Jannah says. "You have news for us?"

"I have *need* of you. The gryphon is attacking my parents' farm. Right now."

"Lead us."

CHAPTER FOUR

The farm isn't nearby. When the gryphon attacked, a neighbor said she'd seen the royal monster hunter pass. The young man had hopped onto the nearest pony and ridden as fast as he could to catch up.

We finally reach the property. The crowd of pitchfork- and ax-bearing laborers tell us the gryphon is still around. We ride across the field, trying not to trample the sprouting crop. Ahead lie the stone buildings and thatched roofs of the farm. An older man runs out to meet us.

"The beast is in the barn," he says.

Jannah's eyebrows shoot up. "The barn?"

He points at the pasture. "It killed two sheep, and the animals ran into the barn. The gryphon followed."

Jannah smiles over at us. "We might have a bit of luck here."

Rhydd nods. "A barn limits the battle arena and gives us the advantage of limited exits."

"Unless it bursts through the roof," I say. "That's possible, isn't it? It might fly up and break out."

Jannah's head tilts as she surveys the barn. "Rowan's right. That roof won't hold if it really wants to escape. So what would you two suggest?"

"Archers on the corners of the roof?" Rhydd says. "The gryphon would burst through the middle, and they'd be safe on the edges."

"Flaming arrows," I say. "That would drive the beast back down."

"It'd also set the straw roof on fire," Rhydd says.

"Could we burn down the barn with the gryphon . . . ? No, there's livestock."

Jannah nods. "If barn-burning was a foolproof plan, I would sacrifice the livestock. It's a good idea, Rowan. We need that creative thinking when dealing with monsters."

She looks at Rhydd. "We also need your clearheadedness. Yes, flaming arrows would set the roof aflame . . . with hunters below. A clever idea but dangerous. We'll stick with regular arrows, archers posted on the corners."

She calls her hunters over and explains the plan. Her two best archers will climb onto the roof while we go inside.

Jannah asks the farmer about the entrances—from here we only see the big door for the animals. He says there's a small one for people around the adjoining side. She sends two hunters to guard the smaller entrance. The remaining two will enter through the large one.

"Guard our horses, please," Jannah tells the farmer. "I'll need your people to stay back."

"Oh, we will, your ladyship. We've seen the beast, and we'll steer clear. My sons will help with the horses." He turns to the unicorn. "I'll personally tend to yours."

Courtois shakes his mane, his iridescent horn glimmering in the morning sun. The farmer steps forward as if entranced. Jannah catches his sleeve.

"That was a warning display, not an invitation," she says. "Courtois will look after himself, and I would strongly advise you not to go near him. That horn is sharp, and he's not afraid to use it. I have a special monster charge for you. Rowan? Let him take your new friend."

I reach around my saddle to where the jackalope has fallen asleep. I scoop him up as the farmer stares. When the jackalope awakes and sees he's going into a stranger's hands, he tries to bite the poor man. I show the farmer how to hold him, avoiding the sharp parts.

Once the animals are looked after, we head for the barn on foot. As we approach downwind, I can see that the livestock entrance is two swinging doors. Both stand open. The sun is on the other side of the barn, casting this entrance into shadow, and we can't make out any details through it.

Jannah stops close enough to see the layout of the barn. Malric thumps down at her side as she surveys it. Then she looks at us.

"And how would you handle our entry?" she says.

"Close the doors," I say. "Sneak up on either side, swing them shut and bar the entrance."

"Only if it's safe to close them," Rhydd says. "If the

gryphon is right there or the doors make too much noise, it'll come running."

"Which could be a good plan," I say. "Jannah and her hunters can be ready to attack, with the archers poised overhead."

Jannah beams and squeezes both our shoulders. "Excellent. You've learned your lessons well."

"So we're ready to be hunters?" I say.

"Ready to *plan* a gryphon attack," Rhydd says. "Not to execute one."

"Your brother is right," Jannah says. "A good plan is important. But following it in the heat of battle is . . ." She inhales. "You'll see."

"We've fought monsters before," I say.

"Not like this."

I nod and promise we'll stay back.

We follow my plan. I could explode with pride at that, but I try not to show it. Rhydd and I stay behind Jannah and Malric, who stand ready to fight if shutting the doors alerts the gryphon. From where I stand, I can't see inside. I strain to listen. Thick stone walls muffle any noise within.

Two hunters ease the big doors shut, and I'm almost disappointed when the gryphon doesn't charge out. They bar the door and guard it while Jannah, Rhydd and I creep around to the smaller entrance. The two hunters guarding that spot join us. One whispers to Jannah that the gryphon is at the far side of the barn. Jannah considers, and then tells us we may enter with her, but we must stay well back from the beast.

Jannah goes first, with Malric at her heels. The two hunters join her; we follow. Once past the doors, Jannah and the hunters fan out, a sword-edged wall between us and the beast.

It's dark and cool inside, and it smells of straw and musk and dung. There's another smell, too, a coppery one that makes me flinch. I can't be a monster hunter and not recognize the scent of blood. To us, it's usually the smell of failure, a monster we had to kill.

Sunlight filters through holes in the thatched roof. The spots of light polka-dot the dirt floor, highlighting a trail of blood to my left. Beyond it lies a mangled sheep. I look away quickly.

There are other livestock in here, too, alive and trapped with the beast. They're trying to be quiet, like hiding children. An injured sheep lies on its side, groaning in pain, and I want to run to help it. Horses press against the backs of their stalls, panting with fear, and I want to rub their noses and tell them it will be fine. I console myself with knowing it *will* be fine. Jannah is here, and the gryphon won't kill anything else.

My gaze slides to the dead sheep. A thought pokes at the back of my mind. Something that tells me to stop and think. But I can't. There's a gryphon in this barn, and I have no attention to spare. I must focus on my surroundings. I'll figure out the answer to this puzzle later.

There's a gryphon in this barn.

An actual gryphon.

I'm going to see a gryphon.

I am only a few dozen feet from one. I can hear it, making horrible ripping and gulping noises as it devours its prey. I can smell it, too, its dank musk overpowering the smell of the livestock.

At the gryphon's stench, again I feel that weird poke at the back of my mind, the one that tells me to stop and think.

Stop and think about what? I'm being careful. I'm staying behind Jannah. I'm not that little girl who longed to see a gryphon, the one who'd want to push past and say hello. Nor am I the one who spat on that tuft of mane from my dead father's pocket, the girl who'd want to rush at this beast and drive my sword through its heart. I may be reckless, but I'm not stupid. That little voice must just be warning me to stay careful.

Jannah motions for us to stay well back of her. We do. Well, Rhydd does, and when I try to creep closer, his hand closes on my arm. So maybe that voice of caution has a reason to be whispering after all.

I'm going to see a gryphon.

A *real* gryphon, just ahead. King of all monsters. It is truly a once-in-a-lifetime experience.

From here, though, all I see is a dark shape. The roof is patchy, with small holes. The light coming through isn't enough to illuminate the beast. The shadowy figure is smaller than I expected, no bigger than an ox. When disappointment stabs through me, I remember stories about the size of the one that killed our father, and I am glad this one's small.

A young gryphon will be much easier to handle. If it's young enough, Jannah might even let us get close.

The beast faces the other direction. Jannah gestures that she'll approach on the left side, by its heart. She glances back at us, and I can tell she's debating. She's assessing the size of the creature and our readiness. Weighing her concern for us against our need for battle experience. When I see her considering, my heart leaps.

I might fight a gryphon. An actual gryphon.

CHAPTER FIVE

Jannah lifts five fingers: *Stay five paces behind me.* That means we'll get closer than I expected, though she won't let us enter the battle. Rhydd must sense my flush of dismay. He gives me a hard look and shakes his head.

I make a face at him. A good hunter obeys her commander. I am a good hunter.

Jannah bears left. We follow, circling wider and staying back. As we move, the niggling feeling pokes at me again.

That smell. That sheep. Think, Rowan. Think.

Think about what? I don't—

Oh. Wait.

I see the shape of the beast now. I see its tail and hindquarters, like those of a giant cat. I see folded wings. I see a thick mane. Exactly as I expect. But something's not quite . . .

The forelegs. They should be talons. Instead, they're paws. The front legs look like the rear ones—a giant cat's.

When the beast lifts its tail, in my gut I already know what I'll see on the end. Not tufts of fur but a trio of spikes.

The dead sheep. Killed and tossed aside. More animals slaughtered outside. Wanton destruction rather than selective feeding. A gryphon—like most predators—kills only what it needs to eat.

Then there is the smell. I've never smelled a gryphon, but I ran across this stench in a den once. A den at the edge of the mountains, where Jannah let us see the lair of a predatory monster almost as rare as a gryphon.

"Manticore," I whisper.

Rhydd looks over, and his eyes go wide. His head swings toward Jannah, his mouth opening as if trying to figure out how to warn her. I shake my head. Our aunt already knows what this is. That's why she didn't make us stay farther back.

A manticore is dangerous. But a manticore is not a gryphon.

It's an easy mistake to make if you're not a monster hunter. Both have the hindquarters and tail of a big cat. Both have manes. Both have wings. But manticores are smaller. They have bat-like wings instead of feathered ones. Their faces are very different. And manticores have the front legs of a giant cat rather than an eagle.

Almost every time a farmer reports a gryphon, it turns out to be a manticore. Jannah always asks people to describe the head, the wings and the front legs, but sometimes they don't get a good look at those. They only see a giant cat-like animal flying overhead or terrorizing their livestock. Also, the gryphon is the more famous monster. So even if the beast is a manticore, they describe a gryphon to Jannah. And sometimes they lie, thinking the royal monster hunter will come faster for a gryphon.

This is not a gryphon. I should be relieved, but in my deepest heart, I'm disappointed. Like Dad, who would come back from yet another gryphon hunt and slump beside my mother.

"Manticore," he'd say with a sigh.

"You should be glad of that, Armand," she'd say.

"I know . . ."

You should be glad of that, Dad.

I wish you'd come home the last time, slumped in that seat, given that dramatic sigh and said, "Manticore."

I wish it so much.

Jannah closes in on the beast. Then she turns to me and mouths, "Shall I ride?" Rhydd's brow furrows. He doesn't understand. But I do, and I nod.

This is Jannah's method of killing a manticore as quickly and humanely as possible. Because we must kill it, unfortunately. A manticore might not be as dangerous as a gryphon, but it's even more destructive, able to slaughter an entire flock of sheep in a night.

Jannah positions herself a few paces from the rear flank of the manticore. It's still busy devouring the sheep. I've always heard that manticores are gluttons—and not terribly bright—and now I see the truth of that. We all stay back and out of sight, of course, but if this were a gryphon, it would have noticed us by now. The manticore doesn't.

Gaze fixed on the beast, Jannah sheaths her sword and hunkers down. Then she runs and vaults onto its back, grabbing its mane in both hands.

The manticore's head jerks back, and I get my first look at the face that has made many a monster hunter stop in her tracks. Stop and wonder if she's seeing a beast at all. The face looks . . . well, it looks human.

It's flat and round with widespread eyes. In our lessons, Jannah would say it looked ape-like. Seeing it up close, I agree. It has a furred face with a wide, flat nose and flaring nostrils. I only get a glimpse of those strange features before the beast bucks.

It twists and rears like a wild unicorn desperate to throw off its rider. Jannah holds tight as she lies across the manticore's back. Malric and the two hunters draw nearer, out of range of the beast's flying claws but ready to attack if Jannah falls.

Jannah does not fall.

She rides the manticore until the beast stops bucking and rearing. It's tiring and the creature on its back seems to pose no threat, so it slows its struggles. When it pauses, she strikes.

The killing blow is not a magnificent and heroic stroke of swordsmanship. That isn't how a royal monster hunter does her job. The hunting part is exciting—the planning, the tracking, the capturing. But if we can't spare the life of a monster then, like putting down a rabid dog, it is duty. Regrettable duty.

It's also quick. Jannah didn't hop on the beast's back for fun. The position just lets her sink in her dagger in exactly the right spot. One hard thrust and the manticore stiffens. Then before it has time to feel more than a flash of pain, it slumps to the ground.

Jannah makes sure the manticore has drawn its last breath before she waves Rhydd and me over for a rare chance to study this incredible creature.

See the claws, how they don't retract like a cat's? They aren't as sharp as a cat's either, for that very reason. See the thickness of the hide? A light blade blow won't penetrate it. Observe the tail, with its spines. They aren't venomous, but see how thin the tail is? The manticore wields it like a whip, driving those spines into an attacker.

Next, she opens the beast up. This is where Rhydd crouches, getting a closer look, asking questions. I know this is important—*notice the size of the heart, the placement of the internal organs, should we ever need to fight one again.* I'm always fascinated by science. But I keep seeing the manticore as a whole. A beautiful and fascinating beast, lifeless on the floor.

When Jannah catches my expression, she nods in understanding. Then she points to the dead sheep.

"A manticore belongs in the mountains," she says. "Not in a farmer's pasture or barn."

"I know."

She hunkers down and runs a hand through the thick mane. "It's not the beast's fault. It spends its life hunting for game, and then it finds an overflowing banquet. Most predators can control themselves. A manticore can't. It is consumed by bloodlust."

"I know."

"If you catch it quickly enough, you can try driving it back to the mountains. The trick is timing and force. If it has only just ventured down and you give it enough of a scare—and a few scars—you can drive it back. But this one had been here too long. It would never be satisfied with the mountains again."

"I know," I say again, and I do, despite my regret at what we had to do.

She rises to squeeze my shoulder. "As future queen, you should go tell the farmer that we saved the rest of his flock. Your mother will reimburse him for the loss of the others. While you do that, I'll take the manticore's hide."

I look about the barn. "Do I need to speak to the farmer right away? Or can I tend to the injured animals first?"

She smiles. "You may absolutely tend to them first, Rowan."

"I'll help her," Rhydd says.

We leave Jannah to skin the manticore. We don't need the hide or the meat, but we'll take them to put to some use, so they don't go to waste on a barn floor. Or, worse, be sold as a trophy in the local market.

A couple of the hunters help us survey the injured animals. Two others go out to reassure the farmer and his gathered neighbors. The remaining two hunters open the main doors to release the uninjured livestock.

There are four wounded sheep and one calf. Two of the sheep must be put down, and the hunters insist on handling that. Rhydd and I assess the rest. The sheep have minor wounds. The calf, though, has a gash that requires immediate attention.

I'm on my knees reassuring the calf when a crash sounds, like a thunderclap right overhead. The very timbers shake, wood falling all around me. I fall back as a flash of light pierces the gloomy barn before the sun goes dark.

An inhuman shriek rips through the shocked silence. A shadow flashes above me—the shadow of the beast that is blocking the sun. The beast that smashed through the roof.

I catch a whiff of something I've never smelled before. It's musky but oddly sweet, too, like honey. Then yellow talons dive, each as big as my forearm.

The talons seize me. I'm trying to scramble up, trying to understand what I'm seeing, before I can even draw breath, the talons lift me and swing me into the air.

CHAPTER SIX

Below me, Rhydd bellows in pure rage. He pulls his sword, ebony and silver flashing. The beast holding me strikes at him. Blood flies. The beast lets out another ear-piercing shriek and slams me into the barn floor, talons pinning me there.

A beak appears, a flash of yellow grabbing at my brother. I scream, and I punch, and I writhe, but the beast doesn't even seem to notice. Jannah and the others shout as their boots pound across the barn floor.

The beak seizes Rhydd and flips him into the air, then lets go. As he falls, the beak grabs him again, this time by one leg. There's a sickening crunch, and I lash out with everything I have, scream at the top of my lungs. My brother is under attack . . . and I'm powerless to help him.

I am supposed to protect him.

I *came* here to protect him.

Now this beast is attacking Rhydd as he tries to protect *me*.

I manage to get my sword out. I can't swing it, though. I'm face down on the barn floor, pinned by huge talons. I manage to jab upward, and my sword hits something solid. I pull it back, and I stab with all my might. The beast drops my brother's leg. Rhydd falls to the floor. Jannah is there with her hunters, running at the beast, their swords out.

Then I'm not on the floor anymore. I'm rising, my aunt and the others sailing past below. I see Jannah's upturned face, the horror on it, her lips forming my name.

She's shouting my name. I know she is, but I can't hear it. All I hear is thunder.

The thunder of wings.

I'm flying upward, and in a heartbeat, I'm through the roof and then I'm . . .

I don't know where I am. I'm lurching and rolling, my stomach heaving, the world a blur below me.

I don't have my sword. That's the first thing I realize.

I have dropped my sword, and I don't know when or how it happened, but *when* and *how* don't matter. What matters is that I have done the unthinkable. I am a warrior in battle . . . and I let go of my weapon.

I have no sword, yet I'm in the grip of . . .

Deep in my gut, I know what has me. Without even twisting to look up, I know.

I still crane my neck. I see feathers. Black feathers tipped with white. And a mane. A thick golden mane.

A gryphon.

I can't even see the whole beast. I only see its chest—an endless expanse of feather and fur.

I am dead.

It doesn't matter if I'm still breathing. I might as well be dead. I'm in the talons of a gryphon, a beast with legs longer than my entire body. It has me in its grip, and it is in flight, and I have no weapon, and I am going to die.

Like my father, I am going to die.

Something whizzes past my face. An arrow buries into the underside of the beast. Then another and another. The beast swoops and screams, more in annoyance than pain. An arrow slices the fabric of my trousers, and I let out a cry. When the gryphon dives, my stomach dives with it.

More arrows strike. One slams into my shoulder. I bite back a yowl and look. My thick leather tunic stopped the arrow from impaling me, but the arrowhead still penetrated, embedding itself in my flesh.

Pain throbs through me. Then the gryphon turns and I am smacked sideways, which drives the arrow in even deeper. I grit my teeth and wrench it free. Then I stare at the sharp arrowhead, dripping blood. I grab the shaft close to the head and stab the gryphon in the leg. The beast doesn't even seem to notice.

Below, Jannah is shouting. I can't make out words, only the sound of her voice. I yank out the arrow and stab again.

"No!" Jannah shouts. "Too high!"

She's telling me not to attack the gryphon when it's flying so high. If it drops me from here, I won't survive the fall.

I don't care. I'd rather die dashed against the ground than ripped apart by a gryphon's beak. I stab again. The gryphon plunges toward the earth, and I stab harder.

Jannah's shouting, but I can't hear her. Blood pounds in my ears, and my vision blacks out every time the gryphon dives or swoops. My mind is blacking out, too. I struggle to focus, to think, and I can't. I want to scream. Just scream for someone to save me.

No one can save me. Not up here. I can't save myself either. An arrow will never bring down a gryphon. It isn't a sword. It can't stab deep enough or slash—

Slash.

A thought flits through my brain, and I try to grab it, but everything's spinning. The world spins below me, and my mind spins with it.

Slash.

Focus on that. I was thinking about arrows and slashing . . .

Yes! The tendon. Slash the gryphon's tendon.

I act without thinking. Instinct tells me where to strike. I grip the arrow close to the head, and I slash the foreleg as hard as I can.

The talons open.

They don't open far enough. The gryphon screams, but it keeps its hold on me.

As it starts climbing, I slash again. The beast gives a terrible shriek. Then I'm dropping. Dropping like a stone, my limbs flailing to break my fall.

Jannah's running for me. I see a blur of her below. Then the sun disappears again. The thunder of wings rips through the sky. A strangled cry rings out.

I hit the ground. Pain slams through me and then . . .

Darkness.

CHAPTER SEVEN

I wake as if slapped. My head snaps up, and I'm gasping for breath. I can't find it. I'm suffocating. There's nothing over my mouth or nose, but I'm suffocating. I can't—

I inhale. A long, ragged gasp scorches my lungs.

I see light, but my mind stays dark. Blank. Where . . . ?

I blink and try to lift my head as I struggle to breathe. There's hay. I'm lying on a stack of hay in a farmer's field. Why . . . ?

Shouts. Running feet. A snarl of rage. A shriek that splits the air. Wind drumming against my back. The ground shaking. Thunder rolls, the wind picking up and—

"Rowan!"

A massive shadow crosses me, and I twist to look up. I see a head. A huge eagle's head with the mane and ears of a great cat.

My muddled brain says, "Is that a . . . ?"

And then I remember . . . just as the gryphon dives at me, talons out.

I roll to the side as fast as I can. Pain slices through me. I tumble right off the haystack and hit the ground with a thud. The gryphon lands, the ground shaking. It rears onto its hind legs, and I'm scrambling out of the way, but my body isn't responding. Pain blinds me. Agonizing pain.

I'm not moving fast enough. I *can't* move fast enough. I'm going to—

A figure runs from nowhere. She leaps. Her sword slashes at the beast's rear flank. An ebony sword. Jannah.

The gryphon wheels on her. Its beak swings her way. I scream, but she dodges it. With my scream, though, the beast remembers me. It rears again, talons extended. I crawl to the haystack and push my way into it. Jannah shouts. Malric snarls. There's a scuffle, and the gryphon screams in pain.

I need to help Jannah.

I don't know where the other hunters are. Everyone scattered after the manticore, and this has all happened so fast. I know they're coming, but they aren't here yet, and I am.

I need to help her.

But I hurt. I hurt so much.

Too bad. I must help Jannah. If Rhydd is safe, then my priority is my—

Footsteps vibrate through the earth beneath me. The pound of them underscores the grunts and growls of the fight. I push through the haystack to be sure it's the hunters coming to Jannah's aid.

It is not.

I do see the hunters. Two stand poised on the remains of the barn roof, firing arrows. Two more run from another direction. But the person coming straight at the gryphon is Rhydd.

My brother is not running. One leg drags as he staggers toward the fight, sword gripped tight in hand. Sweat shines on his face. He's gritting his teeth in pain, and blood drenches his trousers. He is injured. Badly injured. And yet he is coming, ready to fight, ready to help our aunt.

I love my brother more than anyone in the world. I admire him, too, for all the things he is that I am not, all the things I'll never be. And I'm proud of him, for his bravery and his kindness and his pure heart. But when I see him, dragging his leg across that field, clutching his sword, face set in grim determination, that love and admiration and pride surge stronger than ever.

I feel shame, too, for hiding in this haystack. Yes, I'm only here to catch my breath, to force past the pain of my fall, but I'm still here. I am injured and hiding. He is injured and returning to the fight.

I clench my teeth against the pain slamming through me. Then I push my way out of that haystack. I don't exit on Jannah's side, though. She is fighting, and Malric is helping, and the hunters are coming, and the archers are covering her. She is not my concern. My concern is here: my wonderful, brave, stubborn brother, who is heading—bloodied and wounded—into a gryphon fight.

I love him. I admire him. I am so proud of him.

And I need to stop him.

I stagger toward Rhydd. Every muscle aches, but my legs work, my arms work. I need to keep moving. Get to him. Tell him he's amazing, and he's courageous. Then tell him he's crazy if he thinks I'm going to let him fight a gryphon in his condition.

He sees me, alive, and he pauses. Relief washes over his face. He wobbles, as if when he stops, he can't quite get going again. He has to grit his teeth to take another lurching step and—

The gryphon shrieks. Its wings beat the air, the currents of it ruffling my hair. I spin, ready to run to Jannah's aid. But she's fine. She's lunging *at* the gryphon as it takes flight.

It lifts into the air . . . and turns our way.

I stand there as the gryphon hovers, its massive wings keeping it just above the ground. Jannah screams, jabbing her sword uselessly, the gryphon out of reach.

The beast looks right at me, those eyes fixed on me. In a blink, I am a child again, telling my father this is what I want. To stand in front of a gryphon, gaze into these amber eyes and say hello.

What a fool I was. What a silly *fool*.

I square my shoulders, and I raise my chin, and I meet those eyes. Except they aren't looking at me after all. They're fixed behind me. The gryphon lifts its beak, and I see those nostril holes.

The gryphon smells blood.

I spin on my brother, still dragging his injured leg as he heads my way. Blood soaks his trousers. Completely soaks them.

The gryphon shrieks . . . and I run. I ignore the agonizing pain in my chest. I ignore the fact I can barely draw breath. I run straight at my brother. The shadow of the gryphon covers me. The wind of its wings batters me as the creature swoops.

I run into Rhydd. I knock him flying, and I drop on him, flattening myself over him. Behind us, the gryphon shrieks as its dive comes up empty, prey gone. It pulls back for another try. I grab Rhydd's sword from his hand and leap to my feet.

The gryphon starts another dive. Two hunters charge, swords raised, and the gryphon pulls up short. More hunters appear. The gryphon swings around, following Jannah's shouts. It swerves back toward her, the hunters following, one shouting, "Stay here," to me.

Rhydd sits on the ground, catching his breath. When he tries to rise, I hold him down. Then I hear a sound behind me. A snarl of rage and pain. A human snarl.

I jump up and spin to see Jannah on the ground, her sword still in hand. The gryphon is diving at her. Malric leaps right at the beast's head as Jannah jumps to her feet. She swings her sword, but the gryphon's beak closes around her sword arm. Malric hangs off the gryphon's neck. It doesn't seem to care. Doesn't seem to notice. That powerful beak closes with the same sickening crunch I heard when it seized Rhydd. Then it throws Jannah.

Before Jannah hits the ground, it grabs her again, this time by the leg, just like it did with Rhydd.

I'm already running. I don't even realize I am until that moment. I'm watching this, feeling as if I'm frozen in terror, but I'm not. I'm barreling toward the gryphon, Rhydd's sword raised.

The gryphon has Jannah by the leg. It lashes back and swings her . . .

Swings her at a rock.

I see the rock. I see her body, upside down, her skull heading straight for that rock, and I scream. I scream with everything I have as I run full out.

We all run. We all scream.

It doesn't matter.

Jannah's head hits that rock. There is a crunch. A horrible crunch, ten times worse than the beast's beak cracking down. I'm still screaming, my throat raw. Malric is on the ground, racing to Jannah. He throws himself over her prone body.

The hunters attack the gryphon. They've lunged past me and they face the beast, their swords swinging as it backs away.

I race straight to Jannah. She's on the ground, blood streaming from her arm and her leg and her scalp.

My chest seizes, and my eyes flood with tears, and I have to stumble, blind, to her. I drop at her side. Malric gives way, and I lean over her.

Jannah's eyelids flutter. Then they open.

I let out a whoosh of relief.

"You're okay," I say. "Help will come."

"No," she whispers.

"Yes, it will come. I'll get it myself. Hold—"

Her fingers grip my arm. "No, Rowan. Stay."

I look about wildly. The gryphon is in the air. I can't tell if it's backing off. I don't dare leave her if it's not.

Malric slumps onto his belly, his muzzle on Jannah's stomach. Her hand limply falls on his head, and she rubs it.

"You'll watch over her, won't you?" she whispers to the warg. "You'll stay with Rowan?"

"Wh-what?" I say.

— 63 —

She takes a deep, jagged breath, and her hand moves to my arm. "There's not much time, so listen carefully."

"Not much—? No. You're fine. I'll—"

Her grip tightens, cutting me off. "Listen. Please." She fumbles for her sword, fallen at her side. With her good arm, she pulls it over and places my hand on the grip. "Do you still want this?"

"Wh-what?"

"Will you take this?"

"N-no. It's yours. You'll be fine. You'll—"

"After I'm gone, will you take it? When the time comes. When you're ready. Would you give up the throne for the sword?"

"Yes, of course."

Her gaze meets mine. "Even after all you've seen? Here. Today. After what happened to you. You would still trade?"

"Absolutely."

"Good."

Her hand covers mine, closing my fingers on the grip of the ebony sword. "Then it will be yours."

"But we can't. Rhydd is the—"

"Rhydd's leg is injured. Badly. He'll never walk properly again."

"We don't know that. It's hurt, but it can heal—"

She grips my hand tighter. "No, it is gravely injured, and he will never walk properly again. Tell your mother this is the way. This is the answer. Doctor Fendrel will help. He is loyal to his queen and his land, and he knows this is best. Doctor Fendrel must tell the council that Rhydd will never walk properly again. So he can't be the royal monster hunter."

She meets my gaze. "Think about it, as you return home. If this sword is truly what you want—"

"It is."

"Then tell your mother what I've said." She inhales, her breathing shallow now. "And tell her . . . tell her that I love her."

"What? No. You can tell her—"

Her hand rises to my chin. "You will be a glorious monster hunter, Rowan. Seeing you in that beast's clutches, fighting your way free . . . you will be the stuff of legend. I only wish I could be there to see it. I wish I could be there to train—"

Her eyes roll back, her lids closing.

"Jannah!"

Her eyelids crack open, lips curving into a pained smile. "Still here? Good. Go to Wilmot. He will train you. There's time. Plenty of time before you wield the sword. He will help. Beg him if you must. Tell him I begged. Tell him . . . tell him . . ." She's breathing the words now, barely audible as her eyelids flag. "Tell him I'm sorry."

Her eyes close, and her body goes still, and I scream as Malric begins to howl.

CHAPTER EIGHT

My aunt is dead.

My aunt dead, my brother gravely wounded. I am alive ... and so is the gryphon. I hate us both for that.

The gryphon is gone. Because it was already injured, the rush of hunters proved too much for it, and it flew back toward the mountains.

I hurt so much that I barely even feel my injuries. The pain of grief is worse. My insides are empty, rubbed raw, and all I want is my mother. I want my mom, and I want my dad, and I want my aunt, and I'll never see two of those people again, and I can barely breathe thinking about it.

As for my physical injuries, the local village healer says I have a bruised chest, a bump on my skull and the arrow puncture in my shoulder. She's done what she can for me. Compared to my brother, though, I am fine.

His leg is broken. Shattered, according to the village

healer, with three breaks in his calf. He should not have been able to walk onto that battlefield. But he did. He forced himself to walk onto it. And I hid in a haystack and let my aunt die.

That's not how it happened. In my mind, I know that. In my heart and my gut, though, that's what it feels like—as if I spent the entire battle huddled under the hay. My aunt is dead, and that's all that matters to me.

It's a quiet ride home. The healer wanted me in the wagon with Rhydd, but I only do that when my brother needs me. Otherwise, I force myself to ride, with my aunt's sword over my lap and Courtois's reins in my hand as I lead him.

The unicorn follows as docile as a weary nag. Malric walks behind the second wagon, the one that carries my aunt's body. The jackalope snuggles in behind me and never once tries to climb onto my shoulders. The beasts sense the mood, and they are as subdued as the hunters.

Each step seems to take forever. And each step seems to take no time at all, if that makes any sense. Time passes in a blur, and when we have to stop for the horses, I look around, startled at where we are, feeling as if I've slept through the ride. But I don't sleep. I just . . . shut down. Shut down and try not to feel anything and feel *everything* instead.

We don't ride through the castle village. I need to tell Mom what happened before she hears it from anyone else. So I direct the hunters to take a rough side road in, and they obey without question. As soon as the castle spires rise over distant trees, I hand Courtois's lead to another hunter. Then I prod my gelding to a trot.

I take off in a cloud of dust. Behind me, Malric barks, as if startled. His giant paws thunder along the dirt road. When he catches up, he glowers and growls my way. I ignore him and push the gelding to a canter, and Malric runs at my side.

I make it to the castle gates far ahead of the others. A scout spots me, and by the time I reach those gates, my mother is flying through them, Berinon behind her. She has her skirts in hand, running as fast as she can.

I lift the ebony sword in both hands, and my mother's gaze goes from it to the warg at my side. She falters. Then she rocks forward, and Berinon races up to catch her. I lift the sword over my head as tears spill. Then I collapse onto my gelding's neck, sobbing.

We're inside my mother's chambers. I'm on her lap, like I'm a little girl again. I sob on her shoulder as she rocks me and cries softly. When I recover, I pull back, embarrassed, but she holds me there, her arms tight around me.

"I'm sorry," I say. "I'm so sorry. I snuck off to look after Rhydd, and then this happened. We thought the villagers mistook a manticore for a gryphon. After Jannah took down the manticore, I wanted to tend to the injured livestock, and that's when the gryphon struck."

"Drawn by the smell of blood," Berinon murmurs as he crouches beside us. "The slaughter of the livestock."

I nod. "I wasn't ready. I was distracted. The gryphon

crashed through the roof, and it grabbed me. That's how Rhydd got hurt, protecting me. If I wasn't there—"

"Rowan—" Berinon begins.

I hurry on. "The gryphon took me, and that's why Jannah had to go after it. That's why she had to fight it alone."

My mother pales. "T-took you?"

"In its talons. It was flying off with me and—"

Berinon grips my shoulder. "Your mother doesn't need all the details. Not if we ever want her sleeping again." He turns to her. "Rowan got away, Mari. On her own. That's what the hunters said. In flight, she plucked an arrow from her own shoulder and cut the beast's tendon while it was low enough for her to fall safely. That will be a story for the bards."

"I only used the arrow because I lost my sword. I don't know how I dropped it."

He smiles. "Because a gryphon burst through the roof and grabbed you?"

My mother looks like she's going to be sick.

"Mari? She's fine," Berinon says. "As for *making* Jannah attack the gryphon, Rowan, your aunt would have done that anyway, with or without the support of her hunters. The manticore's rampage attracted the gryphon. Jannah believed the villagers had mistaken a manticore for a gryphon. She would have verified that—by speaking to other witnesses—but she didn't get the chance. The gryphon caught everyone off guard. If it hadn't grabbed you, it would have taken Rhydd. You saved your brother, Rowan. The hunters told me you threw yourself over him. You went there to protect Rhydd, and you did, and there is no use speculating on other outcomes. You were wrong to

— 69 —

leave, but you did exactly what you set out to do." His hand grips my shoulder. "We are proud of you."

Mom hugs me. "Berinon is right. You did a foolish thing, but for a good reason. You saved Rhydd. You saved yourself. No one . . ." Her breath catches. "No one could have saved Jannah."

"The hunters say you were with her at the end," Berinon says. "That's a blessing."

"I . . . I guess so. Mom? She wanted me to tell you that she loves you."

My mother looks away, but I can still see her face, contorted with grief.

"And there's more," I say quickly. "That's why I rode ahead."

I tell her Jannah's idea about using Rhydd's injuries to change our fate. To make me the royal monster hunter, and him the king.

When I finish, my mother stares at me, as if struggling to make sense of what I said, her mind still on Jannah.

"What does your brother think of this?" Berinon asks.

"I haven't told him. I can't. It's . . ." I struggle for the right words. "He doesn't want to be the royal monster hunter. He'd rather be king. But he can't say that. He can't even agree to it. That would be wrong."

Berinon nods. "It's asking him to take the crown that is rightfully his sister's. To take the highest position in the land. And give you the most dangerous one."

"Rowan was correct," Mom says. "We can't put this decision on Rhydd. We must make it for him." She looks at me. "Do you understand what that would mean, Rowan?"

"I do. I told Jannah that I agreed, and she told me to think about it. I have. Nothing's changed. I'll give up the throne. I'll take the sword."

"All right, then. Let me speak to Doctor Fendrel."

Doctor Fendrel tells the council that my brother can't be the royal monster hunter. His leg is shattered. He will never walk without a crutch.

The truth is that Doctor Fendrel doesn't know how well my brother's leg will heal. As the physician told my mother privately, Rhydd may be able to forgo a crutch, but he will always have a limp.

"The answer is simple," my mother says after the doctor leaves. "Rhydd's leg does not prevent him from sitting on the ivory throne. Rowan will take up the ebony sword."

"Simple," Heward murmurs. "Conveniently simple."

My mother meets his gaze, her eyes still red from crying. "My sister is dead. My son has been lamed. Nothing in that is *convenient*, cousin."

Berinon clears his throat. "I believe we should count our blessings that a change of plans is so simply done. That Rhydd will be as apt a ruler as his sister. That Rowan will be as skilled a royal hunter as her brother."

"Are you sure about that?" Heward says.

"Rowan saved her brother from a gryphon," Mom says. "She escaped it herself. In *flight*. My daughter is Clan Dacre. She has the gift. Have you seen her new companion? Jackalopes are untamable . . . yet Rowan tamed one without even trying."

Heward sniffs. "It's a very young beast. Orphaned. Starving and desperate."

It takes Mom a moment to answer calmly. From my royal lessons, I know she must. When she stands before the council, she is the queen, not Jannah's sister or our mother. No matter how much she's hurting, she must do this. Just as I must stand by her chair, even as my aching body screams for me to sit. Berinon had offered me a seat, but I had refused to take it. Malric stands as well, at my side, refusing to rest his own injuries.

My mother finds her composure and gestures to Malric. "Jannah's warg has not left Rowan's side since she returned. Courtois allowed her to lead him back. He let her stable him. The beasts know. They understand. As did Jannah, when she handed Rowan the ebony sword, knowing Rhydd's injuries were grave."

"So you believe Rowan is ready to be the royal monster hunter."

My mother's mouth opens. Then she pauses. I watch her carefully. She looks like a beast scenting a trap. When she speaks, it is slow, reasoned. "I believe she *will* be ready. She has already undergone her basic preparation, and with additional training—"

"How much training?"

"By the time she is sixteen—"

"We can't wait four years for a royal monster hunter. You know clan law, Mariela. If the royal monster hunter perishes before the hunter-elect is fully trained, the royal line shifts."

"To your children," my mother says, her voice low with warning.

"Mine are *not* children. My daughter is twenty, my son eighteen. They have been trained for this possibility and they are old enough to succeed you and Jannah right now, in accordance with our law. Since Rowan is not ready—"

"I am," I say.

Mom's hand rises to silence me, but I surge forward, pretending not to see it. I can't, however, pretend I don't see Berinon's face—his expression warning me.

Don't be careless. Don't leap into a fight you cannot win.

"I *will* be ready," I amend. "I can be. Give me one"—I catch Berinon's look—"two years. I can be ready for my ordeals in two years."

Two council members nod as if this sounds reasonable to them.

I straighten. "In two years, I will be a fully trained monster hunter, ready to—"

"Not good enough," Heward says. "We have a gryphon on the loose. One that has already killed a royal monster hunter. I propose that we allow my son to hunt it. If he returns with its head, then we know who has earned the ebony sword."

"That is not—" my mother begins.

"—not necessary," I cut in. "I'm sorry, Mom. I didn't mean to interrupt. But the gryphon has retreated. It's injured, and it returned to the mountains."

"To heal," Heward says. "Then it will come back. They always come back. It will return before winter."

"Perhaps that's where we can meet on this," says one of the council members. That's Liliath—my mother's aunt, and the only one who'd voted against sending Rhydd on the hunt.

"Give Rowan until the first snowfall to train. At that time, if the gryphon returns, she must join the hunting party. If they slay it, then we will grant her two years of training before she must complete her ordeals."

"One year," Heward says. "And with the gryphon, she must strike the killing blow."

Liliath shakes her head. "We will not go that far. We will simply say that she must fight the beast. She can't watch others do it for her."

The two other council members nod their agreement.

There's a long pause before Heward says, "All right. The princess may train until the gryphon returns. At that time, she must fight and slay it. If she does not, then my son will. When he defeats the beast, he will win the sword, and his sister will take the crown."

CHAPTER NINE

The matter isn't decided that easily. The council debates, but ultimately all four agree, and my mother cannot win further concessions. She sweeps out with Berinon, and I follow.

I'm passing my own quarters when something hits the door. Claws scrabble at the wood, and I can hear chattering. As I continue past, another thud shakes my door.

I glance at Malric, padding along behind me. The warg sighs. My mother is right that Malric is sticking close, but it's with the reluctance of a kid forced to babysit a much younger—and terribly annoying—sibling. Jannah told him to watch out for me, and he understood enough to know what she was asking, so he does it. But I suspect, deep in that warg brain of his, he's wondering whether anyone would notice if he snuck out and hightailed it back to the mountains.

Another thud. I push open the door . . . and the jackalope charges out and head-butts my legs.

I stagger back. "Excuse me?"

The jackalope looks up quickly, realizing what he's hit is *not* the door. Seeing me, he chirps in delight and starts scaling my leg. I heft him onto my shoulder. Malric sighs again, his jowls fluttering, and casts a longing look into my quarters.

"Go on," I say. "Rest. You've been wounded, too."

He's dotted with sticking plasters, yet like me, he's ignoring his injuries, as if—compared to others'—they don't bear notice. Still, he seizes the excuse to lumber into my quarters while I take off with the jackalope.

When I near my mother's quarters, her voice drifts into the hall. "Rowan is twelve. *Twelve*. On her birthday, I told her that makes her a woman. It does not."

"Yes."

"Is that all you're going to say, Ber?"

"What else can be said? You are correct. And it does not matter. Heward wants his family on the throne. Now he can achieve that by simply following clan law. I know you don't want to hear this, Mari, but in amending his demand, the council is being somewhat reasonable."

I swear my mother growls at that. Her shoes click on the stone floor, as if she's pacing. Then she says, "I know they are. They're giving Rowan a chance."

"It's possible the gryphon won't return this winter. If so, she has another year to train. Even if the gryphon does return, she won't have to slay it alone. What we must do now is plan. Send her to train with Wilmot, as Jannah wanted."

"Wilmot hasn't seen Jannah in ten years. He has refused all my summons. He will not train my daughter."

"For Jannah—"

"He will not. Jannah made her choice, and he hates all of us for it."

"I don't think—"

"How is a few months of training going to prepare Rowan? That is a gryphon. Armand died facing one. Jannah died facing one. Both were fully trained adult hunters."

"Jannah did kill one, and so will Rowan. She'll be with me and all the hunters. We will not leave her side. With the proper training and battle planning, we can do this, Mari." He pauses. "Unless you wish to give up your throne to Heward. That's where it will go. Not to his children, but to him. The power of both throne and sword in his hands."

My heart seizes imagining Heward in control of our kingdom. My mother would never complain to me about him, but I hear the stories of how he mistreats the tenants on his lands, overtaxing and overworking them. I've met his staff and seen how they look at him, like whipped dogs fearing their master. Even his adult children flinch when he raises his voice.

My mother cannot interfere with the running of Heward's lands and household. That is forbidden by clan law. But what if *all* of Tamarel becomes his?

Inside, it's gone so quiet that I hear the hands of the clock ticking.

"If . . ." Mom says slowly, quietly. "If that happens—"

"No," I say as I push open the door. "It won't happen. Berinon is right, Mom. I can do this."

Her mouth sets, and I know she's ready to argue, so I hurry on. "Please. Let me train. Allow me to try. Give me time."

"Time . . ." she whispers. Then she straightens. "Yes, I need time, and your training will buy me that."

"I—I don't understand."

She smiles at me. "Boring politics. The sort of thing that never interested you. So we will both do what we do best. You will train, Rowan. You will take action and prepare, while I try to get us out of this ridiculous situation."

She pulls me into a hug. "With any luck, you will never face this gryphon. Instead, you will only be training for your future . . . as the royal monster hunter."

I'm in my brother's room. He's in bed, his leg elevated. I'm curled up on a chair. The jackalope is curled up, too, on my lap, purring. I'm petting him, and the warmth of his body relaxes me. Malric has joined us, watching me like a nursemaid who hates children.

"Maybe I can release Malric," I say. "Send him to the mountains."

"He hasn't been in the mountains since he was a pup," Rhydd says. "Releasing him would be cruel."

"You're right. But maybe I could free him from his duties. Let him go . . . do warg stuff."

"Kill chickens and terrorize villagers?"

I sigh. "It's just . . . he doesn't like me."

Anyone else would lie and say Malric likes me just fine. Thankfully, I don't need to worry about that with Rhydd.

"He tolerates you," my brother says. "Which is more than he does for anyone else. Including me. Jannah may have gifted him to you, but he's with you because he knows . . ."

"That I'm the new royal monster hunter."

Rhydd's gaze drops. He's been told about the switch. I wasn't there for that, and when I see his gaze drop, I know I was right to stay away.

"You don't need to take the sword," he says.

"I know. I want to take it."

He shifts, pushing up on his pillows. "I might be fine. Even if I'm not, a limp won't slow me too much."

"As royal monster hunter, you can't be slowed at *all*."

"I could try—"

"I want this, Rhydd."

He shifts again. "I know, but it feels wrong. Like I've stolen something from you. You should be queen. A ruler, not a servant."

"A queen—or a king—is as much a servant of the people as a royal monster hunter. You'll just get the bigger chair."

I smile, but he fusses with his blankets.

"I'm fine, Rhydd. This is what I want. What I've always wanted. You'll make the better monarch. I'll make . . ."

"The better hunter. You can say that, Ro. We both know it." He nods at the warg. "Malric knows it. Your jackalope knows it. Everyone does. You are Jannah's true heir."

"But can I fight a gryphon? That's the question."

He makes a face. "It'll be years before that. No one's going to expect you to . . ." He catches my expression. "Ro . . . ?"

I tell him what the council has decreed. Before I even

finish, he's scrambling to rise. I accidentally upend the jack-alope as I fly across the room to stop my brother.

"The doctor ordered bed rest," I say. "Get up again and I'll order Malric to keep you there. By lying on you."

"He'd probably smother me. On purpose."

"Well, then, don't make me do it. Stay in bed."

I turn back to my chair to see the jackalope reaching one front paw over the edge . . . and tapping Malric's snout. The warg snaps, bearing teeth as long as the jackalope's entire leg.

I race back and scoop up the jackalope. "Really? Is that my new job? Forget protecting everyone from monsters. I need to save them from their own foolishness." I waggle a finger at my brother. "Stay in bed." Then at the jackalope. "Don't tease the giant death-wolf."

I slump into my chair. The jackalope settles back on my lap but not before chattering at Malric. Then he snuggles in, preening himself, and gives the warg a smug look.

"Oh, believe me, Malric isn't jealous," I say. "He doesn't *want* to be on my lap."

The jackalope keeps preening.

"I know you're changing the subject, Ro," Rhydd says. "But we need to talk about this. You are much better at hunt-ing than me, but killing a gryphon? That's madness. I'm not even sure Heward's son has a chance of success at *his* age."

"Is that the answer, then?" I ask. "Let his son try, knowing he'll fail?"

Rhydd considers and then shakes his head. "No, there's a reason Mom hasn't suggested that. Because Heward will cheat. He'll find a way to make sure his son succeeds. I just can't believe Mom would . . . oh." A smile lights his face. "She's buying time."

"That's what Mom said. For what?"

"To sway the council. Make promises. Negotiate. There are ways—many ways."

"See? This is why you should be king. I had no idea what she meant. The only solution I see is action. Defeat the gryphon. Which I . . ."

I pull my legs up and tighten my grip on the jackalope. "If you'd asked me two days ago, I'd have said I could. But I'd never seen a gryphon. I'd never faced one. Now that I have . . ."

I start to shake. At first, it's just one shiver, but then it won't stop. I'm shaking so hard my teeth chatter. Rhydd pushes up, as if to rise again. When I hurry to stop him, he grabs my hand and tugs me over. The jackalope follows, squeaking in alarm.

"She's okay." Rhydd pulls me into a hug. "She just needs this, whether she wants it or not."

"I—I just have a chill," I say.

"And I'm just warming you up." He gives me another hug and then motions for me to sit on the bed beside him. The jackalope perches on my lap, front feet planted on my chest as he chirps into my face.

"Gotta admit," Rhydd says. "He is kinda adorable."

The jackalope bares his teeth and chatters at Rhydd.

I sputter a laugh. "I think he understands you, and he does not appreciate being called adorable." I pick up the jackalope. "He is a fearsome warrior bunny. Not cute at all."

The jackalope chirps again, as if satisfied.

"No wonder you two get along so well," Rhydd says. "Hey, bunny, watch this." He turns to me. "You are an adorable princess—" I raise my free hand, as if to punch him. He wards me off. "Sorry! I meant, you are a fearsome monster hunter, who happens to also be a princess."

I ease back. "Fierce enough to fight a gryphon, though? That's the question."

"You won't have to. Mom will solve this. In the meantime, you get an adventure." He sits up. "So, let's talk about that. Princess Rowan's great monster-hunter-training adventure. Got your field journal packed yet?"

I scoop up the jackalope and settle in to answer.

CHAPTER TEN

Mom still isn't thrilled about me training with Wilmot. I get the feeling she liked him just fine, once upon a time, but that changed when he left to become a lone monster hunter.

When people in Tamarel have a problem with monsters, they come to the castle for help. If it's a serious problem, the royal monster hunter responds herself, alone or with some of her troop. For the minor cases, a member or two of her troop will answer the call. That's a free service, of course.

But coming to the castle could mean riding for days, and if it's a minor problem, wealthy landowners would rather hire someone. By law, the only people they can hire are retired monster hunters.

There are a few of these retired hunters in Tamarel. Wilmot, however, is different. He quit the troop when he was still a young man. I've heard that Mom wanted to stop him from selling his services. The royal family had raised and trained him, only to have him abandon the troop and become a monster-hunter-for-hire. I can see why Mom wouldn't like that. But if the rumors are right, Jannah begged Mom to make an exception for Wilmot, and she did, for her sister.

Jannah and Wilmot used to be friends, and I don't know what happened between them, but obviously Jannah still thought a lot of him if she wanted me to train under him. So I will.

The question is whether Wilmot will accept me as a student. He's refused all contact from the castle for years. If I show up with a royal entourage, it'll be easy for him to send me home. So I won't. I will take two guards, who will wait for me while I visit the hunter and convince him to come back to train me. This is Berinon's idea. Mom doesn't love it.

She loves it even less when Heward insists my guards wait outside the Dunnian Woods, where Wilmot lives. I must travel the rest of the way alone, as part of my training. The council agrees. It's only a day's walk through the forest, and I'll have Malric with me. After my nighttime ride to join the hunting party, this is an easy test that I'll surely pass. Or so I hope.

"It also makes sense," I say to my mother afterward. "It will be harder for Wilmot to refuse a royal princess if she comes alone, a helpless child . . ."

"No one is going to mistake you for a helpless child," Mom says. "But yes, there is an advantage to going alone. Wilmot will be impressed by your bravery. He may also feel some impulse to watch over you, as Jannah's niece." She inhales. "It'll be fine. Just fine."

I only wish she sounded as if she believed that.

At dawn the next day, Mom and I prepare Jannah's body for her funeral. Family always does this part. Mom says I don't have to, but I insist. The royal monster hunter–elect is supposed to help prepare her predecessor's body as a way of acknowledging the danger of her position. This could be me one day, lying on the ritual slab, being washed by my loved ones, my hair being styled as I wore it in life, my body dressed in my favorite clothing and jewelry. If I'm going to be the royal monster hunter, I need to face this reality. So I do.

I cry a lot, too. I'm not the only one. That's another reason Mom and I do it together, with no help from our maids. We have these moments alone with Jannah and our grief and each other.

Once Jannah's body is prepared, Rhydd and Berinon join us. They bring Malric and Courtois, who nudge and nuzzle Jannah before Malric goes to lie below the slab and Courtois to stand beside it.

Jannah's hunters enter next, and we leave them alone with her. After we return, the palace gates are thrown open for anyone who wants to pay their respects. People have traveled all night to be here and tell us about the time they met Jannah. There's the farmer who had called her to chase off a warg that turned out to be a regular wolf—but she'd told all his neighbors it was a young warg, so he could save face. There's the trader whose daughter snuck off during a trade mission to see a hoop snake, only to find herself chased by a warakin— Jannah rescued the girl, and then found a hoop snake to show her. There's the laborer whose dying wife dreamed of seeing a unicorn, and when Jannah found out, she rode all day to show her Courtois.

I'm still recovering from my wounds and standing all day sets my legs on fire. I refuse to sit, though, even when Berinon threatens to plunk me into a chair. Rhydd stands, too, on his crutch, accepting only a stool for his injured leg. This is important. These are the last memories we'll have of our aunt, these stories from strangers, reminders of the kind of person she was, and the kind of royal monster hunter I want to be.

Dusk comes, and the line of mourners does not end. The law decrees that the ceremony must stop before the sun sets, but Mom waits until the last possible moment before halting the procession and promising to throw open her doors tomorrow to anyone who still wishes to speak to her about Jannah.

The ceremony begins with a new bard's song celebrating the highlights of Jannah's career. I imagine her rolling her eyes and whispering to me the true stories behind these "legendary feats." I swear I hear her voice at my ear, smell the musk of her furs, but then I see her body on the slab and I have to lean on Berinon before I collapse in tears. His arm goes around me, and Rhydd takes my hand, gripping tight, and the rest of the ceremony passes in a blur.

When the songs and the speeches are done, Jannah's hunters take her body into the courtyard, where she's placed on a funeral pyre. Rhydd lays her hunter's pack at her feet. I tuck rolled-up pages at her side, sketches I made of her greatest deeds. Then we pause for one last look at her, dressed in her hunter's garb, the ebony sword at her side.

As Rhydd and I step back, Mom moves forward. Her hands slide under the blade. From the crowd, I hear a sharp intake of breath. I follow it to Heward. He rocks forward, as if to protest. Mom's lips curve in the faintest of smiles.

This is the final funeral rite for a fallen royal monster hunter. One I'd forgotten until this moment. Apparently, so had Heward.

Mom lifts the sword lengthwise over her open palms. She turns to face the throng of subjects. The massive crowd murmurs, like the sighing of wind. She steps toward me and Rhydd. Another sound rises from the crowd, this one a buzz of uncertainty, even discontent.

All eyes fix on Rhydd. Our subjects presume he's still the royal monster hunter—elect. They see him on a crutch, his leg badly injured, and are concerned for their future.

Mom lifts her hands, raising the sword over her head. Then she steps in front of me. She lowers the blade and whispers, "Take it."

I grip the handle, my fingers wrapping around ebony worn smooth from generations of royal monster hunters, wood that feels warm, as if Jannah had just held it herself. I lift the sword as my mother says, "I present Princess Rowan of Tamarel, your future royal monster hunter."

There's a heartbeat of silence that nearly stops my own heart.

Then the crowd erupts in a thunderous cheer.

CHAPTER ELEVEN

We eat a late dinner in Rhydd's quarters. Mother has set out a table by his bedside so that we may still eat as a family on my last night home before I leave. I was supposed to stay home another day, but Mom made a statement giving me that sword. One that Heward is fuming about. She wants me safely away on my quest. I'll leave at dawn.

Berinon joins us, as always. He doesn't dine with us. That would be scandalous. We might consider him family, but there are boundaries we cannot overstep. He stands by my mother's right side, guarding her. He also tests her food. The cooks are always pleased by how much my mother eats. It is a tribute to them . . . and not at all because Berinon devours half.

The maid comes in and refills my mother's cup. After she leaves, Berinon takes a deep drink. When he makes a face, Mother only lifts a brow.

"If it's poisoned, please collapse in that direction." She points behind her. "I'd like to finish enjoying my meal."

He rolls his eyes.

"Yes, I know it's not poisoned," she says. "It's cider, and you'd hoped for mead. Such is the price you pay for being the royal bodyguard and not"—she looks over her shoulder at him—"the royal queen."

"Why did Wilmot leave the monster hunters?" Rhydd asks.

Silence falls. Mom stops, with the cup to her lips. She lowers it and says, "That isn't important."

"I think it is," Rhydd says evenly. "Rowan should understand what she's getting into."

More silence, awkward now. Berinon says, his voice soft, "May I explain, Mari?"

Mom nods.

"As a baby, Wilmot was abandoned in the castle forest," Berinon says. "One of the hunters raised him. Wilmot was a year older than your aunt, and he had a knack for monster hunting, so they were natural training partners. Wilmot, Jannah, your parents and I were all roughly of an age, all friends. Jannah and Wilmot, though, were particularly close."

"It became a romance, didn't it?" Rhydd says. "One that ended badly."

Berinon and my mother glance at one another. Then Berinon nods.

"That's why Jannah said to tell him she was sorry," I murmur.

My mother bristles. "She had nothing to be sorry about. *He* left, and she apologizes to him?"

"We don't know the full story, Mari," Berinon says gently. "But yes, it ended badly, and they were both hurt. That happens sometimes. You should tell Wilmot that Jannah was thinking of him at the end, Rowan. Tell him what she said. That will help win him to your side."

A week ago, I stood in the courtyard and watched my brother leave. Now I'm the one leaving, and he's in the courtyard to see me off. They've fashioned a chair for him, one that leaves his leg straight out. He still tries to stand.

"Sit," I say. "Or I'll call the guards over to hold you down."

"I should go with you. This isn't fair."

"That's what I said when they sent you after the gryphon."

"So you came after me. And I can't do the same for you."

"I'll be fine. I'm just talking to a cranky old hunter. I can handle that." I smile, but my stomach flutters, and I'm glad I didn't eat much for breakfast. I keep telling myself I *can* handle this. I must.

Rhydd grumbles. Then he says, "I'll miss you."

"That's why you get to look after my jackalope. He'll keep you company."

He snorts. "Thanks."

"Would you rather take Malric?"

Rhydd looks at the warg, who turns baleful yellow eyes on him.

"No, thank you," Rhydd says with a shudder. "He'd kill me in my sleep."

"Don't be silly. He wouldn't wait until you're asleep."

"Your highness?" One of my guards appears. "The sun is rising. It's time to go."

As a groom brings my mare, my mother joins us. I hug my brother. Hug my mother. Berinon gets a nod—a public embrace would be "inappropriate" even if only the guards are here to see it. When Berinon helps me onto my horse, though, he squeezes my shoulder and slips a pouch into my pocket.

"A jar of honey for Wilmot," he murmurs. "He's unnaturally fond of it. Tell him I apologize for throttling him."

"Throttle—? What?"

"Never mind." Another squeeze. "It'll be fine. He's a good man."

I'm not dropping the throttling comment that easily. As I start to ask, though, a cry sounds from the castle. A crash, like dropped dishes. The scream of a startled maid. Then a brown blur shoots through the open door.

It's the jackalope. He leaps onto Malric's back. There's a pause as the jackalope looks around, as if unsure where he's landed. Malric glances over his shoulder, lips curling, a growl vibrating through him.

The jackalope squeaks in alarm. As he leaps away, he still manages to thump Malric's head with his hind legs. The warg snaps, but the jackalope is gone—he's vaulted straight onto my mare. He hops onto my shoulders and nestles his front quarters on my head.

"Oh no," I say, reaching for him as everyone laughs. "No, no, no."

He hops down and perches on the pommel instead. Then he leans over the mare's neck, ears perked, nose twitching.

"He says you're ready to go now, my lady," Berinon says. "Apparently, you forgot him. A terrible oversight. But he's fixed it."

"I locked him in his crate. I know I did."

A maid appears, holding the gnawed remains of the crate door.

"He loves you," Rhydd says. "You're his very special monster-hunting princess."

"No, I'm just the person who feeds him."

I reach into my pack and dangle dried meat in front of the jackalope's nose. He rises. I toss it to Berinon, who catches it. Berinon walks over, dangling the meat. The jackalope ignores him. When Berinon reaches to pick him up, the beast hisses.

"Just take him, Ro," Rhydd says. "He might find the perfect den and stay there. I doubt it. In fact, I'd bet a gold coin against it. But you never know."

"Fine," I say. "But if he falls off, I'm not going back for him." I lean down. "Hear that, bunny?"

He squeaks and digs his claws into the saddle. I prod the horse forward, and we're off.

CHAPTER TWELVE

It takes three days to reach the edge of the Dunnian Woods. That's where my guards must make camp and wait for me.

I venture in with only my pack, a map, Malric and my jackalope. I can't even take my mare—the woods are too thick for riding. This is the mountain foothills again, much farther north than we went for the gryphon. Wilmot lives out here, among the monsters. To hire him, you either have to venture into this dark forest or leave a message at the nearest village.

I'm okay walking in the forest alone because I'm not really alone. I have my fierce and terrible warg companion, who loves me and will protect me against all dangers. Okay, he doesn't love me . . . or like me very much. I'm not even sure about the protecting part. He walks ten paces ahead, and I tell myself he's clearing the way, making sure it's safe, but I can't help wondering if he's keeping his distance in hopes that if something does attack me, he can pretend he didn't notice.

What? The princess was devoured by a pack of ravenous wara-kins? But she was right behind me, and I never heard a thing. Weird.

Rhydd is correct that Malric tolerates me, and that's more than he does for most people. But I want more. We've been together since Jannah's death, a week now. I've made sure he has a warm bed at night. I've brought him the best food. I've taken him into the castle forest, where he can run and hunt. I even tried to scratch behind his ears. That last one didn't go so well. I still have all my fingers, though, so that's something.

I'm good with beasts. Everyone says so. I'm kind to them, and they are kind in return. All except Malric. Well, and Courtois, but he's a unicorn, and if he was nice, I'd wonder whether he'd been hit in the head.

Mom said that Malric is grieving, just like us. I under-stand that, but I still want to see *something*. Some sign that he's not wishing he could take off into the woods and never come back. And as I'm thinking that, the jackalope takes off into the woods . . . and does not come back.

It's not the first time the jackalope has bounded away, investigating a scent or chasing a mouse or doing jackalope things. Before, though, as soon as I'd start worrying about him, he'd zoom back and climb up to rest on my head, and I'd grumble about that, if only to hide my relief at his return. This time, he does not come back.

After about a half hour, I start to worry. What if he's in trouble? He *is* still a baby. I should go look for him. Unless he's just decided he's done with me. The thought stings more than I expected.

That's when a cry pierces the air. The jackalope's alarm call.

I barrel into the forest as I draw my sword. Malric snarls and wheels to block my path. I growl, "Get out of my way," my gaze locked on the warg's.

Malric lowers his head and growls back. I sidestep to pass him. He pivots, yellow eyes following me, but he doesn't move. When I break into a run, though, he catches my tunic in his teeth.

Slow down. That's what he's saying. *Proceed with caution.*

Malric's right, but my mind runs through the glossary of forest monsters big enough to eat a baby jackalope. The cry seems to come from above. A memory flashes—the gryphon with me in its talons—and my stomach rolls over.

No, the forest is too dense for a gryphon.

Which still means the jackalope could have been seized by a wyvern or a phoenix or a—

Stop. Just stop.

I hear Jannah's voice in my head.

When it comes to potential monsters, acknowledge the possibilities, but don't let them overwhelm you. Be aware. Be prepared. Then move forward. Always move forward.

As I follow the call, I realize I'm running uphill. That's why the jackalope seems to be calling from overhead.

His cry comes again. Two sharp bursts followed by two hollow ones, almost like echoes.

I burst out of the woods into a clearing. We're near the top of a rocky foothill, and I don't see any sign of—

Another cry, definitely followed by an echo. Ahead lies the dark opening of a cave.

Some beast has carried the jackalope into its den.

As I grip the sword, my hands tremble. I can fight off a wild dog or even a wolf. A warakin, maybe. A warg?

I glance over at the one with me. Having Malric here means I *can* fight whatever is in this cave. We'll do it together.

The cave entrance is only waist-high. I crouch to peer in, but it's pitch black. The sun is dropping, shadows swallowing that entrance. I could take out my lantern, but that would mean sheathing my sword.

I slide one hand off the hilt, but only to let my pack fall. It hits the ground with a thump. The cave stays silent. I grip the sword again, take a slow step forward and—

Another thump. This one sounds beside me. It's Malric. He's plunked himself down, as if settling in for a rest. I motion that we're going after the jackalope. He sniffs and lays his head on his paws. I glower, and I swear the beast rolls his eyes.

Okay, so apparently, *we* are not going after the jackalope. I'm doing it alone.

I glare at Malric. He closes his eyes. I swallow again and then fix my attention on the cave entrance, take one step . . .

The jackalope hops into view. I exhale in a long shuddering breath. Then I sheath my sword and reach to snatch him up before whatever is in the cave—

The jackalope hops back inside.

"No!" I shout.

I dive for him before I realize what I'm doing. I hit the ground just inside the entrance. From deep within comes a noise, and I slowly lift my head to see . . .

The jackalope. That's all. The jackalope sits in a shallow and otherwise empty cave. He turns around and, with his powerful hind legs, kicks dried leaves onto a pile. Then he picks up a tuft of old fur and places it with the leaves. He head-butts everything into place and looks at me expectantly. When I don't react, he hops onto the pile and turns around twice, like a dog getting comfortable. Then he squeaks at me.

"A nest," I say. "You've found a den and made a nest." What I'd mistaken for an alarm cry had been a simple alert cry instead. Malric had known that.

I look out at the warg and see the lengthening shadows behind him.

Twilight is coming. Twilight . . . when the monsters hunt.

I was supposed to be at Wilmot's by now. That was the plan. I entered the forest at dawn, giving me all day to walk, so I'd be at Wilmot's before the sun went down.

It can't be much farther. Maybe I can still make it.

I crawl from the cave, ignoring the jackalope's squeaks. I shade my eyes against the falling sun and squint down the hill. There's no sign of a house. No smoke rising from a chimney.

I pull out my map and run my finger along the route. I've traveled only three-quarters of the way.

Was I walking too slowly? Did I stop too long to eat? I recall a pause to sketch a hoop snake that crossed our path. And a brief detour when I heard a waterfall. And then there were the times when the jackalope scampered off, and I slowed so he could find us again.

Maybe I can still make it if we run.

I wander past Malric, still considering. He growls. When I take another step, he's on his feet, lunging into my path. He jerks his muzzle at the cave. Telling me that the jackalope is right. As much as I don't want to stay the night here, I'm safer in that cave than wandering in the twilight when the monsters come out.

I grab my pack and take it into the cave. Arriving at Wilmot's will have to wait another day.

CHAPTER THIRTEEN

After I've eaten, I fall into a fitful sleep, and when I hear thunder, I wake just enough to scoot farther into the cave before the rain comes. The jackalope snuggles up with me, and the beat of his heart starts lulling me back into slumber. I can still hear the thunder rolling toward us.

The sound grows louder and louder. Then it stops.

The thunder stops, but I still feel it in the ground, vibrating beneath me. It's a steady, rolling noiseless thunder. I manage to open one sleepy eye and see only darkness. I can't smell or hear rain, but it must be coming, so I huddle under the blanket and close my eyes.

The thunder stops, and sleep tugs at me again. I'm drifting off when a smell wafts past. It's faint, but familiar. A light musk mingled with something sweet. It's a nice smell, a comforting one and yet . . .

A sudden gust of wind hits my face. Warm wind, carrying that sweet smell.

Did I break Wilmot's honey jar? I try to open my eyes to check, but I'm too tired. I'll check in the morning. The storm is gone, and everything is fine and—

Another blast of warm air. I open one eye to see yellow. A brilliant yellow orb, shot through with brown. An amber jewel with a rich brown center. Almost like . . .

Skin slides over the orb.

I'm looking into a giant amber eye.

The head pulls back, filling the cave entrance. I see an eagle's head. No, a *gryphon's* head, its beak opening, coming straight for me—

I startle awake, my limbs flailing, the jackalope flying off my lap. I leap up . . . and smack my head against stone. I scramble out of the cave as I pull my sword, ready to face . . .

Nothing. There's nothing there. Just Malric, rising and glowering at me for disturbing his sleep. Just the jackalope, chattering at my feet, confused and concerned.

Nightmare.

I had a nightmare.

A droplet of water plops onto my nose, and I jump again. I look around to see that everything's wet. Distant thunder rolls past. That's what I heard in my sleep. Real thunder from a real storm, which sparked memories of the gryphon.

Still, even knowing it was a nightmare, I can't relax my grip on my sword. I back into the cave and lower myself to the ground, my eyes wide, ears straining.

The jackalope squeaks and hops onto my lap. As he

nestles down, I stroke his fur, and I am grateful for him. For the warmth of him. For his little squeaks that sound like reassurance and sympathy.

It's still dark out. So dark and so quiet that I want to cry, grab the jackalope and run all the way back to my guards and say, "I can't do this."

I'm scared. I'm scared of everything right now, and I hate it. I'm the girl who charges into danger, not the one who huddles in a cave, trying not to cry.

Jannah is gone. Dead. I will never see my aunt again, and I loved her so much. I'm not sure I ever told her that. Even at the end, I was so busy listening to her words that I never said my own.

I didn't tell my mother that I loved her before I left. I never do that. Rhydd does, but I don't. I figure she knows.

I didn't tell her. I didn't tell Rhydd. I didn't tell Berinon.

I love you, and if I don't come back, I want you to know that.

If I don't come back . . .

I swipe away a falling tear. Now I'm being silly. There's no gryphon here. It was a nightmare. Of course I'll come back.

I just might not come back with Wilmot. He could refuse me. And then what? Who'll train me?

What if Mom can't fix this and I *do* need to fight the gryphon or we'll lose our kingdom to Heward?

I'm twelve! How does anyone expect a twelve-year-old to fight a gryphon?

They don't. That's the point. Even my mother knows I can't fight a gryphon, so she's frantically trying to fix this so I don't have to.

No one expects that I can do this.

But I need to believe I can. Jannah always said that's the most important thing for a warrior. You must believe you can do it. My father said the same thing. Confidence will take you far.

It can also get you killed, Dad. Get you rushing into a fight you can't win.

Even as I think that, a little voice inside me whispers, *But isn't this what you wanted? To be the royal monster hunter?*

Tears fill my eyes, and I try to blink them back, but they spill down my cheeks.

My aunt is dead. My brother injured. The entire kingdom at risk. But I get to be the royal monster hunter. Exactly what I wanted, what I dreamed of, what I wished for.

Not like this. I did not want it like this.

I fall back against the cave wall and slump to the floor as I sob. The jackalope licks my tears, as if to remind me I'm not alone. I pat his head, and I am, again, grateful for him. Yes, I'm not alone here. I have the jackalope and I have . . .

I look over at Malric. The warg lies outside the cave, his massive head on his paws. He's still glowering from being woken up. Glowering as if to say I'd better not do that again.

Rhydd says Malric doesn't hate me. Yet on this trip, I've seen the warg watching me like this, and I *feel* hated. As if he blames me for Jannah's death. She's gone, and he's stuck with me, and he hates me for it.

I'm a weak little girl who jumps at nightmares. The girl who let *his* monster hunter die. I am unworthy of the ebony sword. Unworthy of him.

Before we went to bed, Malric caught his dinner. A rabbit, which I thought was kind of rude, with the jackalope right there. Malric often hunted on trips with Jannah. He'd bring back his catch, and she'd cook it, take a little for her own dinner, and give the rest to him. So I'd thought that's what he was doing, and I was pleased. I went to take the rabbit . . . and he growled at me. Actually growled at me.

I decided he just didn't understand my intentions. He thought I was stealing his meal. So I laid a fire, letting him see why I wanted the rabbit. When I tried to take it again, he snapped at my hand. Then he took his dinner and retreated to the forest to eat it. Alone.

I wasn't even worthy of sharing Malric's meal. Or *cooking* it for him.

I can't fall back to sleep. By the time the first dawn light seeps into the darkness, Malric's dozing so soundly that he's snoring. The jackalope is, too, his antler prongs twitching with each exhale.

I'm lying on my side, with the jackalope snuggled against my stomach. I ease away, and he shivers, but when I push my blanket closer to him he relaxes and purrs.

I take soap from my pack and head down the foothill to a stream I'd seen earlier. I'm hoping to bathe, but as soon as I draw near, I see the stream is still spring-swollen from mountain run-off, water running fast. I'll wash my hair at the edge. I haven't cleaned it since I left the castle four days ago, and it feels disgusting.

I wash my hair carefully on the bank. When it's done, I flip it back, hearing it slap against my tunic. A noise sounds across the water. I look over to see a deer. A regular deer—a beautiful young doe who came to the stream to drink. When I threw back my hair, it startled her, and she's staring at me, water dripping from her chin. I pause to watch her. And I smile, because it doesn't matter if she isn't a rare monster. Standing there, with the sun rising behind her, she is beautiful.

That's when something hits the back of my head. *Lands* on it. I twist to see brown fur and creamy antlers. A squeak that tells me I haven't been attacked by a monster. Well, I have, but it's only the blasted jackalope.

He must have woken alone and come running, following my scent trail. Seeing me, he took a flying leap at my head. Now he's falling, squealing in panic. I twist to catch him before he tumbles into the stream, but I move too fast. I'm already off-balance from him landing on my head, and when I grab him, I start to fall.

I throw him onto the bank and grab for a rock. My left hand doesn't find one. My right does, but it touches down on a wet, mossy stone. Before I can get a grip, my fingers slide off, and I tumble into the stream.

CHAPTER FOURTEEN

The stream is fast-moving, but the spot I chose for washing is shallow. I'm very pleased with myself for thinking about it beforehand. I'll be fine. Just fine.

The current tosses me, but I manage to get onto all fours. Meanwhile, the jackalope goes crazy on the bank, tearing about and screeching his alert call.

"I'm fine," I shout to him. "Just hold on."

The water isn't even knee deep. I push to my feet and walk slowly. I lift one foot and—

It's wedged under a rock. When I try to free it, I slip and the current grabs me. The next thing I know, I'm on my back with the water rushing over me. My foot's trapped, and water rushes over my face like someone's dragging me backward against the current. I sputter and gag. Water fills my nose and mouth, and I can't breathe.

I can't breathe.

I escaped a gryphon, and I'm going to drown in knee-deep water.

I kick wildly. My foot flies free and I tumble downstream so fast I can't even flip over. My back scrapes over rocks as I spin.

Sputtering and blinking, I spot an overhanging branch.

The branch rushes at me full speed, about to whip past over my head. I reach up and my fingers skim the leaves. One hand smacks solid wood. I grab the branch and I hang there, my body caught in the current and being dragged downstream. I grit my teeth and stretch my other hand up. Water blinds me, and I fumble around. Then my fingers find the branch.

Holding it with both hands, I inch toward shore. One hand slips. I flail, and the current grabs me, ripping the branch from my hand. I drop backward . . . right onto the shore.

My legs rest on the ground, but my upper body still lies in a shallow pool, water spraying my face. I resist the urge to scramble onto land, and I catch my breath first.

When a growl ripples over, I freeze. It comes from behind my right shoulder. I twist, but wet curls plaster my face. I blink and see a familiar form. Blurry but familiar.

"Malric," I say, the word coming in an exhale of relief.

He growls again, his head lowered.

I roll onto the shore. "Yes, yes, I've gotten myself into a terrible mess. Again. But I'm fine."

I flip my hair back as I sit up. "Let's get back to camp—"

I stop as I look over to see . . . *not* Malric. I jump to my feet, hand reaching for my sword, only to realize it's back in the cave where I slept. All I have is my dagger.

The beast lunges. I spin out of its way. My foot hits sand, and I nearly skid into the water. I manage to right myself and back up fast with my dagger raised.

The creature in front of me has a canine body, hunched shoulders and a sloping back. Its fur is reddish-brown with yellow stripes. It has the face of a wild dog and the snout of a boar. A boar's tusks, too. Sharp, deadly tusks.

Warakin.

The beast charges. I dodge—away from the stream this time. I brandish my dagger at the beast, but it pays no attention. I don't blame it. While a warakin isn't as big as a warg, it's larger than a wolf, and it's not at all afraid of a girl waving a blade shorter than its tusks.

So we dance. It charges. I spin out of the way. Charge. Spin. As I move, ducking and dodging, I keep glancing at the stream. I'd be safe in the water. Safe from the warakin. Not safe from that fast-running current.

I see rocks, though. Three big stones cross the stream like lily pads.

The next time the warakin charges, I wait until the last second before dodging. Then I keep running for that first rock. I just need to jump—

Something hits my arm and knocks me off balance. As I stumble, I see an arrow lodged in my sleeve. Where—?

Forget the arrow. There's a warakin running straight at me. I dive to the side and hit the ground in a roll. I'm leaping up when another arrow whizzes past. It hits the warakin in the shoulder. The beast squeals in rage.

"Tree!" a voice shouts.

The warakin rushes at me. I try to dodge, but a bush blocks my way. Instead, I vault over the beast and run.

"Get in the tree!" Running footsteps accompany the voice.

I scramble to a stop. The warakin is right there, its nostrils flaring. I raise my dagger, ready to jab—

A figure bursts through the undergrowth, running at the warakin. The beast swings toward it . . . and the figure leaps the beast like a hurdle, landing on its feet. *His* feet. It's a boy, holding a bow.

"Get in the tree!" he snarls at me.

I see the arrow on the ground—the one that fell out of my sleeve. I grab it. When the warakin charges, I jab it in the shoulder as I spin out of the way. The beast lunges at me. I jab it again.

The boy yells dire warnings of doom. *Angry* warnings. Which is a little annoying. I'm fending off a warakin with a dagger, an arrowhead and fancy footwork. He should be impressed. Instead he's yelling at me like I'm a village child, frozen in terror, about to be gored by the beast's tusks.

"Get out of the way!" he shouts as I dive *away* from the warakin.

The warakin snorts, growing winded. It's bleeding from a half dozen cuts. When it charges again, it's more of a lurch. I lift the arrowhead, and the beast stops short. It looks from me to the arrow, as if considering the odds of goring me versus the odds of adding to its patchwork of shallow cuts.

The beast paws the ground. I brandish the arrowhead in one hand and my dagger in the other.

The warakin looks to the side, ready to bolt, needing only a little incentive. I lunge, yelling, "Hie!"

The warakin takes off . . . just as the boy fires another arrow. While the warakin crashes through the forest, I straighten and prepare to receive at least a grudging show of admiration.

The poor boy can't even seem to form words. Shocked and overwhelmed. I don't blame him. A warakin encounter is a frightening thing.

"What was *that?*" he finally sputters.

"A warakin. It's—"

"I know what a warakin is. You drove it off."

"Yes. The thing to remember about warakins is that they have a low pain tolerance—"

"I was trying to kill it, and you drove it off."

"Killing it was unnecessary," I say, channeling Jannah. "Most monsters can be frightened away, and that is always the preferred outcome."

His face goes bright red. With embarrassment, I think, and I'm about to tell him there's no need for that. But when he speaks, it's through teeth clenched in anger. "I saved your life, and this is how you repay me? Driving off my prey?"

"Saved my life?" I say. "I wasn't *in* any danger until you showed up. I was escaping across the stream."

"It looks like you already fell in it."

"I went swimming."

"In your clothing?" Before I can answer, he stiffens, pulling another arrow from his quiver. "Step away from the stream."

"What—?"

Something crashes through the water behind me. I turn, and this time it is, undoubtedly, Malric.

"Finally," I say. "How long did it take you to realize—"

"*That is a warg*," the boy says, enunciating each word.

"Well, of course it is. Wolves don't grow that big."

"Step away—"

"It's fine. He's my companion. Just don't make any sudden moves. And don't pet him. If you value all your fingers, do *not* even try to pet—"

The boy lunges between me and the warg, bow strung. Malric leaps onto the shore and lowers his head, growling.

"Stop," I say. "Both of you. That's *my* warg. He's—"

The boy pulls back his bowstring. I race between them and throw myself onto Malric, knocking him to the ground and shielding him with my body. Then I twist to ward off the boy, but he's stopped there, staring at me lying on the warg. He blinks.

Then he says, his voice low, "Move slowly. You've caught him off guard, and if you move slowly—"

"He's with me."

"You've eaten something in the forest, haven't you? It's clouded your mind."

"His name is Malric." I steel myself, reach out and carefully pat the warg's head. I'm ready to yank my hand away, but the beast tolerates it, eyes only narrowing. I keep patting him. "Good warg. What a good warg."

I rise and motion for Malric to rise with me. To my surprise, he does. Then he stands beside me, pressed up against my hip. I rest my hand on his head, which is kind of awkward when it nearly reaches my shoulder.

As the boy stares at us, I get my first good look at him. He's about my age. Rhydd's height. A slighter build. Hair that looks nearly black, straighter than ours and longer than Rhydd's. Dark eyes, too. His skin is a deeper shade of brown. He's dressed like a woodsman, in trousers and a tunic and tall boots, with his hair drawn back at the nape of his neck. He carries a bow on his back and a dagger at his hip. Clearly a boy ready to face whatever dangers the Dunnian Woods might offer.

He opens his mouth to speak again, but he's cut short by a frantic squeaking from the other side of the stream. It's the jackalope, racing back and forth along the shore.

The boy squints at the tiny beast. "What is that?"

"Jackalope."

He shakes his head. "Jackalopes have antlers, and they're much bigger."

I walk to the stream and hop onto the first lily-pad rock.

"Wait!" the boy says. "Don't get so close. I think it's a diseased rabbit." His footsteps thump behind me. "See those growths on its head?"

"It's a baby jackalope."

The jackalope leaps onto the first rock . . . and starts to slip off it. I hurry across and put out my arms, and he leaps into them.

I turn to the boy and hold it out. "*My* jackalope."

As I hop back to shore, the boy's eyes narrow, like Malric's did earlier. "*Your* jackalope."

"Yes."

"What's his name then?"

"Jacka—" I stop and struggle for an idea.

"Jacko?"

"Uh . . . yes," I say. "His name is Jacko."

"You named your jackalope Jacko? That might be the dumbest thing I have ever heard."

I lift my chin. "I like it. So does he. Don't you, ja... Jacko?"

The jackalope climbs onto my shoulder and does his head-perch thing. The boy looks from the jackalope to me to Malric. Then he takes a slow step back.

"You're a witch," he says.

I sigh. "There is no such thing as witches. They're the product of overactive imaginations and limited educations."

His face turns a weird shade of red as he sputters, "Excuse me?"

"My mother says that when people lack a firm understanding of sciences, they find alternate explanations for unusual occurrences. That is the basis of superstition." I pause. "I hope that isn't why you were pursuing the warakin. Its tusks don't actually cure indigestion."

"I know that," he snaps.

"Well, when you accuse me of being a witch, I have to wonder. There is no such thing as witches. Monsters are made by nature, not magic."

His face darkens. "I am well versed in the *science* of monsters."

"Are you? Because I just caught you trying to slaughter a warakin who could easily be scared back to the mountains."

"That warakin has been *slaughtering* livestock since the last snowfall. I was hired to kill it."

"You took a bounty on a warakin?" I look around. "Be careful. There's a master hunter who lives in these woods, and he would not appreciate a boy taking his business."

"I—" He shuts his mouth and glares at me. "That is not

— 112 —

your concern. Your concern is that you robbed me of that bounty. I've been tracking that warakin for three days. You owe me two silver."

I pluck at my wet clothes. "Does it look like I'm hiding two silver?"

His gaze drops to my side. "That dagger is worth at least as much."

"Would you like it?" I ask.

His gaze is fixed on the dagger, eyes glittering like a raven spotting a shiny coin. I turn it over in my hands, showing off the fine workmanship. He doesn't exactly drool, but he looks close to it.

I wrap my fingers around the handle and brandish the blade. "Then come get it."

Jacko plunges between us, chattering and gnashing his teeth.

The boy looks at the jackalope. Then at me. "You're kidding, right?"

"Don't fight my jackalope."

"I'm not going to hurt—"

"That was a warning, not a request. He's been trained in eye-gouging."

The boy starts to snort a laugh. Then he looks at Jacko, who is waving his antler prongs. He stops laughing.

"If you want the dagger, you must take it from me. I will ask my beasts to stand down."

"I'm not going to hurt a girl."

"Oh, please. Just *try* to hurt me. And before you do, remember which of us wounded that warakin and sent it running, while soaking wet and armed only with a dagger and an arrow—an arrow you misfired."

"I didn't misfire—"

"So you were aiming at *me?*"

He scowls. "Maybe. And I won't take your dagger. I'm not a thief. I am an honest hunter."

"Excellent. Then you will honestly admit that *you* lost your prey. Now, I have a journey to resume, and I'm sure you have things to do. Like explaining to your client that you have successfully driven off the warakin and, if it does not return in a fortnight, you would like your two silver."

With Malric following, I step onto the first stream rock. I turn and put my arms out for the jackalope. He runs and leaps into them.

As I step to the next rock, the boy calls, "Well, I'm glad to see you don't let it *ride* on your head. That looked completely ridiculous."

I face him. Then I lift Jacko to my shoulders. He settles onto my head. I lift my chin, step onto the other bank, and walk away.

CHAPTER FIFTEEN

I'll need to speak to Wilmot about the boy in the woods. Monster hunting is a dangerous sport, not a way to make a few extra coins. I'm still a royal princess, and I must look after my subjects.

I find the cave where we slept and retrieve my sword and pack. Then I set out along the stream. When the sun is straight overhead, I begin to see landmarks that'll lead me to Wilmot's cabin.

Past a bend in the stream, I spot a wooden cottage, a little smaller than a village home. Outside, a man tends chickens. When I draw nearer, I realize they're young basans, already the size of regular fowl. The birds are red and black, with bright red combs. The legends say they spit cold fire. That's not true, of course. Instead, they spit a mist-like venom that causes mild burns. They also lay eggs. Big, red, delicious eggs.

The man tending them must be Wilmot. My grandparents figured his family came from over the mountains because his skin was so much lighter than ours. His hair is light, too—the color of hay, as Berinon had described it.

I ask Malric to wait at the forest edge. Then I place Jacko on the ground a few feet from the warg. When the jackalope hops after me, I bend and firmly whisper for him to stay. I take another step . . . and he hops to catch up. So does Malric.

Well, the warg doesn't hop, though that'd be funny. Malric walks over and plunks one giant paw on the jackalope, who squeaks. Then the warg grunts, as if saying to me, "Well, go on."

I approach Wilmot, who is still bent over the basan coop with his back to me. As I walk, I brace myself. Berinon has warned that Wilmot is neither warm nor friendly.

I swear the only time I ever saw him smile was for Jannah.

I stop a few feet back, take a deep breath and say, "Wilmot."

He turns. There's a bandage on his left temple, his hair flopping over it. The bandage droops over his eye, but the other one peers at me, bright blue. I steel myself for him to snap and demand to know who I am.

Instead, he peers at me. He tucks the bandage away from his eye. Then his face lights in a smile as he rises.

"Jannah."

I blink. People say I resemble my aunt when she was a girl, but it's impossible to mistake me for a grown woman.

"You're late," he says. "The sun will set soon, and the master archer is waiting."

"I'm . . . not Jannah."

He rolls his eyes. "I know you hate archery, Jani, but you

aren't ducking a lesson that easily. The master won't mistake you for Mari again. Not dressed like . . ." He studies me. "You're filthy. Have you been in the forest all day? Avoiding your studies?"

I open my mouth.

He waves off my reply. "No matter. I'm supposed to bring you to the master and join your archery lesson. Not that I need the practice."

He smiles when he says that, his blue eyes dancing. Then he waits, and his brow begins to furrow.

"Are you all right, Jani?" he asks. "Since you missed the opportunity to insult my archery, then you must be unwell."

He's mistaking me for Jannah. Not the adult Jannah, but the child he knew.

I know when people age, they can get confused. Elderly villagers have mistaken me for my aunt. But Wilmot isn't elderly. Berinon said he's a year older than Jannah, which makes him thirty-three.

My gaze goes to that bandage on his temple. Last year, when a blow knocked Rhydd out, he'd woken asking for Dad, and he'd been confused all day.

Wilmot is smiling, relaxed and pleased to see me. I expected a fight. An argument. Instead, the best monster hunter in Tamarel is waiting for me to come train with him. If he thinks I'm Jannah, is it wrong to take advantage?

"Archery sounds good," I say, "but the master is busy. Would you give me a lesson?"

His eyes narrow. "You aren't Jannah, are you?"

My stomach chills. "I—"

"I'm teasing. I'm just surprised you're actually admitting I'm the better archer. It's about time. Now, where's your bow?"

"I . . . forgot it?"

He sighs. "As usual. Grab one inside, and we'll begin."

I get two steps toward the cabin before someone shouts, "Hey!"

I turn to see the boy from earlier running toward me. My hand drops to my sword, and I back up toward Wilmot to protect the injured man.

"What are *you* doing here?" the boy demands as he slows.

"I could ask you the same thing."

"I live here."

I glance back at Wilmot. His brows knit in confusion. He's been injured, and this boy is taking advantage of that. Pretending to know him—

"Dain," Wilmot says. "Where have you been?"

"Tracking that—" He shakes his head. "Never mind." He turns to me. "I don't know who you are but—"

"This is Jannah," Wilmot says.

Dain's face screws up.

"Jannah of Clan Dacre," Wilmot says. "The girl I told you about. The one who'll hold the ebony sword someday."

"Yes, you've told me lots about Jannah," Dain says, his voice tight. "This isn't her, Wilmot. You—"

A low growl sounds behind Dain. He turns to see Malric, and his hand moves to his dagger.

Before I can leap forward to protect the warg, Wilmot says, "Malric?"

He turns to me. "It *is* Malric, isn't it? I recognize the blaze on his head, but he's grown so much. The last time I saw him he was a pup."

Bushes crackle as the jackalope comes running. Jacko leaps, and I catch him, and Wilmot laughs.

"Taming jackalopes now, Jani?" he says. "When did this happen?"

Before I can answer, he looks at Malric and shakes his head and then touches the bandage by his eye. "I'm confused again, aren't I? Never mind. Dain, take Jannah—"

"This isn't Jannah, Wilmot."

"Did she tell you she's Mariela?" Wilmot sighs. "She does that sometimes. Anyone who knows them can tell the difference. If you can't, just look for the dirt. Jannah is always out scrapping or riding or tearing off on a grand adventure. If she drags her poor sister along, at least Mariela cleans up afterward." He nods at me. "This is not Mariela."

"I'd like to speak to her," Dain says.

Wilmot nods and heads for the house. "Do that. I'll get the bows. You could use some practice, too."

Once Wilmot goes inside, Dain grabs for my arm. Malric snarls, and Jacko gnashes his teeth.

Dain lowers his hand and motions for me to follow him. I do. He waits until we're away from the cottage. Then he spins on me.

"He is injured," he says. "Can you not tell that? Coming here and telling him you're Jannah—"

"I told him I *wasn't*. I'm—"

"Princess Rowan." He waves at my sword. "That gives it away, which is why you hid it earlier."

"I didn't hide anything. I don't bathe with my sword."

"In these woods, you should do *nothing* without that sword. And you shouldn't misrepresent yourself, princess."

"How did I misrepresent myself? I knew how to handle a warakin. I have a warg and a jackalope. Clearly I'm Clan Dacre. You saw all that and decided I'm a witch. The ridiculous answer instead of the obvious one."

"I didn't expect to find a *princess* wandering the forest alone."

"I'm not alone. I have my warg and jackalope. And guards wait for me at the forest edge."

"Where's your brother? Your aunt?"

When I struggle to answer that, Dain's eyes narrow. "You haven't run away, have you? Please don't tell me you came here to reunite your aunt and Wilmot. A silly girl with silly, romantic—"

"Jannah is dead."

That stops him. He studies my expression as if I might be making a horrible joke. When he sees I'm not, he gives a gruff, "My condolences."

"Thank you."

He shifts his weight and looks over his shoulder. "If you came to tell him, it'll have to wait. He wouldn't understand."

"What happened? Is it the blow to the head?"

His face gathers in a scowl. "A blasted pegasus. There's a meadow to the north of here. I don't know if the beast is orphaned or lost, but there's a young pegasus filly there. Wilmot tried to capture her. To help her. And she kicked him for his trouble. She could have killed him. Instead, the blow addled his mind." He straightens. "But it's temporary. It happened only last month, and at first, he didn't even know who I was. So he's been getting better. It's just all . . ."

"Muddled," I say. "The past and the present."

He nods. Then he says, "What happened to your aunt?"

"A gryphon."

"Gryphon? Isn't that what killed . . . ?"

"My father, yes. A gryphon killed my dad, and then Jannah killed it. Now one has killed her . . . and I must kill it."

He stares at me. Then he says, "I hope that's a joke. Tell me you did *not* run away from the castle to get Wilmot's help on this fool's quest."

"No, my mother sent me here—"

"To get Wilmot's help killing a gryphon? Are you nuts? Are you *all* nuts? Your father *died* fighting a gryphon. Now your aunt has. Wilmot says they were both incredible hunters. And now *you're* going to fight one?"

I could say that I might not have to—that the gryphon might not return or Mom might find another solution—but that won't convince him I need training. So I say, "I don't have a choice."

He looks off to the side for a moment. When he answers, his voice is softer, gentle even. "If your mother sent you on this mission, then you need to speak to the council. In her grief, her mind's as muddled as Wilmot's. You aren't even the hunter-elect. That's your brother. You're meant to be queen."

"Not anymore. My brother was injured. He'll be king. I'll wield the ebony sword. But only if I kill the gryphon when it returns. Otherwise, Heward will give his children the throne and the sword, and rule through them. He'd be a tyrant. He doesn't care about anyone but himself."

"Then your mother needs to find another way to keep her throne. You can't kill a gryphon. I've been training under Wilmot for five years now. While I may not have Clan Dacre blood, Wilmot says I'm a natural hunter."

"Okay, so—"

"That isn't bragging, princess. I'm making a point. Six months ago, a young gryphon was sighted just off the mountain. I wanted to go after it, and Wilmot locked me in the cabin until the beast was long gone. If he wouldn't let me face a young gryphon, there's no way you can fight a full-grown one."

Time to change my tactics and admit the truth. "My mother hopes I won't need to. She's working on that. In the meantime, though, I must train. That's why she sent me here. To train with Wilmot. You could help. You say his mind is improving. Help me train with him while we convince him I'm not Jannah." I meet his gaze. "Your kingdom needs you."

I expect that last part to sway him. When I say the words, though, his face darkens.

"You want me to help my kingdom?" he says. "Of course. Because it has helped *me* so much. My parents lost their farm when they couldn't pay their taxes, princess."

"What? No. We don't—"

"The Crown took our farm, and I was sold into servitude. I'd barely begun school, and instead I was sent off to work as a rat catcher. If it wasn't for Wilmot, I'd still be chasing rodents and hoping to buy my freedom before I died of disease."

"That's—that's not right. We don't take homes for taxes, and we don't allow indentured servitude."

"Are you calling my parents liars?"

I almost say yes. Luckily, I stop myself. I don't know what happened here, but I can't accuse his family of lying.

He leans toward me. "Go away, little princess. Solve this problem yourself. Wilmot doesn't need your kind of trouble . . . and neither do I."

CHAPTER SIXTEEN

It's midday, and I'm sitting on the forest floor, leaning against a tree. Jacko is stretched over my lap. Malric lies with his rear end toward me. Turning his back on me, disgusted by my failure.

I want my brother. I miss my mother, too, and Berinon, and I don't even dare think of how much I miss Jannah and Dad, or I'll collapse into a puddle of blubbering tears. Right now, though, it's Rhydd I miss the most. We've been together since before we were born, and we've never been separated for more than a night. In the last four days, I've wanted him by my side, but I haven't *needed* him there. I need him now.

I've messed this all up, and I don't know how to fix it. Wilmot's injured, and there's this boy who hates me, and I don't know what to do next. I want to talk to Rhydd. I want his advice, but I also want *him*, because I'm scared and I'm trying not to freak out.

Jannah told me to get Wilmot's help. Those were her dying words. Get his help, and tell him she's sorry. I couldn't do either. I failed my aunt, and I failed Mom, too. If I couldn't even manage this first task, how am I ever going to become the royal monster hunter?

I huddle beside that tree, face buried against my knees, head whirling with panic . . . and that is not going to help at all. None of it helps. I can't wish my brother into appearing and telling me it'll be okay. I need to do that myself. I need to make it okay. Stop panicking and think.

So this boy, Dain, hates me. For good reason, given what he believes my mother did. I know she didn't—I was training to be queen, so I understand our laws and how we govern.

I'm sure his family *did* lose their farm and obviously he *did* become an indentured servant. But my mother doesn't take homes and farms for unpaid taxes, and indentured servitude is illegal. The only explanation is that his family were tenants of Heward—or some other corrupt lord. I can't tell Dain that—he'd say I was naive, blaming others to prove my mother innocent.

I can't even imagine what that life must have been like for him. At the age of five, he'd been living with strangers, forced to catch rats for a living. When *I* turned five, I got my first pony and my first sword, and then I got mad because I wasn't allowed to go on a proper monster hunt, so Dad released two colocolo in the barn. That was my "rat catching," a game set up by a doting father, with a barn full of family and staff to cheer me on, and a plate of honey cakes and jam for when I captured the rat-headed lizards. I'm sure Dain didn't get honey cakes and jam at the end of his day.

Dain might hate me, but I don't hate him. I think about his life, and I wish I could get to know him better. That isn't happening, though, and the important issue is that Dain is stopping me from training under Wilmot. I understand he doesn't want me taking advantage of a sick man, but I *need* that training and Wilmot needs to get to the castle, where our doctors can help him.

Maybe that's the answer. Dain obviously cares for Wilmot. I have to convince him that this is best for Wilmot.

I leap to my feet, startling Jacko. I heft him into my arms and hurry back toward the cabin, leaving Malric lumbering after us.

I find Dain out behind the cabin, practicing archery. Earlier, I insulted his skill because he'd hit me with one of his arrows. As I see him work, I realize my mistake. If he hit my sleeve, then he intended to—probably to warn me he was there. I watch Dain fire arrow after arrow at targets, knocking them over as easily as if he'd run down and shoved them off their perches.

"You're good," I say.

He wheels, bow rising. I lift my hands and walk toward him.

"I'm sorry I mocked you earlier," I say. "You're *really* good. I've never quite gotten the hang of archery, but I've never had a teacher who emphasized it, either. Our hunters are swords-men first."

He says nothing, just lowers the bow as I walk over, still talking.

"I would love to learn better marksmanship, and you are exactly the sort of teacher I need. The troop doesn't have a single hunter who can shoot like you. I would be honored—"

"Stop."

"I'm just saying—"

"Stop. Please. It's a good thing you are no longer destined for the throne. Flattery is not your strong suit."

"It's not flattery." I pause. "Okay, it's not *just* flattery."

He makes a noise, and it takes me a moment to realize it's a laugh. A genuine one. "Your honesty is admirable, princess. Another reason why you shouldn't sit on the throne." He walks to the targets and plucks out his arrows. "You need my support in this harebrained scheme with Wilmot, so you're complimenting my skill in hopes it'll woo me to your side."

"Yes, but I'd also *like* to learn better marksmanship."

He eyes me over his shoulder.

"I mean that," I say. "I've always wanted to be the royal monster hunter, and everyone says I'll make a good one."

"You're a princess. They flatter you."

I bristle. "I tamed a jackalope without even trying. Believe me, no one *wants* a jackalope companion."

Jacko squeaks and chatters up at me.

I set him on the ground and wave at Malric. "Yes, Jannah gave me her warg, but he chooses to stay. He tolerates my companionship."

"Tolerates?" Dain scoffs. "That's not exactly high praise, princess."

"No? Try getting within three paces of him. Even my brother can't."

"You may have a connection with beasts, but that doesn't mean you can fight. You're too young to face a gryphon."

"I *have* faced one. I was there when my aunt fought the one that killed her. I snuck along to protect my brother. We came across a manticore, which seemed to explain the reports. Then the gryphon crashed through the barn roof and grabbed me. It carried me into the air, and I escaped, armed only with an arrow, which I plucked from my shoulder. I waited until it flew low, and then I cut its tendon so it would release me."

As I tell the story, even I'm impressed. It *will* make an excellent bard song. I sound so much more heroic than I'd felt.

I expect to see respect in Dain's eyes. Maybe even a touch of awe. When I don't, I say, "There were witnesses. Many witnesses."

"An arrow?" he says.

I straighten, swelling with pride. "Yes."

"What happened to your sword?"

"I—"

"And you were caught off guard. You allowed yourself to be taken."

"I—"

"Yes, you did well, princess. For a *child*."

"Child?" I sputter. "How old are you?"

"I'll be thirteen this summer."

"And I'll be thirteen in the fall. I'll admit I can't fight a gryphon alone. But for the sake of the kingdom, I must train. I must prepare. If you bring Wilmot to the castle, our skilled doctors can treat his injuries while he trains me."

"No." He heads for a small barn.

I jog after him. "But it's best for Wilmot."

"No, princess. It's best for *you*. I will not entrust Wilmot's care to the queen. He is improving daily and has no need of your physician."

"But—"

"I said no. Now leave or you'll see exactly how good my marksmanship is. And this time, I won't aim for your sleeve."

CHAPTER SEVENTEEN

I have an idea. It's crazy, of course. All the best ideas are.

Dain calls me a child, but if I am, then so is he. I need to show him that I may be young, but I have what it takes to be a royal monster hunter. He doubts I have a way with monsters, so I'm going to prove it by capturing a beast. A very specific one.

First, I send Malric back to my guards with a message. Mom hoped that Wilmot would agree to train me, and that we'd return to the castle together, but she acknowledged neither of those things would be easy. She warned he might insist I stay there and train for a while, testing me, and I'd need to use that time to also persuade him to come back with me, since I couldn't spend the entire summer at his cottage.

If I had to stay awhile, Malric was supposed to return to the guards bearing news, so they could go home while I began my mission. In my message, I don't lie. I just . . . stretch the truth. I say that I'm with Wilmot and I'm fine, and they may return to the castle for a fortnight. That will keep them from coming after me while I complete the mission that will win me my training.

Next, I find a place to camp. We're close enough to the mountains for me to locate a good cave. For safety, I will stay within sprinting distance of Wilmot's camp until Malric returns. That night, instead of curling up with me, Jacko sits in the cave mouth, as if guarding me while Malric's gone. I wake once, and he's still there . . . fallen over and fast asleep.

I must be more exhausted than I realized, because by the time I wake again, the sun is high. As I'm washing—in a cove with *no* rushing water—I hear the thump of running paws. I leap up, and Malric bursts through the trees.

"You must have run all night," I say.

He gives me a look as if to say, yes, *he* didn't sleep away the night and half the day. There's a bundle harnessed to his broad back. It's the rest of my supplies—a little extra food but mostly clothing, packed under the presumption that Wilmot would feed me. I tuck the clothing into the cave for later and pack the food.

"We're off, then," I say. "Off on a grand and wondrous adventure with hardly any danger at all."

Malric shakes his massive head and pads after me as we set out.

I spend the rest of the day climbing trees. Well, not exactly, but it feels that way. I walk with my compass in hand, and every time I find a tree towering over its sisters, I climb as high as I can. I'm scouring the forest for a large clearing. Small glades are common enough. A large clearing mid-forest, though, is rare, occurring only when something has happened there to clear it, like a past fire.

I spend an uneventful night in a thicket, protected by Malric. Then I begin my hunt again. That morning I spot a grove that's big enough to be what I'm looking for. I ask Malric and Jacko to stay where they are. Malric does. Jacko does, too, once Malric's giant paw pins him to the ground.

As I creep up on the clearing, my heart hammers. All those years ago, when I told my father and Jannah that I most wanted to meet a gryphon, it wasn't entirely true. I wanted to see a gryphon. Hear one. *Experience* one. The beast I wanted to meet most, though, is very different. It's the one I hope to find in this clearing.

I sneak up downwind. Then I peer into the clearing and see . . .

It's empty.

Well, not exactly *empty*. There are tall grasses. Wildflowers. A few small trees and bushes. A spring burbles into a glassy pond. A place of magic, with the sun dancing and the grasses swaying in the breeze, flowers perfuming the air.

It does not, however, contain any monsters. I square my shoulders and tell myself I simply need to keep looking.

When I call Malric, Jacko comes bounding through the tall grasses, the warg lumbering behind. I walk to the pond. We'll enjoy an early lunch in this meadow before we resume our quest.

Crystal clear water flows from an underground spring in

the pond. When I stoop to fill my waterskin, Jacko's frantic squeaks nearly topple me in again.

He doesn't leap on me this time. He's hopping along the pond's edge, squeaking. Malric snuffles the ground beside the jackalope, and the tiny beast leaps clear over the warg's head in his excitement.

"What is it?" I say as I walk over.

I see the answer to my question. Prints in the soft ground at the pond's edge. An animal has come to drink before us, one with dainty hooves the size of my fist.

My heart leaps. Then it jams in my throat.

I think I know what these hooves belong to. If I'm right, then it means this *is* the clearing I was seeking. It also means I'm too late.

I hunker down to examine the hoof marks. The shape is wrong for a deer or mountain goat. These are equine. They aren't horse, though, and certainly not unicorn. This is indeed the beast I came for . . . a beast that is no longer here.

I touch the tracks, hoping they'll be fresh. The edges are hard, long dry.

I ease onto my haunches as my chest tightens. I'd told myself that the pegasus filly would still be in her clearing, a month after she kicked Wilmot.

She is not.

And I don't know what to do now.

This was my plan. Dain said Wilmot forbade him to come after this filly, and Dain agreed that he wasn't ready for her. So this seemed my answer. I would find and tame the pegasus filly and then parade her back and prove myself to Dain.

I am Clan Dacre. I should carry the ebony sword. I am worthy of Wilmot's training.

And now . . . ?

Now I want to cry.

I want to cry, and I want to scream. I want to throw a tantrum and not care because there's no one here to see me.

Except there is someone here. There's Malric, who already thinks I'm a spoiled little girl. And there's Jacko, who seems to think I'm awesome, and while I doubt I've earned that, I don't want to disappoint him.

I crouch, hands planted on a rock, hair hanging in a curtain around my face as I take deep breaths. Then I scoop water and splash it on my face.

Okay, so my plan failed. I need a new one. I have no idea what that will be but—

A shadow passes over me. I hit the ground and roll, hand on my sword, images of the gryphon flashing before my eyes. Instead, a cloud floats down from the sky. Or that's what it looks like. A wisp of white cloud settling on the far side of the meadow.

It's not a cloud.

It's a pegasus.

The young winged horse lands with her back to us. I motion for Malric to keep Jacko away and slide onto my belly. When the pegasus lowers her head to graze, I creep toward her until I'm fewer than twenty paces away. Then I stop and stare.

Two mornings ago, I'd paused to admire the beauty of that doe at the stream. This filly, though, is . . . incredible. I've seen paintings and illustrations of pegasi, but that's like all the times I've seen a monster and tried to draw it in my journal, and I can't quite capture what my eyes see.

The filly's coat is white as new-fallen snow. Her silky mane and tail and fetlocks are roan red. Her wings look like those of a gigantic dove, white with roan-red tips, folded delicately over her slender back. She's much smaller than a unicorn. More finely boned than my mare. A creature made for speed and flight.

Unicorns are very difficult to tame. Pegasi are said to be nearly impossible. Clan Dacre legends tell of two monster hunters who found and tamed one while it was young. The male hunter could never ride his—he was too big—but the woman could.

I remember those stories, and I look at this filly, and I have never wanted anything so much in my life. She is alone, lost or abandoned, and I will take her. I will care for her, like I'm doing with Jacko.

I back into the forest, so I don't pop up like a gopher and startle her. Then I approach on foot, slowly, keeping my voice low as I speak. "Hello," I say.

She lifts her head with a whinny, and her wings unfold.

"It's okay," I say as I stop, my hands raised. "I'm not going to hurt you. I want to help."

She dances in place, wing tips fluttering.

I hold out my hand. "I've brought an apple."

I crouch and roll it to the side so she doesn't think I'm throwing a rock at her. She still whinnies and stamps.

"You're alone," I say. "I can help. This is a lovely meadow, but it's in the middle of a forest full of monsters. It's not safe. I'm sure you know that by now."

How much of this does she understand? Maybe none. I keep my voice soothing and encouraging. This will take time. I can't ride out of here on her back today. She's too young to be ridden at all. When we do leave, I'll be leading her on a rope. But we need to build a trust first.

I keep talking as I head to retrieve the apple, which she's ignored. I pick it up and roll it through the grass to her . . . and she runs straight at me.

I dive, hitting the ground. A whoosh and a whinny, and when I look up, she's in the air.

I lift my empty hands. "I won't hurt you. Here, I'll sit down. I'll just sit and talk to you. That's it. I'll talk and—"

She dives. It happens so fast I don't even realize what she's doing until I see those roan-red hooves streaking straight for my head. I roll out of the way and scramble up, my hands raised. She flutters back and lands, rearing now, her hooves flashing.

"Okay. I'm leaving your meadow. I'll stay outside it. Just let me—"

She charges. I backpedal, stumbling over my feet. A squeal from my left. Jacko races through the long grass and launches himself at her.

"No! Don't—!"

He lands on her back. She flies up with great flaps of her wings, and Jacko clings to her, squealing. She dives, and he tumbles, and I scream. Then he's dangling from her mane, his claws tangled in it.

The pegasus tosses her head, and Jacko goes flying. I race to catch him. He drops into my arms with such a thud that I stagger backward . . . and trip over Malric. The warg wobbles, and we fall on top of him in a heap.

When I look up, the pegasus is gone. Malric shakes us off and stalks away, glowering over his shoulder. I smack the ground with my fist, hard enough to make Jacko jump, squeaking in alarm. That makes me take a deep breath, shaking off my anger.

"I'm sorry," I say, picking him up and hugging him. "I'm just mad at myself." I scratch behind his antler prongs. "Are you okay?"

He chirps and rubs his nose under my chin, purring. I cuddle him and then realize Malric is sitting there, watching me with baleful yellow eyes.

"Sorry to you, too," I say. "I was just trying . . ."

Trying to fix this problem with Wilmot. Failing to fix it.

"We'll get her," I say. "I just need to be patient. I'll win her over. I know I can."

CHAPTER EIGHTEEN

I spend three days in that meadow, sleeping in a nearby thicket and returning from dawn to dusk. Yet I make absolutely no progress. I give the filly all my apples. I bring her tender young ferns. If I pile my gifts on a rock, she accepts them. But if I try to hand them to her, she doesn't want them. If I toss them near her, she doesn't want them. If I speak to her, no matter how soothingly, she flies off, like I'm a boring dinner guest who won't stop talking. If I approach her, she flashes her hooves in warning. If I linger too long in her meadow, she charges.

I'm tired, and I'm hungry. I ran out of food on the second day. I've been eating berries and drinking water whenever the pegasus flies off and I can get near her spring. I've caught one grouse and one squirrel, but I gave most of the meat to Jacko. Malric has been off hunting several times, and when he returns, the blood on his muzzle tells me he's eaten, but he brings nothing for me.

I can't even win over this warg, and I've known him all my life. How will I tame a pegasus in a few days?

On the third night, after finishing the filly's sketch in my field journal, I drift off to sleep in the thicket. I'm dreaming when Jacko nuzzles my cheek. My eyelids flutter open, but it's pitch black. I feel that nuzzle again. A velvety nose prods my cheek and then snuffles it. I shift . . . and feel Jacko against my stomach, his body rocking with deep snores. I go still, every muscle tensing.

Warm air blows against my cheek. Then another prod, and I realize it's not an affectionate nuzzle, but a sniff. Something is sniffing my face. Something is standing right over me.

I slowly swivel my head and find myself looking into two big round eyes. I blink. The eyes blink. Mine adjust to the moonlight, and those eyes become reddish-brown, velvety and soft, with long lashes. The eyes pull back, and the nose comes at me again. A black nose on a long snout covered in white hair.

The pegasus filly is right here. Standing over me. Sniffing me.

I lift a tentative hand and touch her nose. Her nostrils flare, and her front hooves dance in place, but she doesn't move. I stroke her nose and murmur under my breath. She nudges my hand, encouraging the attention, and my heart soars.

I've done it. My patience has paid off. My kindness has paid off.

I don't see Malric. He must be off hunting. Maybe she was waiting until he left so she could come to me safely. The warg must frighten her. He's a predator big enough to take down a young pegasus. I've been keeping him away from her, but it wasn't enough. She needed him to be gone completely.

I keep stroking her nose and telling her how beautiful she is, how good I'll be to her. Then I reach into my pocket and pull out my last bit of food. It's a carrot I've been saving for her. I hold it up, and she nibbles the end.

She makes her way through the whole thing and her lips tickle my hand. I laugh. Her ears twist at that, but she doesn't move away. She nudges my hand again, and I pet her. Then she rears. For no reason at all, she rears. Her hooves fly at my head, and I drop as fast I can, Jacko squealing as he's startled from sleep.

I hit the ground and roll, and when I come up, those hooves are right over me.

She's going to trample me.

I roll again and then scramble to my feet. I grab Jacko and race into a part of the forest where the foliage is too thick for her to follow. She still tries. She charges and snorts . . . and another snort answers.

It's Malric. He's tearing through the woods, a game bird in his mouth. He tosses his meal aside and barrels straight for the filly. She turns on him, her hooves flashing. He doesn't stop. He's charging right at her, and she's reared up. She's going to hit him. The second he's close enough, those hooves will slam into his skull, like they did with Wilmot.

I run and plow into Malric's side. One of the filly's hooves glances off my shoulder—the same one still recovering from the arrow. Pain sends me staggering. Malric lunges, and the filly turns tail and gallops back to her meadow. Malric follows just far enough to be sure she's going. Then he returns to me.

I catch my breath, pull out my sword and stomp toward the meadow. Ahead, I see the pegasus trotting around, shaking her mane, her head high. Proud of her trick. I stop there, seething.

They say pegasi are gentler than unicorns. Kinder. More timid. They are not. They can play the role, but it's a ruse, a deadly one. The filly came to *me*. She approached *me*. I was sound asleep, and she came to me and pretended to be won over. She let me pet her. She accepted the last of my food, straight from my hand. Then she attacked. One blow of those hooves could have killed me.

I thought she came to me because Malric was gone. That's true—she waited to attack when he wasn't here.

I slam my fist into a nearby tree. Pain jolts down my arm, and I don't care. I kick the ground as tears of rage fill my eyes.

I was kind. I was gentle. I was respectful and generous and patient. I gave her most of my food and went hungry myself, and this is how she repays me?

I was *too* kind, *too* gentle. This isn't how Jannah tamed Courtois. Pegasi and unicorns are pack animals, like horses. They only obey a strong leader. That's what Jannah says. To tame a wild horse, people capture them and break them. Show them who's boss.

I wanted to win another way. Everyone says I have a special connection with monsters, and I wanted to persuade the filly rather than force her.

I tried to be nice and that failed. I will no longer be nice.

I grab rope from my pack. Then I take out a needle and fill it with sedative. I'll knock her out, and then after she's roped, I'll give her enough to keep her docile as I lead her to Dain.

It's not what I'd wanted, but she's left me no choice.

The trick, of course, will be sneaking close enough to inject her. Then I have to get out of the way before she attacks. She will attack. If you punch a needle into anyone—human, animal or monster—it's not going to be happy.

Inject, flee, hope the sedative works. Then hope it keeps working long enough for me to bind her.

It won't be easy. Jannah always said more hunters died trying to sedate a beast than fighting one. Which is why we don't run around armed with a needle instead of a sword.

I retreat into the forest with Malric and Jacko. I let the filly think we've given up and gone home. Then I climb a tree so I can see into her clearing, and I wait.

It takes half a day, but finally the filly falls asleep. I circle downwind through the forest. I ask Malric and Jacko to stay behind, but even Malric refuses. He lets me go on ahead, though. When Jacko tries to jump onto my shoulders, Malric grabs him by the nape of the neck and carries him. Jacko chatters and grumbles, but thankfully, he soon goes limp and lets himself be carried.

To stay downwind, I need to come up alongside the filly. I creep as quietly as I can, stopping every few paces to listen. I watch her ears. If they so much as flick, I'll retreat. They don't. Soon, I'm close enough to smell her, a clean smell like newly harvested hay.

I ready my needle. I know where to aim. Hit her in the flank, and then back away fast.

Two more steps. Lift the needle—

The filly jumps to her feet. She spins so fast that I know she was faking sleep.

She wheels and rears. One hoof hits that sore shoulder again. I stumble, and I see another hoof coming straight for my head. My arm flies up. Her foreleg is delicate enough that I knock it off course.

As I scramble out of the way, she comes at me again. This time, she grabs my tunic in her teeth and whips me off my feet.

Jacko squeals. He leaps onto her back and digs in all four sets of claws. She rears up but doesn't release me. Malric snarls. He's trying to lunge, but she's moving too fast.

The filly whirls me around. I see her haunch, a wall of white, and I thrust the needle in. I hit the plunger but only get it half-depressed before she throws me.

I land hard on my rear. The filly wheels to charge. Then she stops. Her eyes go wide and roll. She bucks, kicking, and the needle falls out, but she keeps twisting until she starts to stumble. She rears . . . and nearly topples over. Then she stands there, panting, breath streaming into the chilly air as her eyes continue to roll.

She has no idea what's happening to her. And she's terrified. I see that look in her eyes, and I feel like one of those hooves struck me in the stomach.

The filly staggers back. Her tongue lolls. Then those long wings unfurl.

"No!" I say, rushing forward.

She stumbles but manages to lift off, her hooves skimming my head. Then she screeches. A screech of absolute panic and fear. I wheel as she crashes to the ground, the earth shaking under me.

I run to her. She lies there, legs splayed and bent, her head drooping. She's still awake, breathing hard, those beautiful eyes wide.

I reach her, and she doesn't move. Doesn't even seem to know I'm there. She just keeps panting.

I could capture her now. The looped rope hangs from my belt, lariat tied. I could slip it over her head, and she'd be too weak to fight.

The thought makes me sick. Makes my gut seize so hard I double over. I look at her, confused and terrified and panting, and then I can't see through my tears.

What have I done?

Gotten angry, that's what. I got angry, and I lashed out, and I swore to take her by force. Why? Because she wouldn't let me take her nicely. Because she resisted me and tried to drive me off.

I can say I only meant to help her, but that's a lie. I wanted her so I could prove myself to Dain. And I wanted her . . . well, because I wanted her.

That is wrong. It's disrespectful and unforgivable.

I can't force Malric to like me. I know that. Twice I've thrown myself on him to protect him, but that doesn't mean he owes me his dinner. Or that he owes me kindness.

I didn't steal Jacko away from his den. He chose to follow. He chooses to stay.

That's how it must be, just like it would be with a human companion. I can't force Malric to hunt for me. I can't force Jacko to stay with me. I can't force Dain to help train me. All this, I understand. As I should have with the pegasus filly.

"I'm sorry," I say.

She just keeps heaving, struggling to breathe as she fights to stay awake. I reach out carefully and touch her neck, and she seems to relax a little. I stroke her, and she falls into a half sleep, drowsing. Then I move to pet her legs, worried that one might have broken in her fall. They all seem fine.

I rise and locate the needle so she doesn't jab herself with it later. I lead Malric and Jacko from the meadow. Both are quiet. I don't leave yet, though. I ask the beasts to wait for me while I gather new ferns and shoots and take them back to the filly. Then I wait at the edge of the forest with Jacko and Malric.

The filly wakes. She seems to rise easily, uninjured, but I need to be sure. So I keep waiting. Soon she's prancing around the meadow as I watch from the forest. When she finds the pile of shoots and ferns, she whinnies and dives in.

"I'm sorry," I say again. And then I leave.

CHAPTER NINETEEN

I head to Wilmot's cabin. I take a direct route now, and I'm
there before nightfall. As I approach through the forest,
I see Dain and Wilmot on the porch. Dain's changing
Wilmot's bandage while the older man eats.

I intended to plead my case with Dain again, but now, as
I watch them, I know that's wrong. Dain needs to care for
Wilmot, and part of that is making sure no one takes advantage of the old hunter while he's hurt and not thinking straight.
Tricking Wilmot into training me is as bad as capturing the
pegasus filly. I'll return in a couple of months, when Wilmot
might be well enough to agree to train me. So I slip away
before either of them sees me.

I walk until the sun drops. I head straight east, out of the
forest, so I won't be traipsing through it at twilight. As soon
as I reach the edge I stop to rest. It's too close to the Dunnian
Woods for sleep. I should keep going, but I'm so tired and so

hungry. My pack seems to weigh a hundred pounds, making my steps drag. I'm still upset at what I did to the pegasus and feeling sick at the thought of going home and telling the council I failed.

I know my mother hopes to find another way to save her throne—one that doesn't involve me facing a gryphon—but even if she manages that, it'll only be a temporary fix. I *will* need to fight a gryphon or perform some other spectacular feat to prove myself, and to do that, I'll need the best training. Without Jannah or Wilmot to provide that . . .

I could lose the kingdom. If Heward seizes power, he'll be such a terrible ruler that the other clans will revolt in civil war. I've read about such things. I know how horrible they are. That could happen to Tamarel, and it would be all my fault.

I need to rest and clear my head and come up with a new plan. Just close my eyes for a few minutes, until I can get farther from the forest.

When Malric takes off to get his dinner, I try very hard not to think about how hungry I am. I might be a hunter but I don't have a bow or snares. While I did manage to fashion traps to catch the squirrel and grouse, it's too dark to do that now. I'll try in the morning and, if I can't, I'll be out of the forest soon, where I can buy food.

I'm dozing when something drops onto my leg. It's wet, and it's wriggling, and I jump with a yelp. Jacko bounds straight up in the air. He lands on my head, I fall flat on my back and, somewhere over my shoulder, Malric sighs.

A fish flops on the ground beside me. I squint up into the sky. Malric sighs again.

"Oh," I say as I blink. "You brought this?"

He rolls his eyes as if to say, *Well, it didn't drop from the moon.*

I rub my eyes. "I'm half asleep, okay? I was *completely* asleep when *someone* dropped a live *fish* on me."

Jacko chatters, as if seconding this. He hisses at Malric. Then he pounces on the fish. I grab him off before he rips it to inedible shreds.

The fish has gasped its last and lies still on the grass. It's a big trout, as long as my arm.

"Did you want me to kill it for you?" I ask Malric. "It's dead now. You can take it."

He walks to my pack, picks it up and brings it to me.

"You want me to carry your fish?" I say.

He gives me a look. Then he noses inside the pack and knocks out the tiny box containing my sulfur sticks and striking stone. Apparently, Malric would like his dinner cooked. I could grumble about that, but I might be able to take the leftovers. So I start a fire, then clean and cook the fish. When I try to give the pieces to Malric, though, he lies down, muzzle on his forepaws.

"Is it . . . for me?" I ask.

I lift a piece to my mouth, watching for him to growl. He only grunts. I eat my fill, sharing with Jacko. There's plenty left, more than half the fish, but when I give it to Malric, he only accepts one piece. I wrap the rest, and I thank him, and then I pack up and we head out again into the night.

I walk until morning, only stopping when I find places to safely rest for a bit. I stay close to the forest. I have the fish, and I found a huge berry patch, so I can avoid villages. Even if I hide my sword, I'm still the royal princess, traveling without an escort. Better to avoid people if I can.

It's early morning, and I'm tramping along a narrow dirt road. It's empty, being too close to the Dunnian Woods for most travelers. Malric has loped off into the forest to hunt. He'll catch up. Jacko sleeps nestled on my head, snoring softly.

When I hear voices ahead, my gaze darts to the trees, and I'm ready to hide there when the distant voices turn to cries of panic, and then desperate shouts for help.

My hand drops to my sword, but I hesitate. I don't want to wave around my silver-and-ebony sword if I don't need to. I pull out my dagger instead. Then I take Jacko off and set him on the ground with a murmured apology. He only squeaks and hops beside me as we continue on.

I soon see the problem. There's a hill in the road, and a small tree has fallen at its base. A wagon came roaring over the rise . . . and its driver failed to see the fallen tree below. The wagon lies on its side. A woman shouts for help while a man tries frantically to pull apart the broken vehicle.

I duck off the road and shove my sheathed sword into a tangle of undergrowth. Then I jog toward the travelers. The woman sees me and comes stumbling my way, tripping over her long skirts.

"Help us, please!" she shouts. "My little girl is trapped inside!"

I break into a run. The woman doesn't seem to notice Jacko. The moment I start running, she flies back to help her husband. When I draw near, I see the wreckage of the wagon. Already old and rickety, it couldn't handle the crash and collapsed in on itself.

From deep within the wreckage comes the whimper of a child. The man tries valiantly to free her, but he can't break through the wood.

"You need an axe," I say as I arrive beside him. "Do you have one?"

"And risk hitting our baby?" The woman's voice rises.

The man backs up and wipes his brow, smearing dirt through the sweat. He eyes me.

"You're a tiny thing," he says.

I straighten. "Maybe, but I'm strong. I can help."

"No, I mean it's good that you're tiny. You can get inside."

He waves for me to come around the side. There's a gap in the wreckage, one too narrow for the man or his wife.

I peer in and see a flicker of white. "Can't she crawl out?"

"She's a *baby*," the woman snaps. Then she rubs her face. "I'm sorry, child. I was afraid no one would come, and she's our only child. Please. Just get her out. We don't have much, but I'll give you everything."

"That won't be necessary," I say.

I study the hole. It's underneath the wagon, and I'll need to crawl into it. I lower myself to the ground. Jacko chatters behind me, and the woman lets out a cry. The man grabs a piece of broken wood, wielding it against Jacko.

"No!" I say, leaping up. "He's mine."

"That . . . that's a jackalope," the woman says, staring.

I laugh. "No, it's a joke. He's just a regular rabbit, but my friend glued tiny horns to his head, and I can't get them off."

She hesitates, but then the baby wails, and she forgets Jacko and drops to her knees beside the broken cart.

"We're coming," she says. "Just hold on. Mommy is coming."

I get on my stomach again and begin wriggling into the hole. As soon as my head disappears, Jacko starts his alert cries.

"I'm fine!" I call back.

He keeps squealing. I ignore him. He'll be fine once he can see me again.

Ahead, I hear the baby whimpering. I wriggle in farther. It's dark, and it stinks in here. Did the baby soil herself? Probably, but I can't worry about getting dirty. That'll wash off.

I squirm in a little more, until I can lift my head. I see that white again, the swaddling clothes of the baby. I reach out for her, saying, "It's okay. I've got you."

"No," a voice says. "I've got *you*."

A hand grabs my hair. My fist punches right through the rotting boards. I see a face. It's a young man, hunched up. A young man wearing a white tunic and a bandana over his mouth and nose, hiding half his face.

He wrenches me by the hair. I try to swing at his face, but there isn't enough room. I yank out my dagger and slice his arm instead. He snarls. I slash the blade as I back out.

Someone grabs my leg. Hands grapple at me from the wagon wreck. I twist to see the "father." Behind him, the "mother" holds Jacko upside down by his rear legs. Scratches cover her bare arms.

I kick at the man gripping my feet. I try to slash him, too, but he jerks my leg and I can't get close. Then someone plucks the dagger from my hand. It's the young man. Still holding my hair, he yanks me away from the older man.

"Looks like we have a fine prize here," he says.

The ground shakes. Running feet. No, running *paws*. I twist to see Malric tearing up the road, and I have never been so relieved to see his scowling warg face.

These are three villagers, armed only with my dagger. All Malric needs to do is help me get free, and we'll defeat them. Better yet, if they have a speck of common sense, they'll let me go, seeing him bearing down on them.

"That's a warg," I say. "My warg. He's battle trained and he—"

The young man whistles. Men rush from the forest. Men armed with axes and knives and staves. They run toward Malric. The warg skids to a stop as the men surround him.

"No!" I say. "Please, no. Don't hurt him. I'll tell him to go away. I can make him—"

The young man shoves a sack over my head. I scream under it. Scream and kick and punch. As he hauls me away, my feet tangle, and I fall. He keeps dragging me, the sack cutting into my throat. I hook my hands in it as I struggle to breathe.

The last thing I hear is the roar of the men as they charge Malric.

CHAPTER TWENTY

I wake in darkness. When I try to spring up, my head smashes against something firm.

"Careful, your highness." It's a girl's voice, and I twist toward it.

"Who are you?" I snap. "What have you done with—"

"Shhh," she says. "If they hear you, they'll come. I can't help you if they come."

I blink. My eyes adjust to the dim light, and I see that I'm in a tent, the hide flapping in the night breeze. A moonbeam shines through the smoke hole.

That roof isn't what I hit when I stood, though. I reach up and run my hand over solid wood slats. I follow one board to the end, where more rise vertically to join it.

I'm in a cage.

I feel around. There isn't room to lie down, to stand, to do anything except sit with my knees drawn up.

At a noise beside me, I remember the girl. I look over to see a shape crouched a few paces from me. I move to that side of my cage and press my face to the slats. She's in another cage. A fellow captive.

"What are we—" I stop. "You called me 'your highness.'"

She nods, and as she moves, the moonbeam washes her hair in light. I recognize the clip fastening it back. It's mine. My hand flies to my braid, but even as it does, I know it didn't come from there. The clip in her hair is my favorite, and I'd never wear that on a trip into the forest.

My brain's all fuzzy, and I blink hard, trying to think. An image flashes. Me, pulling that clip from my hair and handing it to . . .

The girl raises her face, and the moonlight glints off her blue eyes. Eyes that match the clip's sapphires, which is exactly what I thought when I first gave it to her.

"You're the flower girl," I say. "From the morning the hunting party rode to find the gryphon."

"Yes, and we need to get out of here. They know who you are, your highness. They know who we both are."

"How—? Wait, they know who *you* are?"

"It's a long story. I'm not as valuable as a princess, but I'm not a flower girl, either. They captured me three days ago. I've been trying to get free ever since. When they brought you in, I managed to sneak this from one of their pockets." She holds out a thin metal rod. "I can use it to spring the lock."

"You know how to open locks?"

"It's not difficult, your highness. Most girls can do it. At least those who are not raised in castles."

It seems an extremely specific skill. One they don't teach princesses or flower girls or anyone who doesn't make their living in a very illegal way.

"Who's captured us?" I ask.

"I have no idea. Does it matter? They aren't planning to escort us to the queen's ball."

"The woman took my jackalope. And they attacked . . ." I suck in breath, my heart stopping at the memory. "They attacked my warg. Armed men attacked him, and I think they . . ."

I can't breathe. *Malric.* He came to my rescue, and they—

"I heard howling," she says as she works on her cage lock. "After they brought you. Don't worry, your highness. They wouldn't harm him. A tame warg is valuable."

I wouldn't exactly call Malric "tame," but I don't say that. I hope whoever captured us thinks he is.

"And my jackalope?" I ask.

"I'm sure he's fine. They'll keep him to sell."

"But you haven't actually *seen* my beasts?"

"I'm in a cage, your highness. I haven't seen the *sun* in three days. I'm sure both your beasts are fine. Now please let me concentrate on opening this lock."

For someone who's supposed to know what she's doing, she spends a great deal of effort trying to find the hole. I can see it easily, but she pokes the rod around the edges and grunts with exertion.

I'm about to tell her to turn the lock sideways so it'll catch the light. Then I look from the rod to her hair.

"Why didn't you use the clip?" I ask.

"What?" She shoves stray hair from her eyes.

"The clip I gave you. It has a metal prong just like that . . . What *is* that rod?"

"How should I know? It was in a man's pocket. I don't understand man things. I'm a girl."

"Well, you don't understand girl things very well either if you didn't realize you could use the clip."

"Are you hoping to wake the guards with your chattering?"

No, but I do have a lot of questions. Including why a very valuable clip is still in her hair when she's been taken captive. I don't ask, though. I just think. I think very hard about this whole situation.

I ease back to watch. She doesn't hesitate now. The rod goes in and with an expert flick of her wrist, the lock opens. Then she rests on her haunches and exhales as if requiring rest after the effort.

"I need my dagger," I say as she opens her door.

"You don't need anything, your highness. You're escaping captivity, not checking out of an inn."

"I'd like my dagger and my jackalope and my warg."

"And I'd like a unicorn with a golden horn."

"No, actually you wouldn't. Not unless you want gold-dusted holes in your body."

She waves me to silence and works on my lock. When it's done, she swings open the door.

I don't budge. "Dagger. Jackalope. Warg. I'm not leaving without them."

Now, at this point, she should throw up her hands and say, *Fine, then apparently you're not leaving.* Instead she only studies me, her eyes narrowing. Then she says, "I might have seen them put your belongings over there. To sell later."

She directs me to the spot, where I find my dagger, along with my cloak and travel pack. As I go through the pack, she comes up behind me.

"Are you really taking inventory?" she whispers. "If anything's missing, I'd suggest you don't rush out there, demanding it back."

Which isn't what I'm doing at all. I'm just curious. So many things about this situation are curious. Like the fact that no one took my very valuable dagger into safekeeping. Or that they didn't remove the sedative needles from my pack. Or that they left the entire pack just outside my cage.

By now, I have a very good idea of what's going on here. That's why I'm in no hurry to escape.

"I still need my jackalope and warg," I say as I shoulder my travel pack.

"You really are a princess, aren't you? You have absolutely no concept of the word *danger*. Or *hurry*. Or *fleeing life as a slave*."

"But we don't have slavery in Tamarel. They'd need to take us over the mountains, which is extremely treacherous." I pause. "Unless they're Clan Bellamy. That's it. They must be part of Clan—"

"Absolutely not," she says, straightening. "These are mere thieves. Pickpockets and scoundrels. Clan Bellamy is a noble family of—"

"Bandits."

Her face darkens. "They are a nomadic people who have learned special skills to survive in a harsh climate."

"Skills like springing locks? Picking pockets?"

"They—" She pulls back. "I wouldn't know. But these scoundrels are not from Clan Bellamy."

I head to the back of the tent. There, I lie on my stomach and lift the tent edge. Outside, it's dark. Quiet, too.

I watch for a few moments. When it stays quiet, I take my dagger and slice through the hide wall. The girl yelps softly.

I look over at her. "Are you complaining because I'm damaging our captors' tent?"

"Of course not. Just be careful."

I peel back the newly created flap and push my head through. There's another tent beside ours, but it's dark and silent. I catch a pine-scented breeze coming in from my left, and I follow it to see the forest.

I crawl through the flap. One slow look around. Then a step right. *Away* from the safety of the forest.

The girl tries to grab my arm, but I keep walking. When I reach the edge of the tent, I peer around it. Far off to my left, a campfire burns. The glow of it lights up another tent. I peer into the sky to see the smoke swirling up at least twenty paces off. I turn the other way and squint into the darkness.

A squeak sounds. Then a chattering drifts over from a wagon parked to my right.

I start in that direction. When the girl reaches for me again, I duck around her and keep going. She tries to pull me back, but I brush her off.

I reach the wagon. No one's guarding it. In the distance, a figure stands with his back to us. I slit the hide cover on the wagon. Inside, it's pitch-black, but Jacko chatters, letting me know he's there. I climb onto the wheel and then wriggle through the ripped cover.

I follow the jackalope's chattering to a metal crate. It's closed with a simple latch, which I undo, and he leaps into my arms. I comfort him as I climb out of the wagon.

"There," the girl says. "Now can we—"

"I need my warg."

I keep Jacko in my arms, and to my relief, he actually stays quiet. I head back the way I came. The girl runs in front of me.

"They're holding him in the middle of camp," she says. "Over by that bonfire."

I find the rising smoke and continue toward it. Once I'm near enough to smell the fire, I creep around a tent until I can see it. And there's Malric. He's wearing a collar chained to a wagon. He's also sound asleep. Three men sit at the fire. There's no way I can get to the warg without them seeing me.

"I need to wake him," I say. "He can easily break free. I'm sure he can."

"Which means he doesn't sleep a natural slumber. Otherwise, he *would* break free. They've drugged him."

"I need to—" I begin.

"He's fine. There's no way of getting to him. They haven't hurt him, but if you wake him and he fights, they might need to."

I hesitate. She's right. This situation is, I suspect, not as dangerous as it seems. But my captors won't hesitate to kill Malric if he poses a threat.

I already feared I'd lost him. As difficult as this is, I must accept he's temporarily safe. Walk away for now, and return soon to free him. Very soon.

Once we're away from camp, I march to a nearby outcropping of rock and climb it. From there, I can see the landscape. The Dunnian Woods is to our right. Then I spot a gnarled tree I recognize.

I take off at a jog; the girl protesting as she follows. Sure enough, I find the road. Ahead, I see the hill where the wagon "crashed." I root around at the roadside until I unearth my sword.

The girl catches up as I buckle on my sheath.

"Now we may go," I say.

She wants to head to the nearest village. I ignore her and climb a wooded hill right near the forest's edge. At the top, I find a clearing and sit. She shivers as she lowers herself to the ground.

"We should start a fire," she says.

"And let the smoke tell them where we've gone?" I shake my head.

"We shouldn't be in here," she says. "These woods border the mountains. They're full of monsters."

I stroke Jacko as he settles on my lap. "Then it's a good thing you're with the next royal monster hunter."

She dips her chin. "I'd heard that. My condolences on the loss of your aunt. Still, you are a hunter in training, and perhaps we shouldn't stay inside these woods."

"It's fine. I've been in here before. So have you, I suspect, in your journeys over the mountains."

She starts to protest.

"You were going to tell me who you are," I say. "Or did that change when I called your clan bandits?"

Silence.

"You're Clan Bellamy," I say. "And you *are* bandits. You waylay travelers and relieve them of their belongings. What else would you call that?"

"A lesson," she says hotly. "We teach them to better protect their goods. To hire guards to help protect them."

"Guards from Clan Bellamy?"

"We can, as you said, cross the mountains. We may not hunt monsters, but we know the paths to avoid them. We share that knowledge for a price. Just as Clan Dacre shares its monster skills for a price . . . the price of a throne."

"The people chose that. We united the clans and offered them our services in return for the throne."

"As we offer our services in return for gold."

I snort. "After you've robbed people and shown them the need for protection. That would be like Clan Dacre capturing monsters in the mountains and freeing them in the villages."

When she opens her mouth, I cut her off. "I'm not arguing that Clan Bellamy doesn't provide a service as mountain guides. It's the raiding and thieving that's the problem. Right now, though, my concern is you. You didn't show up at my castle by accident. You were spying."

I expect her to deny it, but she raises her chin and says, "My father is about to negotiate with your mother, and he wanted a better understanding of the royal family. I gave him a good account. I said you were kind and generous. He was impressed."

"Your father?" I think fast. "So your father is Everard, Warlord of Clan Bellamy."

"Yes."

"And you would be?"

"Alianor."

"So tell me, Alianor, why did you—?"

Something moves deep in the forest. When I go still, Alianor turns to me. "Did you see something?"

I peer into the darkness. Then I shrug. "Just trees blowing in the wind. Before we continue, though, I need a moment of privacy. I was in that cage a very long time."

After a pause, she realizes what I mean. She nods, and I slide Jacko off my lap. He hops quietly after me as I creep into the forest.

Alianor's busy looking down the hillside toward the encampment. I'm sure I saw someone in the forest. When I notice movement again, I duck into a cluster of bushes. A slender figure moves toward Alianor. A male figure. He stops and leans each way as if looking for me.

When he turns, I hide again and watch him through the branches. His gaze travels past me. As he starts forward, he steps into a patch of light, illuminating his face.

Dain.

As soon as I wonder why he's here, I know the answer. He must be working with the bandits. They didn't just happen to find a royal princess tramping across the fields. Someone told them I was coming.

I know it was Clan Bellamy that captured me. Take the princess captive and then have Alianor "free" me and win my mother's gratitude before negotiations begin. Quite a plan. When we'd climbed onto this hill, I'd watched for one of Alianor's clansmen to slip after us. None had. Because Dain was already nearby. Already waiting.

He creeps toward Alianor. He's noticed I'm gone, and he wants to speak to her privately. I slip after him. He's still twenty paces from her when I charge. I hit him square in the back, and he lands face-first with an *oomph*.

I try to pin him, but he's twisting, and he manages to get onto his back and throw me aside. That's when Jacko attacks. He jumps onto Dain's face and digs his claws in, legs wrapped around Dain's head.

Dain yowls and tries to yank the jackalope off, but Jacko only grips harder. Then the jackalope squeals and jumps off. I think Dain bit his stomach, which is really rude. But I suppose if I had a jackalope on my face, I might do the same.

Dain grabs my leg. I kick free. He starts to rise, but I jump onto his chest, forcing him down. He hits the side of my head, and my cloak hood falls back. I pin his arm and press my dagger to his throat.

His lips curl in a snarl. Then he stops. "Princess?"

"Don't act surprised," I say. "You knew exactly—"

Jacko sails from nowhere. He lands on Dain's lap and sinks his teeth into the boy's stomach. Dain yelps and goes to throw the beast off, but I grab Jacko before he can.

"Serves you right," I say to Dain. "You bit him first."

"Because he was attached to my *face*." He glowers at Jacko. "I should have known that's what it was. Blasted jackalope."

"*Good* jackalope," I say, scratching around his antler prongs. I lean down and croon, "Who's my brave little guard-bunny?"

Jacko purrs and rubs against my hand.

Dain shakes his head. "That is the weirdest—Wait, where's Malric?"

"He's fine. Just . . . temporarily absent. He—"

"Tell me later. Right now, the important thing is that girl you're with. She isn't a friend. She's—"

"Alianor of Clan Bellamy. Her people took me captive, pretending to be slavers. Then Alianor pretended to rescue me. It's a ruse to win my mother's favor."

He stops and stares at me, blinking. Then he says, "Oh."

I peer down at him. "You really do think I'm a little fool, don't you?"

"No, I just thought . . . I thought you needed help."

"You were here to rescue me?"

He squares his shoulders. "You're the princess, and you were in the clutches of bandits. It is my duty to help."

I sigh and roll off him. "Could you *stop* helping me, please? First the warakin, and now this. One minute, I'm handling a crisis perfectly well. Then I have a hunter barging in, determined to rescue a princess who does not require rescuing. The only thing you're doing, Dain, is making situations worse. Now, let's talk to . . ."

I look over at the spot where Alianor was sitting. It's empty.

CHAPTER TWENTY-ONE

I slap my dagger into Dain's hand. "Take this. There, you've been compensated for the loss of the warakin. That's worth more than two silver, so it also pays you for your 'rescue.' Now go. Please."

He shoves the dagger back at me. "I don't want your dagger. Or your money. I spotted you at the cabin the day before last, and I was concerned. You don't have a guard. So I followed you. I saw you taken captive while trying to help those villagers. I was figuring out how to rescue you when you escaped with that bandit girl. I knew she was up to something, so I tried to help— because it was the right thing to do. You're the royal princess."

I eye him, looking for the lie in his words. He's bristling with anger and honest indignation. Seeing that, my own anger evaporates.

"Okay," I say. "You had the best intentions. You just aren't very good at this sort of thing."

He starts to sputter, but I cut him off.

"I appreciate your help," I say, "but you can go back to Wilmot. I have a bandit to catch."

"Why? You're free. Just let her go."

I shake my head. "Her father had me kidnapped. I need to talk to her and get all the answers she can give."

He crosses his arms. "Okay, then, princess. Which way did she go?"

I scour the hillside.

He points at trampled grass and then strides in that direction. I hurry after him.

I spot the next sign—a broken twig. Dain pushes ahead until he sees a footprint in soft ground. A smeared footprint.

I point left. He points straight on.

"The footprint is smudged," I whisper. "It shows she turned here."

"No, the ground is *slippery*. That smudge means she slipped here."

I march left. He growls in frustration and follows. We get about five paces before reaching thick bramble, no signs of recent passage.

"So I was correct, princess?"

"Yes."

We head straight on from where Alianor slipped but get no more than fifty paces before we hit another ambiguous sign. This time, it's grass trodden in two directions.

One is Alianor. One must be some other creature passing through.

I say that the signs to our right look old, that the grass is already springing back up. Dain disagrees. I let him have this one. We turn right . . . and discover we're wrong and need to backtrack again.

We track Alianor for another hundred paces—while fighting to be in the lead—before I pluck at Dain's sleeve.

"This isn't working," I say. "We're both trying to prove we can track. Competing is slowing us down."

He's quiet for a moment. Then he says, "You're right. As the royal monster hunter, you should lead."

I shake my head. "You're better at tracking. I'll watch and learn." I pause. "Though if you're mistaken, I'll mention it."

"I'm sure you will," he says, but his lips curve in a faint smile. He walks a few steps. Then he slows and glances over his shoulder. "You *were* doing a good job."

"Thank you," I say, and we continue on.

We catch up to Alianor. In trying to be sneaky, she'd headed deeper into the forest. I presume she was going to loop around the hill and head back to camp, but at some point, she lost her way.

I can't blame her for that. Clan Bellamy are able to guide travelers through monster-free routes because they use those routes themselves. They know them. They don't know this forest.

Eventually, we spot her up ahead, where she's slumped at the foot of a tree.

"Taking a break?" Dain murmurs with a shake of his head.

"She must realize she's lost," I say. "She figures she's safely away from us by now, so she's waiting for daylight. It's what I'd do."

He considers and then nods. "All right. Of course, it'd be even smarter to—"

"Climb a tree and see where she is?" I stop myself. "Sorry. That's showing off again, isn't it?"

That faint smile again. "It might be. But I think I started it." He peers around. "We're hours from sunrise. We should leave her for now and find higher ground to assess the situation. She isn't going anywhere."

CHAPTER TWENTY-TWO

I n this part of the forest, "higher ground" means a tree. Our goal is to scope out the landscape around Alianor and plot our approach. We want to take her captive and question her. Her father kidnapped a princess, and my mother must know that. We can't just say I'm safe, therefore no harm's been done.

My plan is to question her and then march her back to the castle. When I tell Dain, he considers it, which tells me I'm making progress—at least he doesn't jump right in to tell me my plan won't work.

"Come morning, there will be an entire bandit clan hunting for their warlord's daughter," he says. "I'm not sure we want to haul her on a three-day ride." When I open my mouth to protest, he says, "Let's see how it goes. The important thing is getting her confession."

I find a big oak tree and set my pack at the base.

Dain looks up it. "This doesn't have enough branches. We can't . . ."

I'm already on the first branch, climbing to the second.

"You can stay down there with Jacko." I wave at the jackalope, who circles the trunk as he searches for a way up.

Dain grabs the lowest branch and heaves himself onto it. Jacko starts leaping and squeaking.

Dain looks down at the jackalope. "You need a rope to tie him down. Also possibly a muzzle."

"That would be wrong."

He watches Jacko bounding, each leap taking him a little closer to the tree limb . . . which remains at least two feet out of his reach.

"Gotta admire his perseverance," I say.

"Or his stupidity."

The jackalope hunkers down, leaps as high as he can . . . and sinks his teeth into Dain's boot.

"You know I can't feel that, right?" Dain says.

Jacko latches on with his claws, pulls himself onto the boot and sinks his teeth into Dain's calf. Dain cuts off a yelp, slapping his hand over his mouth. I climb down and rescue my jackalope before he goes flying from a kicked foot.

I settle Jacko onto my shoulders and resume climbing. Dain struggles to follow.

"You can stay down there," I say, as he tries to figure out how to get onto a branch.

"I'm fine, princess."

"My name is Rowan."

"And you're a princess. One form of address takes precedence over the other."

Before I can answer, Jacko starts to slip, and I straighten to rearrange him before climbing again.

"Are you sure you aren't part monkey?" Dain calls up.

I keep going until I'm almost where I want to be. Then the moonlight dances through the leaves, illuminating something overhead, and I go still.

"Princess?" Alarm sparks in Dain's voice. When I don't answer, he says, "Ro—" Then he spots me and stops.

"See, you *can* say my name," I say.

"No, I was calling the jackalope." Dain's head appears, at least five branches down. "Ro*dent*. I called him a rodent."

An acorn bops off Dain's nose. "Hey!"

"Wasn't me," I say.

Jacko chatters. I shimmy along the limb I'm straddling.

"The bandit girl is that way." He jabs his thumb in the opposite direction.

"I know. I see something in the tree."

"Leaves? Branches?"

"Ha ha."

"Spiderwebs?" He lifts one web-sticky hand and makes a face.

I shake my head and peer up into the dark tree. That moonbeam still illuminates what I saw. It's a feather. A bright orange-and-red one that glows like a lick of flame.

Beneath me, Dain grunts with effort as he makes his way out onto a branch several down from mine.

"Is that . . . ?" He places one hand on the trunk and rises to his knees for a better look.

"Firebird feather," I say.

I grin down at him, and I get a smile in return. He's not looking at me, though. He's staring at that glowing feather.

"Wilmot told me there are firebirds in a mountain to the west," he says. "I keep bugging him to go, but it's too dangerous just to catch a glimpse of a bird. Not worth it."

"Not worth it to *him*," I say. "*I'd* climb a mountain to see a firebird. And I'm definitely going to climb a tree to get that feather."

I expect Dain will object, but he just says, "Careful, princess. You're already on thin branches, and you have that blasted rodent on your shoulders."

Jacko chatters at him.

"Since you seem to understand me, rodent, maybe you can do the princess a favor and hop off while she goes after that feather."

Jacko settles in on my head, his back claws digging into my tunic shoulders.

"Jannah always said monsters understand some words but mostly our tone," I say. "A keen intelligence rather than actual magic."

"Yes, and I've already had your lecture on magic. I suppose you'd like to explain the flaming feather over your head."

"The feather will reflect any source of light, but it won't glow in total darkness."

"Do you spoil everything?"

"A scientific explanation isn't 'spoiling' anything. Figuring out *why* a firebird glows or a basilisk paralyzes its prey is far more interesting than just calling it magic. The fascinating thing about firebird feathers is that they amplify light. That feather needs only a pinprick to glow like that." I look down at him. "Don't you think that's interesting?"

"Get your feather, princess. You can grind it up with a chemist's pestle to see how it works."

"Don't be silly. I'm going to make a pen of it. So I can write in my field journal even when it's dark. I might also use part in a hair clip. It'd look amazing at night festivals." I pause. "However, if I ever find a second feather, I will grind it for analysis."

He shakes his head. "You are—"

"Correct. That's all you need to say. *Princess, you are correct.* Now, let me fetch this feather while you do what we're supposed to be doing: survey the landscape."

I lean to look the other way. I've been checking as I climb, making sure Alianor is still in her spot. She is. She has her eyes closed. Dain might mock her for sleeping, but I think she's only resting. Either way, she's in no hurry to leave, so I have time to fetch this feather.

Firebirds look like peacocks but with glowing feathers of orange, yellow and red. They aren't as rare as phoenixes, but they're still one of the least commonly seen monster birds, which makes this feather worth the effort.

I climb two more branches. Below, Dain makes a warning noise in his throat but says nothing. I am on a branch that's thinner than I'd like, so I take Jacko off my shoulders and set him in a crook by the trunk. He curls into it and watches me.

The feather is just overhead. I can either climb one more limb or stretch for it. The branch above me really is too thin, so I get my balance on this one. From below, I'd thought the feather was caught in the leaves. Now I see that it hangs in midair, swiveling in the night breeze like a dancing flame.

As I reach for it, my hand passes through sticky strands of spiderweb. Mystery solved. I tug on the feather. It sticks more than I would expect from a mere spiderweb. When I pull the feather free, strands cling to it.

I lay the feather on my hand to admire it. It is truly a wondrous thing. Jannah had several. She'd fashioned them into arrow fletchings so she could see their flight path at night. I guess that's a more fitting use of firebird feathers for a royal monster hunter. Still, this is my first, and if I want a new quill pen and a hair ornament, that's what I'll make of it. My second one will be for arrows. No, my second will be for research. My third for arrows. I'll travel to that mountain pass, and I'll bring back as many feathers as I can find. That will make the trip worthwhile.

Of course, first I need to convince Dain and Wilmot to train me. Then I need to slay the gryphon and *become* the royal monster hunter so I can travel to the firebird pass. And before all that, I need to question Alianor, rescue Malric and figure out what to do about the bandit clan trying to kidnap me.

Until then, I have this one feather. I lift it, still smiling. When I lean over to show Dain, he smiles back . . . and then tells me to stop leaning and climb down. I tuck the feather under my tunic. The spiderweb sticks to my fingers. As I brush it off, I see the strands are thicker than usual, about the size of fine thread. They're also black.

Thick black spiderweb. That pokes at my memory, but I'll figure it out later. For now, I wrap the strands around the feather quill so I can save some for further examination. Then I tuck the feather away, turn to leave . . . and see another flame dancing overhead.

I lean, earning me a warning from Dain and a chatter from Jacko. Above, the spider's web has caught another firebird feather. I'd missed it because leaves had blocked my view.

This one is a tail feather the length of my arm. Silky fronds end in a glorious eye of red and orange and black. I'm so close. I can reach it. I know I can.

It'll just take a little maneuvering.

"Are you coming down, princess?" Dain says.

"I see another feather. A tail one right here."

His sigh ripples up. "Okay. Be careful."

I grip the slender branch above mine. I use it to pull myself up so I'm standing on the limb below.

"Princess . . ." Dain says. "That isn't safe."

"I'm steady, and I'm not going any farther. Just give me a moment."

"Quickly." He pauses. "No, not quickly. Slowly and carefully. Please."

I inch along the limb. At the first ominous creak, I stop. Jacko chatters. Dain says, "I thought you said you weren't going any farther."

I stop. When I stretch, I'm still a forearm's length short. The tail feather twists in the breeze, taunting me.

I snap a dead twig off the branch over my head. Then I use it to catch the strands of web and lift the feather with them. Holding my breath, I draw the feather closer, little by little.

When it's almost within reach, it slips. I give a tiny jump and grab my treasure. As I hold it between my fingers I see a big spider that's come along for the ride. It's the size of my fist, hairy and dark yellowish-brown.

I know spiders freak out a lot of people. So do snakes and bugs. But to me, a spider is just another animal, maybe not as cute as a puppy but no less interesting. I resist the urge to examine the spider and figure out what kind it is. Really not the time. I shake the feather over the limb, and the spider falls onto it and scampers off.

I'm watching that spider go when another one drops onto my arm. That makes me jump, my boots sliding. Jacko squeaks. I catch myself and the spider drops onto a branch below and then skitters away.

Two huge tree spiders. That's odd. Spiders are solitary creatures. There must be a good food source around, and this tree has attracted them. I peer into the canopy of leaves overhead. Is there a dead firebird up there? I hope not. I'd like to think these feathers fell off a live one.

I push the tail feather into my tunic along with the first. The end sticks out, and I'm rearranging it with one hand while my other clutches the branch above. I've almost got it tucked in when I feel something on my arm.

Another spider? Really?

I look to see *three* spiders running down my arm.

I accidentally let go of the branch. My arms windmill for one heartbeat of sheer terror before my brain kicks in, and I grasp the branch again. One spider reaches my shoulder. I fling it off. As I shake away the other two, I see a whole stream of them coming down the dangling, broken web.

It's like I stumbled into a nest, but that's impossible. Spiderlings are tiny, and these are the size of my fist. I take deep breaths, trying not to freak out. I might not be afraid of spiders, but that doesn't mean I want a mass of huge ones crawling all over me.

I squeeze my eyes shut and tell myself this is an interesting phenomenon, from a purely scientific view. A tree full of fist-sized spiders. I'll have to make a note of it to research later.

There. I've tucked this experience away as nothing more than a fascinating scientific interlude, and now I can face—

A spider drops onto my head. I yelp, scrabbling to claw it off.

There are spiders. A tree full of huge spiders. Dropping on me.

This is *not* okay.

I reach for Jacko just as a spider falls onto him. He jumps with a shriek and starts to fall. I drop to my knees and manage to catch him, but I lose my balance. I fall. I grab the branch below with one hand, the other still around Jacko. My body stops short with a shoulder-wrenching jerk. I stifle a gasp of pain. Jacko scuttles up my tunic, freeing my other arm, and I heave upward and grab the branch.

I'm hanging there, with Jacko glued to my head, chattering in terror. One of the spiders lands on my hand, and I have to force myself to keep gripping the branch. Then something touches my boots. I start to lash out, but Dain says, "If you kick me off this tree, I can't help you down, princess."

I look to see him sitting on a branch, higher than he was before. He's holding my lower legs.

"Am I allowed to rescue you?" he says. "Because I wouldn't want to get in trouble again."

"S-spiders. L-lots of spiders."

He chuckles. "Disturbed a nest, did you? Okay, let's—"

He looks up . . . and one lands on his face. He frantically brushes it off and manages to keep hold of me with one arm. Spiders crawl down my body. Dain sees that and his eyes widen in horror.

"Jba-fofi," he whispers.

"What?"

"Monsters. They're monster spiders."

"Monstrous sized, yes, but these aren't—"

"Princess, you need to get out of this tree. Now."

"That's what I'm trying to do."

A strained chuckle. "I'm going to move your feet." He does that, and I feel the branch below. "Now let go, and allow me to lower you."

He helps me onto his branch. I grab Jacko and tuck him under my arm as we both swipe off the spiders. They're still coming, racing along the tree trunk. We scramble down as fast as we can, and we're halfway to the bottom before the spiders stop following. I lean against the trunk to catch my breath. Jacko climbs down onto the branch. Dain turns . . . and a lump twitches under his tunic.

"Don't move," I say.

He freezes. "Where is it?"

"Under your tunic."

He starts pulling at his shirt, but I stop him.

"Can we leave it in there?" I ask. "I'd like a live specimen to study. You just need to keep your tunic tucked in for a few days . . ."

I expect a sarcastic retort to my joke. But he just says, in a strained voice, "Please remove the spider, princess."

"Hold still," I say.

I reach up under the fabric and pull out the spider. As I do, he yelps and bats at the back of his tunic. Another lump scuttles underneath. Then Dain yelps louder, in pain now.

"It's *biting*—"

I drop the one I have and pull out the other. I hold it up by the abdomen, watching its pedipalps wave.

"Princess, put that down."

"It's all right. Even at this size, spiders aren't dangerous."

"That's a baby."

I look up at him, the spider still in my hand. "What?"

"Didn't you hear me earlier? They're jba-fofi."

I shake my head. "Jba-fofi are extinct, if they ever existed at all."

"Princess?" He speaks slowly, as if to a child. "That is a baby jba-fofi. I've seen one in this forest. Wilmot has seen a few. Now you have, too."

"You—you're serious?" I stare at the spider. "A baby jba-fofi? I was joking about keeping it, but now I have to. Do you know what this means? It's a huge discovery—"

"No, princess. It means there's a mama jba-fofi some-where below us."

"Okay, but . . . Oh."

"Yes, *oh*." He takes the spiderling from my hand and sets it on a branch. It scuttles away. "May we leave now? Or do I need to explain why we don't want to meet his mommy?"

Before I can answer, something moves in the undergrowth off to our left. We both go still.

According to the legend, only baby jba-fofi live in trees. The adults are too big for that. They're the size of dogs, and they build trapdoors on their burrows. When any unsuspecting prey passes, they jump out and drag it in.

The noise comes again. I pull myself onto the next branch for a look. Something moves through the trees. With an exhale of relief, I realize it's only Alianor. We are high enough that she doesn't notice the commotion in the treetops, but she must have heard Dain's yelps. She's twenty paces from the base of the tree, looking around with her dagger in hand.

That's when I remember the mother spider.

"Alianor!" I call.

She gives a start and looks around.

"Don't move!" I shout.

Exactly the wrong thing to say. She thinks I'm telling her to stay there so I can take her captive . . . and she bolts.

"No! Jba-fofi!" I yell. "There's a jba-fofi! Stop!"

She doesn't stop. She won't know what a jba-fofi is— I barely do. I leap down a few more branches. I'm very near the bottom now. Both Dain and Jacko are waiting on the last branch, Jacko sounding his alert squeaks. When I join them, the jackalope jumps onto my head, and I start to topple. Dain grabs my shoulder and braces me. Together, we vault to the ground.

As I grab my pack and start to run, Dain calls, "Watch—!"

"I know!"

A jba-fofi lair will be a patch of open ground covered only in grass. So I stay close to trees and bushes, avoiding empty areas.

"Alianor!" I call. "Please! There's a spider. Just stop. Please stop."

She slows and then halts. "Spider?"

"A jba-fofi. It's a giant ground spider. We disturbed the nest, so we know the mother is around."

She brandishes her dagger. "Stay right there."

"I will."

I stop and put out my arm to warn Dain to stay back.

"Who's that with you?" she says. "I heard you two talking on the hill."

"It's Dain. He's a monster hunter. We need to speak to you."

"I heard what you two said. You think I tricked you."

"I *know* you tricked me, Alianor. Your father made you pretend to be another captive and help me escape."

"My father didn't do anything. This was—"

Something looms up behind her. I let out a cry and lurch forward. The ground opens, and a giant spider grabs her leg.

"Alianor!"

She falls face-first as the spider drags her into its lair. The ground closes, and they're gone.

CHAPTER TWENTY-THREE

We race over to where we last saw Alianor. Her dagger lies on the ground.

"Someone else who drops their weapon at the worst possible moment," Dain grumbles as we drop to our knees, patting the earth beneath us.

"I'd like to see you keep your grip when a gryphon yanks you into the air," I say. "Or when a jba-fofi drags you into its lair."

The ground where she disappeared looks like a moss-covered patch of earth. There's no sign of the trapdoor. I'm feeling around when my hand sinks into the moss, and I feel an edge beneath it.

I pull, and it moves. Dain catches his side, and we lift together. It really does look like a door—it's round and con-structed from dead vegetation and earth, woven with spider silk. More silk latches the other side so the spider can push it open, grab its prey and disappear back inside, with the door slapping shut behind it.

We heave it up to see a burrow beneath. From deep within comes a scuttling sound and muffled screams.

I hand Jacko to Dain.

"What?" Dain says. "No. You're not going in there alone."

"I'm smaller. I'll fit."

Before he can answer, I drop my pack and dive into the burrow. I crawl down the steep incline as fast as I can. Behind me, Jacko chatters, and Dain grunts, struggling to hold him. A gasp of pain and two heartbeats later, the jackalope head-butts my rear end.

"Princ—" Dain calls. "*Rowan*. Get back out here . . ." A grunt as he comes in after me.

I keep crawling. It's pitch-black, and I'm creeping my way forward by sound and feel. I hear the jba-fofi and Alianor ahead, and I'm moving fast when something hits the top of my head. I fall back, reaching up to ward off . . .

Wood. My head hit a long wooden tube. I can wrap my hand all the way around it and trace it down to where it plunges into the dirt.

It's a root. I feel around to find more of them blocking my path. There must be a way through—the spider managed—but I'm blind down here. When I try to move forward, a root tip pokes me in the eye.

The faintest hint of moonlight seeps through the open trapdoor behind me. It's not enough to see by, but it gives me an idea. I reach into my tunic and pull out the smaller firebird feather. It reflects that light, and its dim glow reveals the tangle of roots in my path. With my dagger, I hack at the smallest. Jacko begins gnawing at another.

By the time Dain taps my foot, I've cleared enough. I stick the feather in my hair, sheath the dagger and continue on. Jacko tries to creep under my belly, but we reach a tight turn, and he backs away to let me get around it. Then he pops through. The burrow narrows after that, and I have to wriggle on my stomach.

"I can't—" Dain's voice echoes behind me. "I can't get around this bend."

"It's even tighter up here," I say. "Back up and wait outside. Please."

He doesn't like that, but I keep moving. Jacko bumps my legs as he tries to keep up. The feather no longer does any-thing—we're too far from the light. I put it back into my tunic and wriggle forward and—

My hand touches down on air. I stop and pull back. Then I feel around. Thankfully, I'm not teetering on the edge of a hole. The tunnel just drops steeply after this. I inch forward and then—

And then I'm skidding face-first down the incline. Behind me, Jacko yips and squeaks and bops into my legs as he tum-bles after me. I'm trying to get my arms out in front of me when I slam into the bottom, my face landing in soft earth.

When I inhale, though, I don't smell earth.

I've landed on a cylinder that is both soft and hard at the same time. Soft outside with a solid core. I'm feeling it when I remember that I have sulfur sticks in my pocket, along with my striking rock. I pull them out and light one. It catches fire with a hiss. I lift it to see the cylinder and . . .

I yelp. It is a fawn wrapped in black spider silk. The corpse is desiccated—drained of blood. I shiver as I shift the carcass aside.

I've fallen into a chamber. I can't see far—the sulfur stick casts only a small bubble of dim light, leaving the chamber black beyond it. As I shimmy in, Jacko nudges a smaller black object. Another web-shrouded victim of the jba-fofi. I shine the flame around to see the entire chamber is littered with the wrapped bodies of its victims.

The second bundle is a rabbit, and Jacko nudges it again with his antler prongs, chattering in distress.

Shoving the burning sulfur stick into the earth, I pick him up in a hug. "You're fine. Everything's okay."

I hope it's okay. I'm telling myself that same thing, trying not to freak out at the thought of Alianor with the spider. I can't be far behind them. I need to save her. I will.

I set Jacko down at the tunnel mouth, facing the other direction. "Go back to Dain. He'll take care of you."

Jacko climbs onto my lap instead.

"Okay then, stay with me. But we need to keep moving. I have to find . . ."

I don't hear Alianor. That's what I realize as I'm about to say her name. I don't hear the jba-fofi, and I don't hear Alianor.

My stomach seizes as I look at the mummified bodies all around us. I see those bodies, and I think of Alianor.

Do not freak out.

I can't save her if I'm freaking out.

I scuffle across the chamber on my hands and knees, Jacko creeping beneath my stomach. I pick my way around the bodies and, yes, sometimes I have to crawl over them. I hate that, but there's no other way. The cavern ends in . . .

Three tunnels.

Oh no.

I stop and look frantically from one to the other. Which is the right one?

I strain to hear, but the burrow stays silent. Then I catch a whisper of movement down the tunnel to my far left. A sound, like a muffled cry. Behind me, my sulfur stick goes out. I blink in the darkness and then feel my way into the tunnel.

Ahead, I hear a clacking that makes Jacko hiss. The spider. I try to catch some sound from Alianor, but even the jba-fofi has gone quiet.

I continue along, climbing upward now. Then the ground drops again. This time when I reach down I'm touching a soft-and-hard bundle that I know is wrapped prey. I try to keep going, crawling over the bundles, flinching as the dried bones crackle within.

Soon I'm in the middle of another cavern, and I can't feel a wall on either side. I don't know which way to go, so I take out another sulfur stick. I strike it.

The stick lights with a hiss and a sizzle. The exit tunnel is just ahead and off to my left. I veer toward it. Jacko's sniffing madly. His nose works, neck stretching as if to pick up a smell. Then he freezes. He goes perfectly still, fur rising on his entire body.

The jba-fofi is ahead. It must be just—

A clacking sounds behind me.

I look over my shoulder to see the beast right there, pedipalps waving, fangs clacking.

It has six glossy black eyes, and each leg is longer than one of mine. It rears up, showing a purple-streaked belly. I fall back as I pull out my sword. The jba-fofi springs. It's on me before I can even free my blade.

I drop the sulfur stick. It lands on one of the wrapped prey bundles, the dried silk igniting with a whoosh.

Don't freak out.

Do not freak out.

Jannah always joked that that was the monster hunter's motto. When a beast attacks, just keep repeating it in your head, because it doesn't matter how long you've been fighting monsters, the first thing you'll want to do? Freak out.

I'm alone with a baby jackalope who needs me to protect him.

Alone with a ginormous spider that wants to add our bodies to this heap.

I hear Jannah's voice in my ear.

Think it through. Don't just swing your sword and hope to hit something. Think.

There's no room to swing my sword. I grab my dagger instead and stab at the jba-fofi, but it's a blur above me, and I'm striking wildly.

Don't just swing your sword and hope to hit something.

Great advice . . . if I wasn't lying on my back, in the dark, with a killer spider *on top of me.*

The spider's front two legs wrap around my chest. It pulls me toward its jaws, and Jacko shrieks, leaping on the beast.

— 187 —

I start another wild strike. Then I stop. I know where those front legs are—I can feel them—which means I have a target.

My dagger slices into one of the legs. The spider drops me. I scuttle backward as fast as I can. As I do, my foot strikes another of the spider's mummified creatures, pushing it into the one already ablaze, and the second lights up.

Fire.

Oh yes. *Fire.*

I grab a small bundle—a rabbit or squirrel—and throw it on the flames as I back-crawl behind the fire, toward the tunnel where I hope Alianor is, leaving the jba-fofi on the other side. I'm about to pitch another mummy on the blaze when Jacko jumps onto the spider, sinking his fangs into its back.

"Jacko!" I put my arms up for him. "Jacko! No! Come here!"

The spider bucks and twists to rid itself of the jackalope. Finally, Jacko looks over and sees my outstretched hands. Then he notices the fire.

Jacko leaps over the flames and into my arms. A tuft of his belly hair ignites. I pinch it out and set him down. Then I shove more mummies into the fire, stretching them in a line between us and the jba-fofi.

Soon a curtain of fire blocks us from the beast. The spider's legs appear and disappear, as if it's trying to reach through. It shrieks as the flames lick at it.

I keep pushing over dried bundles until the wall is complete. Then I grab Jacko and run, hunched over, to the tunnel. I push Jacko into it and follow, prodding him along.

Behind me, the spider screams. As the tunnel inclines, I

strain to hear Alianor, but the jba-fofi's fury drowns out all other sound.

Had I picked the wrong tunnel back in the first cavern? There's nothing I can do about that now. An enraged spider and a wall of flame block the way back.

I'm sure I'd heard Alianor.

But what if she was in that cavern I just left?

What if she was one of those mummified bundles?

My heart stops. I swear it does.

No, Alianor couldn't have been back there. The jba-fofi didn't have time to wrap her in webbing.

Keep going. Just keep—

Again, the ground stops in front of me. I lie on my belly, allowing the light from the fire to shine through ahead of me. It's still dark, but I can make out another cavern here. As I crawl into it, my hands touch something warm. I pull back my fingers to see a trouser leg riding up a sturdy calf.

My gaze travels along the leg to Alianor's tunic. I grasp her bare calf and shake it.

"Alianor," I whisper. "It's Rowan. Come on. We need to go."

She's not moving. Why isn't she . . . ?

Where's her face?

I don't see anything above her tunic. I claw my way overtop of her. Then I see her head, completely wrapped in black webbing.

CHAPTER TWENTY-FOUR

I grab the webbing and pull. It sticks to my fingers and holds fast, refusing to break. With my trembling hand, I pick up my dropped dagger. I feel for her mouth, find it and slice the webbing as carefully as I can.

Jacko runs up to Alianor's head and begins gnawing at the web. I work fast, cutting and peeling until her face is free.

She's not moving.

She's not breathing.

I open her mouth. There's more webbing in there. I yank it out and then press my hands against her chest and . . .

Alianor coughs.

I push her so she's sitting upright. She keeps coughing until a wad of webbing flies from her mouth. Then she's doubled over, catching her breath. I pat her back and tell her she's okay.

When she's breathing fine, I crouch beside her. "I've

trapped the jba-fofi—the spider. There's a tunnel behind you. It should lead out. As soon as you're ready, we'll go."

"You still came after me, knowing what I'd done?"

"You made a really dumb mistake. It doesn't deserve death-by-giant-spider. You can explain the rest once we're out of here."

I climb over the mummies to the exit tunnel.

"You go first," I say. "If you don't hear me behind you, just keep going. Oh, and take this." I press my dagger into her hand. "You dropped yours."

"Thank you."

I prod her into the tunnel. Jacko hops in behind her, and I follow them. The burrow soon slants up. When we reach a second tunnel, Alianor stops. I squint and see a trace of light ahead.

"Keep going straight," I say.

I'm right behind her until my sword hilt catches on a root. I back up to free it. That takes more effort than it should, the darkness leaving me fumbling. As I start crawling again, Jacko chatters behind me.

"Yes, yes," I say. "I'm moving."

I reach forward to continue on . . . and my hand touches a furry, warm flank. I go still. A warm nose nudges my finger. A tiny tongue licks at it. Then Jacko's prongs poke my hand, telling me to keep going.

But if Jacko is in front of me, what's chattering behind . . . ?

"Go!" I say, pushing the jackalope.

Rough hair brushes my ankle. I yank away and crawl as fast as I can. Something wraps around my leg. As I fight, it pulls hard, and I'm flipped onto my back. I try to get my sword out, but it's too tight in here, and I'm lying on the scabbard. I kick as hard as I can. The spider squeals. I crawl back on my elbows and heels.

I'm flipping over when powerful fangs grip my leg. I scream. Jacko jumps onto my stomach. I hear the gnashing of his teeth. It's pitch-black, and I'm kicking and punching, hoping to hit the spider and not my jackalope. I get my sword out, but all I can do it thrust it downward, where I'm sure I won't strike Jacko.

The sword jabs something. The spider squeals. I grit my teeth, put both hands on the pommel, drive the sword down into flesh and then yank it out.

I'm scrabbling backward. I can see light. I just need to get a little farther—

The spider's fangs sink into my leg again. I kick hard, and it screeches.

Above me, the ground vibrates. Dirt rains down. It hits my face and fills my open mouth. I sputter and shake my head, and then something shoots through the earth. Something white. That's all I see. Something long and white slicing down like a sword.

The spider screams. I shout for Jacko. He leaps beside me, and I thrust him over my head as I twist onto my stomach. The passage is collapsing, and the spider is shrieking in rage, and I'm crawling as fast as I can.

Moonlight shines ahead. Then it's gone, and something grabs me. I yank away, but a voice says, "I'm rescuing you, princess, whether you need it or not."

Dain yanks me out of the burrow. Alianor is there, but she's staring at something behind me. I turn to see a blur of white ten paces away. That's all I can make out in the darkness. It's huge, and it's white.

Dain grabs my arm and yanks me in the opposite direction. A screech bursts from the earth, and I look over my shoulder to see the spider crawl out of the ruined burrow. And the huge white *thing* . . .

It's not a thing. It's not even huge. It's the pegasus filly, her wings flapping as she attacks the spider. I twist out of Dain's grip and run to her, sword ready. I can't get close, though. She's a blur of flying hooves. So I focus on the spider, ready to attack if it grabs her. It can't. Every time it rears up, she comes down.

Her hooves strike the jba-fofi over and over until it scurries back into its ruined burrow. Even then she tries to trample it through the ground. That's what I'd seen in the tunnel—her leg coming through a thin layer of earth. Stabbing the spider with one slender, sharp hoof.

When the jba-fofi is gone, she noses the hole. Then she snorts, satisfied she's driven it off. There's dark ooze on her forelegs. Spider blood. The jba-fofi has retreated to tend to its wounds, and it will not be back anytime soon.

The pegasus filly shakes her head, her roan-red mane rippling. She's very pleased with herself, as she struts along the caved-in burrow, kicking at the earth and trampling it down. Then she looks at me.

"Thank you," I say.

She tosses her head and whinnies. Then she prances toward me. I stay perfectly still, not daring to breathe. She snuffles my hands. Then my pockets. A snort as she backs up and does a little two-step dance, head shaking in annoyance.

I turn to Dain and Alianor. "Does either of you have an apple? A carrot? Anything?"

Alianor just gapes at the filly. Dain lifts my pack, brought from where I dropped it. I shake my head. He pats his pockets and pulls out a small, bruised apple. I hurry over to grab it and then stop.

"May I?" I ask.

He nods and hands it to me. I hold it out to the filly. She snatches it, gobbles it down and comes snuffling for more.

"Hold on," I say.

I turn to the others. "Help me gather young ferns, shoots, anything tender."

I give them sulfur sticks to help search in the dark, and Dain jogs into the forest. Alianor follows, slower, still gaping at the filly. I head in another direction. As I'm pulling shoots, Jacko chirps, and I see him unearthing something with his front paws, dirt flying. I hurry over to find a patch of wild carrots. I dig up a bunch. I offer him one, but he gives me a look as if I'm trying to feed him dirt.

I chuckle and offer him a scrap of dried meat from my pocket instead. "More later."

I run back with the carrots. The pegasus filly is still in that clearing. The surrounding forest is too dense for her. I wipe off a carrot, and she slurps it from my hand. I keep feeding her until the others bring fresh sprouts, which they pile in front of her. She takes a few bites of those. Then she lifts one dainty, blood-spattered foreleg and rubs it against some long grass, but it's not coming clean.

I grab a handful of broad leaves, speckled with dew. Then I approach.

"May I?" I ask.

She snorts and sets her hoof down and waits. As I approach and bend toward her, Dain says, "Rowan? That's the filly who kicked Wilmot."

"I know."

"She tricked him into thinking she'd accept the halter. Then she kicked him. She can't be trusted."

"I know."

I look the filly in the eye. Then I begin to bend again. I brace for a blow. She might very well lash out. But I have to try. I have to trust her ... and show that she can trust me. This isn't her meadow. I'm not trespassing on her territory. She came here, and I've been nothing but kind, and so I must have faith that she realizes that.

She came to me for a reason. Probably more apples and carrots. Yet she fought that spider, and there are much easier ways of finding food.

She followed me, and she drove off the jba-fofi for me. I am repaying her. I can only hope she understands.

When she lifts her foreleg, I stop, ready to fall back if she pulls it in to strike. But she only holds it there daintily, like a noblewoman raising a dirty foot for her lady's maid to clean.

I wipe the spider blood from one leg. Then she gives me the other. Dain brings me more damp broad leaves, and I clean every bit of spider blood from the filly. When I finish, she whinnies, as if in appreciation. Regal appreciation, a haughty noblewoman thanking her maid.

When I stand, she nudges my arm. I stroke her nose and scratch behind her ears, and she accepts all that as if it is her due. Then she looks at me. Just looks, with those big red-brown eyes.

"Thank you," I say.

She whinnies.

"I'm not going to harness you," I say. "I'm not even going to ask you to come along. I'll only say that you're welcome to. That's your choice. It must always be your choice."

Another whinny, and a nudge. I pat her again. Then I gather more carrots. I show her that I have them as I stuff them into my pockets.

"Yes, that's a bribe for you to come back," I say. "But you can't begrudge me that."

I pick up Jacko and place him on my shoulder. Then I wave for Dain and Alianor as I head into the trees. Dain falls in step beside me. It's a few moments before Alianor runs to catch up.

"That—that's a . . ." she sputters.

"Pegasus."

"And you're just leaving it there? It let you *pet* it. You could rope it. You just need to distract it and give me some rope. I know horses. I can do it."

"No."

We take a few more steps in silence. Then Dain says, "I was running around, trying to find another way in, when the filly landed in that clearing. She came for you. You know her."

"I found her after I left Wilmot's cottage. He couldn't catch her. You didn't dare go near her, so I thought if I brought her back that would prove I'm the rightful royal monster hunter. That I'm worthy of training."

"What happened?"

I shrug as I adjust Jacko on my shoulders. "She tricked me and nearly killed me. I got angry and sedated her, and I nearly killed *her* because she tried to fly and crashed. I realized that she was right to attack me—I was on her territory. I was wrong to get angry and even more wrong to try capturing her. So I apologized and left."

He shoves his hands into his pockets. "After she hurt Wilmot, I went after her. I wanted to kill her for what she did to him. I saw her in that meadow, and I felt sick. Like you said, she didn't do anything wrong. She was defending herself. Wilmot always said whatever happens to us, we can't blame the monsters. They are doing what they do. Finding food, protecting territory, protecting their young . . . I never understood what he meant until I saw that pegasus."

After a few steps, he glances over. "Which doesn't mean you were right about the warakin."

"Had to throw that in, didn't you?"

He smiles. "Of course." Then his face goes serious. "You thought it was about the two silver. It wasn't. That beast is a proven menace. If I wounded him and drove him off and he came back and snatched a child, that would be my fault."

"Then you were right to want to kill it. I didn't know the whole story, though, so I was right to drive it off."

"Agreed."

"I have no idea what you two are talking about," Alianor says. "But you were hand-feeding a *pegasus*, Rowan. It let you clean it. It let you pet it. It came to *help* you. You could have taken it. It's yours."

"That's not how it works."

"I don't understand."

"Because you're not a monster hunter," I say, and Dain and I exchange a smile as we continue on.

We find a glade far enough away that we don't need to worry about the jba-fofi popping up. As Dain starts a fire, I take out my feathers. They're a little rumpled, but Alianor marvels at them. I don't tell her this is what almost got her killed. It isn't really. I climbed the tree to spy on her, not to get the feathers. We'd have disturbed the spiderlings even if I hadn't gone after them. Or that's what I tell myself, whether it's *entirely* true or not.

It isn't dawn yet. That seems impossible, considering how much we've done. But we escaped the camp not long after sundown, and while it might feel as if we've had two solid days of excitement, it really has only been one night.

"So," Dain says to Alianor once the fire is going, "your father's men set a trap for Princess Rowan. They took her captive . . . so you could free her, and your father could claim the glory. Rescuing a princess. That must be worth a reward."

"Is that why *you* helped her?" she says.

"I'm a hunter, not a bandit."

"And I didn't do it for the reward either. I did it for my clan. To help with their negotiations. My father had nothing to do with the plan. He's already at the castle. This was my idea."

I shake my head as I pet Jacko. "Your plan? You expect us to believe that your father placed you in charge of a clan camp? How old are you?"

"Thirteen. It's my brother's camp. One of our scouts spotted you near the forest. That warg gives you away, princess. I came up with the idea. If it had succeeded, I'm sure Lanslet would have tried to take credit. Now that it's failed . . ." She pokes a stick into the fire. "He'll be sure to let Dad know it was all my idea."

"Your brother still allowed it," I say. "Which means he approved the plan. Despite the fact it was really, really stupid."

She stiffens. "It was a perfectly sound plan. I didn't expect . . . they say your brother is the smarter one."

"That doesn't mean I'm dumb. Just that Rhydd is very, very smart."

"It was a cruel trick you played on the princess," Dain says. "I heard what you did. You made her think someone was trapped in a crashed wagon."

"A baby," I say. "She knew I'd fall for that. She posed as a flower girl outside the castle, and I gave her that hair clip she's wearing."

"You—you took advantage of the princess's *kindness?*" Dain sputters.

"It wasn't like that." Alianor's face goes bright red. "Yes, I knew she was kind, and so I set a trap she'd fall for. But a *safe* trap. One where she wouldn't be hurt."

"One of your clansmen dragged me from the wagon by my hair," I say. "He put a sack over my head—just as I saw a dozen armed warriors charging Malric. I thought they were going to kill my warg."

Dain stands. "Enough of this. I'm surprised the princess didn't let that spider devour you."

He pulls his dagger so fast that Alianor gasps and scrambles to her feet.

"I'm not going to hurt you," Dain says. "Not unless you try to run away again. I just don't want you sharing my fire, acting like you're a friend of the princess. You are not. You are her captive."

"Wh-what?"

"We're taking you to my mother," I say. "You can explain what your father—"

"My father knew nothing about it. Please. I swear it." Tears spring to her eyes. "It was stupid. I just . . . I wanted to help the negotiations. To show him I *can* help. You said my father would never leave a child in charge of a camp, but I'm the one who's *been* in charge. Lanslet couldn't lead a raid on a chicken coop. That doesn't matter. He'll still be the next warlord."

"Because he's older than you."

"No. I have a sister who's older than him. But girls can't be warlords."

I screw up my face. "Why not?"

"That isn't how it works in my clan."

"Well, that's dumb."

"I agree, but that's the old way, your highness. Clan Bellamy women *can* fight. We can lead raids. But we can't be warlords. It doesn't matter if my father's only son is a terrible leader. It doesn't matter that my sister or I could do better. They won't even consider us."

"And you want your father to change that?"

It takes her a moment to answer, and when she does, she speaks carefully. "For now, I simply want him to listen to me. I want to be able to say that my brother is dangerous for our clan and have my father pay attention. To do that, I must prove myself. I'm sorry if you were hurt. I'm sorry if you were scared for your warg. We wouldn't have injured him. We respect Clan Dacre."

"That's a fine way to show it," Dain mutters.

"I want my warg," I say. "Now."

CHAPTER TWENTY-FIVE

Alianor doesn't dare just walk into camp and take Malric. Her brother would stop her. So we need to sneak him out. It's too late to do this under cover of night. Dawn lights the sky as Alianor's clansmen rise from sleep. As soon as everyone is awake, they'll start cooking breakfast at the main campfire . . . which is right beside Malric.

Alianor leads us to a stand of trees near the camp. "I told Lanslet to cut these down if we were camping here. They're the perfect spot for enemies to hide. He said Clan Bellamy has no enemies to fear."

"I'm quite certain your clan has plenty of enemies," I say.

"But none we need fear. That's his point. Yet an unnecessary battle still means unnecessary injuries for our people. Lanslet doesn't see that. He only sees the chance for a fight."

She positions us where we can see the campfire through the tents.

"They'll change guard soon," Alianor says. "You need to get the warg before they do. The night guards are sleepy, and they'll be easy for me to distract."

Dain stays behind. He's not thrilled about that, but three of us entering camp is too much. When Jacko tries to follow, Dain hoists him by the back of the neck and holds the jackalope with his claws and teeth out of striking distance. I don't get far before Jacko stops struggling. It's been a long night, and he's little more than a baby. When I last catch sight of him, he's dangling from Dain's hand, his eyes already closing.

As Alianor and I approach the camp, I wonder if they've discovered their prisoner missing. Then I remind myself that their prisoner is *supposed* to be missing. No one will be alarmed to find my cage empty.

"They're breaking camp," Alianor says. "They can't risk being seen here. They're heading out and leaving clues suggesting it was slavers. That was my idea."

She can't keep a note of pride out of her voice. I'm not sure she truly realizes what she did. Yes, I told her I'd been scared. Yes, I said her clansmen dragged me by the hair and threatened my warg. But I feel like she thinks I'm exaggerating all that. It was still, in her mind, a reasonable plan.

As we approach camp, we split up. She tells me to wait until I hear her distraction. Then I can free Malric.

I hide behind a storage wagon at the edge of camp. No one guards it. You'd think bandits would know better, but I guess it's like Alianor said—Clan Bellamy believes no one would dare steal from master thieves. I'm almost tempted to raid the wagon myself, to prove them wrong. There's no time for that, though I do slip out a few apples as I wait.

I'm stuffing one last apple in my pocket when I hear Alianor calling for help, her footsteps thundering over the hard earth.

"Alianor?" someone says.

"It's the princess." She's panting, out of breath. "Princess Rowan's hurt. We were attacked by a jba-fofi spider in the forest. It bit her, and she's paralyzed. I've tried to treat her, but I don't know anything about giant spiders."

Shouts follow. Shouts for the healer and a party of warriors to go with Alianor back to the princess. I sneak closer to the fire. Two men stand guard. They can hear the commotion but not the words. One says he's going to see what's going on. As soon as he leaves, a man running past tells the remaining guard he's needed for a rescue party. He jogs off.

Malric is alone.

I hurry along the tents. Once I'm close enough, I peek out to be sure I haven't missed a guard. I haven't. They're gone, and the way is clear. I still creep carefully, my sword in hand, gaze scanning my surroundings. The ruckus continues to my left, and the campfire area stays clear. That won't last long. I need to hurry. Alianor said the chain binding Malric is fastened with a clasp. I just need to unscrew that, and he'll be free.

Malric lies on the ground just ahead. Fast asleep. With all this noise? Is he still drugged?

Of course he is. They wouldn't want to risk him attacking anyone.

I bend in front of his massive head. "Malric?" The rise and

fall of his chest tells me he's alive, but he doesn't move. I lay my hand on his outstretched paw.

"Malric?"

I squeeze. He still doesn't budge. I lift my hand to the chain on his collar. I'll free him first, then wake him.

I unscrew the clasp. The chain falls and—

Malric leaps awake. Fangs grab my arm. When I yelp, he releases me and stares, blinking in confusion. Deeply sedated confusion.

Oh no.

I bend in front of him. "Malric? I need you to stand—"

He growls, his jowls vibrating. A thread of drool hangs from his lip. His eyes don't focus.

"Malric? It's Rowan. I've—"

Those gigantic jaws snap a finger's breadth from my face. I fall back. He starts to rise, swaying as he does. He can only get his forequarters up, and he wobbles there, still growling.

"Malric, please. I'm trying to—"

"Princess," says a voice behind me. "That's funny. You don't *look* poisoned. You do, however, look as if you're trying to get your face bitten off by that warg."

Still kneeling, I twist to look over my shoulder. My breath catches. It's the young man from the wagon. The one who pretended to be a baby. The one who dragged me out by my hair and threw a sack over my head. He's a few years older than me, with straight light-brown hair and a smile like Malric's snarl.

I push to my feet and lift my sword, showing him I'm armed. He is, too. He holds a finely crafted sword with etching on the blade. A stolen heirloom, no doubt, taken from a noble family. From the way he lifts it, though, I can tell he knows how to use it. He also wears a tunic of hardened leather that doubles as simple armor.

"You don't want to fight me, little princess," he says. "I owe you for a cut from your dagger, and I repay my blood debts tenfold."

He moves forward. I back up, my sword raised to block his blows.

"You tricked my sister, didn't you? Pretended to be poisoned by a giant spider."

Sister? This must be Lanslet, Alianor's brother.

I shift my grip on my sword and think quickly. "Yes, I tricked your sister. I faked being paralyzed and then escaped. That's fair, considering you two tricked *me*. Now we're even, so I'll take my warg and—"

"Do you really think that'll work, little princess?"

I straighten. "Yes, because your plan failed. I won't be telling my mother that Alianor rescued me. I won't be telling her that I was captured by slavers. I know the truth, and Clan Bellamy can't win my mother's gratitude."

Lanslet steps closer, looming over me. "Maybe I don't want your mother's gratitude, little princess. Maybe I want her throne."

I laugh at that. I can't help it. It's entirely the wrong thing to do, though, which I realize as his face darkens.

"You say my plan failed," he says. "It didn't. It just needs an adjustment. One that ensures you never get the opportunity to tell your mother what happened. Apparently my sister *did* rescue you . . . only to have you succumb to your injuries on the way home."

He lunges at me. I leap forward to counter, and that isn't what he expects. Our swords clang. I dodge his next swing and come up on his other side. My sword strikes his arm. He never even flinches, just draws his sword back and—

An arrow hits his shoulder.

Lanslet snarls and plucks the arrow from his leather sleeve. He pauses to see where it came from, and I lunge. He retreats. Then he swings. I block, but his blow is too hard, and it sends me staggering backward. I manage to stay on my feet. His sword sails up, undercutting, and I spin fast.

Another arrow hits, this one striking Lanslet in the back. He stumbles, but again, it's only lodged in his armor, and he comes out of it swinging. I dodge. His sword blade still slices through my tunic sleeve.

It takes only a few moments for me to realize I can't win this fight. Lanslet is an expert swordsman, and he's armored, and Dain's arrows do nothing but distract him.

I hear Berinon's voice at my ear, and he doesn't need to whisper more than a word, because I already understand.

I am outmatched. I see that, and I must recognize it. I can't be like Dad with those bullies. I must do what he couldn't. Retreat. Flee.

I'm fighting for my life here. My actual life.

Yes, I was fighting for my life with the gryphon and the spider, too, but somehow, this is scarier. This is a *person* who wants to kill me. Murder me.

Lanslet swings again. His sword tip cuts more than fabric this time. Pain slices through my side. I duck and strike. I hit his leg, drawing blood, but that only enrages him and he comes at me even harder.

Run. Just run.

I would. I really would. I know I can't win, and I'm not too proud to flee. But if I do, Lanslet will turn his fury on my warg—my heavily sedated, defenseless warg.

I abandoned Malric once. I will not do it again.

I swing. Lanslet counters with a blow that rings through my arm. I dodge and dance to the side. My foot strikes a stray fire log, and I stumble over it. Lanslet gives a grunt of satisfaction, his blue eyes lighting up as he—

A blur of motion behind him. Malric hits Lanslet square in the back. The young man goes down with the warg on top of him. Malric's teeth sink into Lanslet's collarbone, ripping away the leather. Lanslet screeches, and running footsteps sound as someone shouts an alarm.

Lanslet rears up. Malric should be able to pin the young man. That's what Jannah taught him. Never kill people. Subdue and pin them. But when Lanslet rears, Malric loses his grip. He slides off and then he stands there, his paws too far apart, as if struggling to stay upright.

He's still sedated. We need to get out of here. Fast.

Lanslet rises, one hand to his bleeding shoulder. It's his sword arm. He's kept hold of his weapon, but when he lifts it, his face screws up in pain. He swings the blade at Malric. I counter with my sword. Then I give Malric a push away from the campfire, telling him to run. He teeters. I wrap my hand in the thick fur behind his head and drag him as he blunders along after me.

"I'm sorry," I whisper. "But we need to get out of here."

I expect Lanslet to charge, but he's turned toward the guards running our way. I drag Malric. The warg finds his footing and begins a stumbling run just as a clansman bursts from behind a tent. An arrow whizzes past, and the man pulls back. Malric and I run, covered by arrow fire.

"Get them!" Lanslet shouts.

"But—but that's the princess," the man says.

Lanslet snarls at him. I don't hear what he says. We're moving as fast as we can. Soon Malric is running full-out, and I am, too, as the noise from the camp fades behind us.

CHAPTER TWENTY-SIX

I reach Dain and Jacko sooner than I expect. Dain left his post to get closer when the fight began, and he was almost to us by the time I started running. One clanswoman comes after us, but when she sees Dain and I both brandishing weapons—and Malric at our side—she thinks better of it and retreats.

I put Jacko on my shoulders, and we flee. When we're safely away, we pause to regroup, and Malric snarls. Something's coming through the trees. Dain pulls his sword and slips off to investigate before I can stop him. Malric and I stay where we are, the warg poised for attack, me ready with my sword.

A moment later, there's a gasp. A scuffle. I run over as Dain appears, pushing Alianor in front of him.

"She was spying on us," he says.

"Spying?" she yelps. "I was *walking toward* you. I wanted to help you get away."

Dain snorts. "I didn't see you running in when your brother was trying to kill Rowan."

She turns to me, eyes widening. "Lanslet?"

"Unless you have another brother," I say. "He called you his sister. He's about sixteen years old. Light brown hair. Blue eyes. Carries a sword etched with wolves. I wasn't sure what was on the blade at first, but I got a close-up view when he tried taking off my *head* with it."

She stares at me, her face paling. "He must have just been trying to stop you."

"No, he was trying to *kill* me. He said that was the way to fix this. Make sure I can never tell my mother what happened. Pretend you rescued me, and I died on the return trip." I turn away. "Go back to your clan. I'll keep my promise. You helped me get Malric, so I won't tell my mother I was kidnapped." I look at her. "I won't lie to her, though. If it comes up somehow, I can't deny that it happened."

"I understand, your highness. But my father needs to know. I have to tell him before Lanslet does. He'll be at the castle already for the negotiations. That was my plan—I bring you after he arrived, and the queen would be grateful, and my father would see . . ."

Her shoulders slump. "I'm sorry, your highness. I didn't mean to doubt you about Lanslet. He can be cruel, but I never thought he'd harm a princess. I beg your forgiveness, and I swear, you aren't in danger from the rest of my clan."

I suspect she's right. I remember Lanslet pausing when the others approached. He didn't dare kill me in front of them—he wanted to do it before they arrived.

Alianor continues. "Please let me go with you to the castle. I need to confess to my father before Lanslet gets there. I can guide you back. If I give you any reason to doubt me, you have my permission to tie me to a tree and leave me there."

"We wouldn't do that," I say. "But if you trick us again, I will tell my mother what you did. She won't negotiate with your father after that."

"I understand."

We must get away from Lanslet's camp and avoid any trackers he sends after us. But we also have to rest, or we'll be bumbling around, easy prey. Alianor says Lanslet will expect us to head into the forest. The problem is that we *need* to go there. Dain can't leave Wilmot alone for long in his condition. As much as I might want his training, I need to worry about that later, and it'll be easier to get it if we bring Wilmot to the castle.

The solution is misdirection. We'll leave a trail suggesting we're making straight for the nearest village. Then we'll loop south, where we'll re-enter the Dunnian Woods closer to Wilmot's cabin.

Everyone's exhausted, and Malric's still dopey from the sedative. No one complains, though. Even Jacko valiantly tries to hop alongside us rather than sleep on my head. But we're going to collapse soon. So I must take the initiative. I am the princess. If I say we rest, we rest.

I find a spot with enough trees to hide us. Then we take turns dozing. Two sleep while the third stands guard. When it's my turn to guard, I wander about while munching an apple and dangling pieces of dried meat to make Jacko jump for them.

We're enjoying the moment, staying close to camp, eating and playing. Then a huge shadow passes overhead. Jacko squeals and jumps on my leg. I scoop him up and run for the trees. When I see what's casting the shadow, I skid to a halt.

The pegasus filly circles once, spots me and then lands gracefully, tucking her wings in before trotting over.

"Smelled the apples?" I say.

I hold out my half-eaten one. She noses it, her nostrils flaring. Then she nudges my pocket.

"What? You want a whole one? I'm not the only princess here, am I?"

I set Jacko down and take out an apple. She tries to snatch it, but I throw it in the air and catch it again. She tosses her mane like a girl tossing her hair. I can't help laughing at that.

"You want it?" I ask.

She prances with impatience.

I throw it as far as I can. She takes off at a gallop, catches it and chomps down the apple before trotting back and eyeing my pockets again.

"One more," I say. "That's it."

This time I throw the apple high. She runs and spreads her wings to sail up and grab it in midair. When she returns, I'm crouched, petting Jacko.

She walks up to him and lowers her head, coming nearly eye to eye with the jackalope. He lifts one paw, claws extended, as if in warning. She exhales a blast of air that bowls him over backward.

I'm still laughing—and cuddling Jacko to restore his dignity—when Alianor and Dain appear.

"Pegasus, jackalope, warg . . ." Alianor motions at Malric, watching us from the grove. "Princesses really do get everything, don't they?"

"She doesn't get them because she's a princess," Dain says.

"I know," Alianor says. "Sorry. I was teasing. She's a monster hunter. She has a special connection with animals."

Dain walks closer to the pegasus filly, getting a good look at her while staying out of kicking range. "The monster hunter blood helps, but they trust Rowan because she respects them, and she is kind."

Alianor makes a face.

Dain looks at her. "She saved your life. Was that not kindness?"

"She saved me because she's a good fighter. It was kindness that got her captured in the first place. Compassion is a luxury a warrior cannot afford. Tamarel could have lost its princess because she tried to save someone who betrayed her."

My brows shoot up. "Are you saying I should have let that spider kill you?"

"No, I'm just warning you, Rowan. You need the teachings of Clan Bellamy. Others will take advantage of kindness."

"Like Clan Bellamy does?" Dain says. "Robbing and raiding strangers?"

I can see this is leading to a fight, and I step between them.

"Alianor?" I say. "Would you mind scouting before we go? Make sure our path is still clear? I want to be at Wilmot's before sundown."

She nods and leaves. Dain watches her go. Then he takes

a carrot from his pocket and holds it out. The filly ignores him and looks at me. Dain sighs and hands it over. I feed it to her.

"I'm bringing Alianor along because Lanslet is dangerous," I say. "If he gets to their father first, it means trouble for the peace negotiations. Also, when she speaks to her father, I intend to spy on her. I want to be certain this was her idea, and he knew nothing about it."

Dain smiles. "You wouldn't have been such a bad queen."

"A queen is supposed to send someone to spy. I want to do it myself."

I grab a handful of young ferns and feed them to the filly. As she eats, Dain circles her, getting a close-up view.

"Speaking of kindness," I say, "Wilmot was kind, taking you in."

Dain chuckles. "I'm not sure it was kindness."

"Will you tell me about it?"

"On the way, yes."

I'm not sure if he means that or he's putting me off. I search around, gathering more shoots for the pegasus.

"What she really wants is another apple," he says.

I sigh, take one out and pitch it high. The filly leaps into the air, wings unfurling … Before she can grab the apple, Dain shoots it down with his bow.

I laugh as I jog to retrieve it. "Show-off."

I pluck out the arrow and toss the apple to the pegasus. As I return to Dain, he's smiling, his eyes glinting with mischief, and I can't believe this is the same boy I met chasing the warakin.

I've proven I'm worthy of his trust and his companionship, and I didn't need to tame a pegasus to do it. I did it just being myself.

"I meant it when I said I'd like to learn how to shoot like that," I say as I hand back his arrow. "I wasn't just flattering you."

That smile twitches. "Not *just* flattering me. Sure, I'll teach you to shoot . . . in return for that pegasus filly."

I must look horrified because he laughs.

"I'm joking," he says. "You can keep your monsters, princess."

"Are you certain?" I lift Jacko, who's hopping around my feet. "I can offer a lovely young jackalope."

"Sure, I'll take him. And, by the way, dinner tonight will be rabbit stew."

Jacko hisses and gnashes his teeth at Dain. I'm about to say something when Alianor announces that the way is clear. It's time to go.

"She's still there," Alianor says, glancing over her shoulder.

I look back. Sure enough, the filly is prancing along after us. When she sees me watching, she gallops over . . . and butts Jacko, who is riding on my head. He swipes at her, chattering. She continues past and then looks over her shoulder, as if expecting Jacko to come after her. He grumbles and settles in on my shoulders.

We're nearly at the forest, and the filly has followed us the whole way.

"She knows I have one more apple," I say. "Let's just get this over with."

I throw the apple. She soars up, snatches it . . . and brings it back, dropping it at my feet.

"Uh, okay," Alianor says. "She doesn't want the apple."

When I try to keep walking, the filly noses the apple, flip-ping it toward me. I pick it up. She prances past and looks back expectantly.

"I think she wants to play fetch," Alianor says.

I throw the apple. The pegasus flutters after it, tosses it in the air, catches it again and then trots back to me.

"She's lonely," I say. "I don't know what happened to her mother, but pegasi live in herds, like horses and unicorns."

"So we're her herd now?" Alianor says.

"Temporarily maybe?" I look toward the forest. "But we need to go in there, and it's too dense for her."

"I know another way," Dain says. "There's a dried-up riverbed a little farther north. It'll take us close to Wilmot's cabin. We just don't usually use it, because it cuts along a mountain ridge."

"And mountains mean monsters." I shake my head. "No, that's dangerous. We can't change routes for . . ."

I look at the pegasus. She's prancing around Malric now, bowing and trotting, trying to entice him to play. He's pre-tending he's still sleepy from the sedative. When she nips at his hindquarters, he wheels, snarling. She darts out of the way . . . only to charge and feint to one side when he snaps again. He gives me a look.

"Sorry!" I call. "But look on the bright side, Malric. Being pestered by a playful pegasus is better than being held hostage by bandits, isn't it?"

His grunt says he's not so sure. But the next time the peg-asus comes at him, he gives her what she wants—chasing her clear across the field. Jacko squeaks, leaps from my shoulder and races to join in.

"Guys, no," I say. "We need to keep moving."

Malric lumbers back, looking at me as if to say *he* didn't start it. In the field, Jacko tears around with the pegasus.

"We . . . we need to leave her behind." I force out the words. "She'll have to find me later. I can't take a more dangerous, roundabout route to suit her. Not when she might just want to play for a while and then take off again."

"She might," Dain says. "She probably will."

My shoulders slump. That's not what I want to hear. He's right, though. The filly isn't like Jacko, who's had to be peeled from my side since the moment we met. The filly was living fine on her own. She came to me for extra food and attention and companionship, but once she's had enough, she'll take off, like she did after saving me from the spider.

"But . . ." Dain says. "There's a problem. She's accustomed to people now. Wilmot always says there are two reasons for relocating a monster. One, if it's a threat to livestock. Two, if people are a threat to it. We're as much a danger to monsters as they are to us. Maybe more. Capturing a young pegasus would be like finding a crate of gold coins. People *will* try to capture her. They'll get hurt trying, and she might get hurt, too."

"So you must let her follow you," Alianor says. "For her own good."

This is a gross exaggeration. The filly won't even take food from Dain's hand. She's not going to swoop into a villager's yard hoping for handouts. Dain knows that. He's giving me an excuse.

I want to seize it.

I want to say, *Yes, you're absolutely right, Dain. I cannot, in good conscience, abandon this beast.*

I would love to keep this filly. I picture myself on her back, racing across fields. I imagine us in the air, flying over forests. This is a dream come true, and I want it so much it hurts.

That doesn't matter. My mother taught me that being a princess is a privilege. I serve the people. I must put their needs first.

Dain and Alianor have chosen to come with me, like Jacko does, like the filly does. They put their safety in my hands, and I can't risk it because I dream of riding a pegasus.

"I . . . I can't," I say, forcing the words. "I shouldn't ask you to—"

"You're making a request," Alianor says. "Not issuing a royal command. We already agreed, so it's settled."

"And it's not too dangerous," Dain says. "Wilmot only avoids that path because there's no reason to take it. I've only ever seen centicores there and, once, a khrysomallos."

Centicores are mountain goats with sharp horns, one out the back of their head and one out the front. Those horns are dangerous, but only if you force the beast to defend itself. A khrysomallos is a flying ram with golden fur. It's a beautiful creature, like a firebird, and no more deadly than a regular sheep.

When I still hesitate, Alianor says to Dain, "Which way is it?"

He points, and she sets off. Dain jogs after her . . . and I follow.

I tell myself I don't have a choice, but I do. I choose to follow.

CHAPTER TWENTY-SEVEN

We reach the old riverbed. It makes a natural road into the Dunnian Woods. At first, that's all it is—a wide trail through the forest. Then we come to the foothills, and the path turns into a canyon cut through rock.

The pegasus filly is still with us. She's calmed down, and she's trotting along, sometimes behind, sometimes in front. Jacko had been hopping with her, but his baby legs gave out long ago, and now he's dozing on my shoulders.

As we walk, I marvel at the red-striped canyon walls looming above us, higher than the castle spires. Every now and then I spot a mountain goat. Once I think I see a centicore, but it's too far away to be sure. Whatever beasts are in this canyon, they hear us coming and stay clear.

There are caves, too. Natural ones worn into the rock by the river that once ran through here. I imagine the mighty waterway must have run all the way up these canyon walls.

"Oh, I know what this is!" I say. "It's the Michty River. I studied it in history and geography. Long before the clans united under Clan Dacre, this was a huge river flowing from Mount Gaetal. It was the widest and fastest river in the land. The most treacherous, too, full of rocks and monsters. Clan Hadleigh were the only people who knew how to navigate it. That's my father's tribe. He used to tell family legends about it. They could bring people clear through the mountains on this river."

"What happened to it?" Alianor asks.

"I was hoping you could answer that."

"Me?"

"Clan Bellamy are the people of the mountains. All my father knew is that the river stopped running. One winter, it froze over for the first time ever. Then, when spring thaw came, all that melted water rushed down to the lake . . . and the river emptied, like someone pulling the plug on a bath basin. No more water flowed from Mount Gaetal. His clan tried to travel to the source, but no one ever returned. While they continued being river guides elsewhere, once this river was gone, so was their fame and their fortune."

"We don't know how the river stopped," Alianor says. "Our people stay far from Mount Gaetal. Once, when I was little, I declared I would go there one day, to prove my bravery, and my mother told me the story of—"

Thunder cuts her short. For a heartbeat, I ignore it. Every time I've heard a loud noise or felt a wind or seen a shadow pass overhead, I've scurried for cover like a frightened mouse. And it has turned out to be nothing. So when the thunder claps, I only glance into the clouds, expecting a downpour.

Then Jacko bolts upright on my shoulders. The pegasus filly whinnies. The sun vanishes as a massive shadow creeps over us. I squint up to see a white head and feathered wings, and I think it's a pegasus. The filly's mother has found her.

That's when I see the beak. A yellow beak and yellow talons.

"Cover!" I scream. "Take cover!"

Even as the words leave my mouth, I realize they're pointless. We're in a canyon. There *is* no cover here.

"Rocks!" I say. "Get behind—"

The gryphon swoops straight for the filly. I pull my sword and run at it. Jacko leaps from my head before he falls. Dain fires an arrow. It hits the gryphon in the neck, and the beast changes course. It flies over our heads. Then it lands with a thud that vibrates through the canyon floor.

The gryphon lands fifty feet away. That's still close enough for us to see its tongue when it opens its beak. Close enough to hear the clack of its talons on the rocky riverbed. Close enough to spot blood on one foreleg, where I cut its tendon last week. The beast limps but only slightly, its three good legs compensating.

I see the gryphon coming at me. I smell it. I hear it. I swear I feel its talons wrap around me again, dragging me into the air. I see it throwing Rhydd, and I live that moment again, when I thought my brother was dead. I see Jannah on the ground. I watch her dying right in front of me.

We're going to die. We are all going to die.

"Rowan?" Alianor says.

I barely hear her. I'm frozen there, unable to move, unable to even blink.

Alianor says my name again, her voice rising in fear. I catch it that time, and I numbly look over to see her staring at me, her eyes wide.

Staring at me because I am the royal monster hunter. Saying my name because I am the royal monster hunter. And this is a monster.

I swing my gaze back to the gryphon. It's still advancing, its feline tail flicking, like a cat spotting trapped mice. It's still thirty feet away, in no hurry to get to us.

"We need to drive it off," I say, my voice quavering. I swallow hard and come back stronger. They need me to be stronger. "Don't try to kill it," I say. "We just need to drive it off."

"How?" she says.

"Dain and I will handle that. You shoo the filly away. She can fly faster than a gryphon. Get her gone. That's what the beast wants. The pegasus."

Alianor runs for the filly, shouting and waving at it. The pegasus whinnies, but I keep my attention on the gryphon.

"How many arrows do you have?" I ask Dain.

"Only four. I used the rest on Alianor's brother. But I have a slingshot, too."

"Use that then. Save the arrows."

The gryphon is still taking its time, amber eyes fixed on us.

Malric charges. The gryphon rears like a horse, its talons flashing, but Malric feints to the side. When the gryphon twists to parry, Malric leaps, teeth sinking into the beast's foreleg.

As the gryphon writhes, I grab a rock. I race closer and whip the rock at its head. It bounces off the gryphon's beak but still makes the creature squawk. Dain launches a rock from his slingshot. It hits just below the gryphon's eye, and the beast shrieks. Malric still hangs from its foreleg, his jaws clamped tight.

I glance over my shoulder, hoping to see the pegasus long gone. She's still there.

Alianor runs at her, yelling, "Hie! Hie!" The filly only dances past, snorting in annoyance. Then she runs for me. Straight for me. Straight toward the gryphon.

"Keep firing!" I shout to Dain.

I charge at the filly, my arms waving. She stops and tosses her head.

"Go!" I say. "Please! Get out of here!"

She whinnies and dances. She's decided to stay with me, and she isn't going anywhere. But I need her to leave. If she doesn't, the gryphon will kill her.

I told Alianor we'd drive the gryphon away, but it's obviously not going to be that easy. Instead, I need to drive *her* away—the pegasus filly. If we distract the gryphon while the pegasus leaves, it might give chase, but the smaller and faster filly will easily escape.

My gut seizes at the thought, and a little voice inside me screams that I don't need to do this, that she can defend herself, that the gryphon might not go after her. Even if I drive her away, the gryphon could stay and attack *us*. What if the gryphon actually wants me? What if it knows I'm the one who hurt it?

No, I wasn't the only person who hurt it that day. A human might want revenge, but a predator only wants dinner, and that would be the pegasus.

I finally won the filly over, and I want to keep her, and that doesn't matter. It can't. I earned her trust, and if I don't do this, I betray that trust. I made her a promise. That I'd keep her safe. I need to do that . . . even if it means losing her forever.

To save her, I must give her up.

I reach down for a rock. Then I heft it.

"I'm sorry," I say . . . and I pitch the stone at her.

CHAPTER TWENTY-EIGHT

The filly backs up fast, her wings fluttering. The rock glances off her shoulder, and she turns on me with a look of shock.

"Go!" I shout, my voice thick. "I don't want you anymore. Get out of here!"

I reach down for another rock. She whinnies and stamps.

Dain shouts behind me. Alianor shrieks, "Rowan!"

I turn to see the gryphon charging. It has thrown Malric off, and it's running straight at the pegasus.

Sword raised, I plant myself between the charging gryphon and the pegasus. The beast lowers its head and rushes at me. Then it rears, shrieking. It whips around, and I see Malric, the huge warg lifted in the air as he clings to the gryphon's rear leg. The gryphon grabs him with its beak.

I run and slash at the beast. I know better than to stab its thick hide. But I slash at its foreleg, right where it's bleeding from Malric's initial attack. The gryphon swings on me. Its giant beak strikes my shoulder, and I fly through the air, thumping down flat on my back.

I lie there, dazed. Then I remember where I am, and I bolt upright just as the gryphon flies at me again. I leap to my feet. A stone hits the gryphon square in the eye. It shrieks. Alianor pitches a bigger rock and strikes it in the throat. I race out of the beast's path. Malric jumps at it again. As the gryphon twists to deal with the warg, I see a shadow far off to my left. It's the filly, disappearing over the canyon walls.

"I'm sorry," I whisper.

I tear my attention from her and grab a rock. Alianor and I keep at it, throwing stones as Dain slings them, and Malric lunges and bites. Even Jacko dashes in, distracting the beast when it goes after the warg. The filly is gone, but the gryphon isn't leaving.

"Shelter!" I shout. "We need to take shelter."

Alianor points to the canyon wall. High above us, a dark patch marks a cave entrance. It should lead into a series of tunnels—a perfect escape route, too small for the gryphon to follow.

"Go!" Dain says. "Take Jacko and run. Malric and I will distract it."

"No, you need to come—"

"We'll be right behind you."

Alianor and I back toward the cave while pitching rocks at the gryphon. I hold Jacko under one arm, and we keep pelting the beast while we retreat.

We must climb to reach the cave mouth. Alianor goes first. I want Dain to follow, but he insists I go next.

I position Jacko on my shoulders. Then I grab a rock ledge. That means putting my back to Dain and Malric. It feels like escaping. Like I'm turning my back on my friends. Like I am, once again, hiding in that haystack as Jannah fights the beast.

The more I hesitate, the longer we are all exposed. The longer they are in danger.

As I heave myself onto the ledge, the gryphon snarls behind me. Dain's rocks thump off its thick hide. Malric roars. A cry rings out. A canine cry of pain, edged with a whimper.

"Malric!" I shout, and I twist, hanging from the ledge, Jacko sliding on my shoulders.

"Keep going!" Dain yells. "He's fine!"

Malric is not fine. He's lying on the rock, thrown there by the gryphon. The gryphon is bearing down on him ... just like it did with Jannah.

Malric whimpers and lifts his head. My hand tightens on my sword. As the gryphon advances on the warg, Dain runs for the canyon wall. He runs right past Malric, not pausing to help the warg at all. I tense, ready to leap down.

"No!" Dain shouts. "He's fine! Keep going!"

Fine? *Fine?* Malric lies battered on the rock, unable to do more than lift his head and whine. The gryphon has launched itself into the air. It's poised over the wounded warg. I have to—

The gryphon drops. I scream ... and Malric nimbly leaps out of the way. He runs in the other direction. Then he staggers and falls again.

Below, Dain says, "Move, princess! Malric's not wounded. He's—"

A screech of frustration from the gryphon drowns out Dain's words. The gryphon has dived, only to find its prey gone *again*.

Malric is drawing the gryphon off. He's faking injuries to lead it away as we climb. Dain smacks the bottom of my boot and says, "Move, princess!" I climb as fast as I can. When I near the top, Alianor bends to lift Jacko off my head. He chatters at her but lets himself be taken as I get up onto the ledge. I reach for Dain. He grabs the ledge with both hands and heaves himself onto it.

"Show-off," I say.

He passes me, heading into the cave as I crouch on the edge and shout, "Malric!" The warg sees that we're up and comes running. Behind me, Dain whispers, "No!" His footfalls pound deeper into the cave.

"What's wrong?" I say.

As soon as I turn for a better look, I see the problem. From below, the opening looked just big enough to let us through. That was an illusion. What we find is a massive cavern . . . one that the gryphon can fly right into.

I jump to my feet. "We need to go! This won't—"

"Over here," Alianor says. She's running for a hole off to the cavern's right side. She leans into it. "This one's too small for all of us to fit inside."

Dain's at the back of the cavern, on his knees, peering into another opening. "Here! This'll work!"

I look down the canyon wall. Malric has leapt onto a ledge. He hunkers down and jumps but doesn't make it to the next. His claws scrabble against rock as he slides. The gryphon is in flight and coming straight for him.

I pitch a chunk of rock as hard as I can just as the gryphon swoops for Malric. The rock hits the top of the gryphon's head. It shrieks and loops back.

Malric reaches the ledge. He crouches and leaps for the next one. This time, he makes it. Then he jumps again. His paws hit the one I'm on. They hook it, but he's fallen short again and he's slipping.

I drop to my knees and grab one paw. Dain runs over to grab the other. Alianor reaches to seize the scruff of Malric's neck. We drag him up onto the ledge just as the gryphon flies at us.

We fall back in a tumble of legs and fur. Then we scramble to our feet and run for that hole in the back. I push Alianor in as Dain grabs Jacko and motions for me to follow Alianor. Malric comes after me.

The warg is too big for the opening, and Dain has to shove him as I pull his ruff. Finally, Malric pops through. Then Dain passes the jackalope to me. He starts through . . . and then I hear the gryphon scream. In a flash, its beak closes on Dain's leg. I drop Jacko and grab Dain by the shoulders. I yank as hard as I can, and Dain flies in, one foot bare.

The gryphon drops Dain's boot. Its beak pokes into the hole as we all scramble back. It manages to get its beak inside, but it can go no farther. The air fills with the sweet smell of gryphon breath. It hisses and growls, but we're out of reach, and after a moment, the gryphon withdraws into the cavern.

We take a moment to catch our breath. As Alianor checks Dain's foot—and declares it unhurt—I lie on my belly, far enough from the opening that the gryphon can't grab me. I watch it in the cavern. It has enough room to move around, to be comfortable. But there's not enough room for us to sneak by it.

I look over my shoulder. Past the low opening, the rear cave expands. It's big enough to fit all of us. We can even stand up if we move farther back. We cannot, however, go anywhere. There are no passages to crawl through. It's a blind cave.

We're trapped.

No, not trapped. *Safe*. For now, we are safe. We can breathe. We can rest. After that . . .

After that, I don't know.

The gryphon isn't leaving. It's smart enough to realize it has its prey cornered.

"It'll get hungry eventually," Alianor says, an hour or so later, as we watch it lounge on the cavern floor.

"Gryphons are like wolves or mountain cats," I say. "They can go a week without eating."

"And we can't," Dain says grimly.

"We actually can," I say. "But we can't go a week without water."

We check our water skins. They're only half full.

"What about the gryphon?" Alianor asks. "How long can it last without water?"

"Longer than us," I say.

"Then we'll wait until it sleeps."

I shake my head. "Gryphons sleep like birds. It'll doze, but as soon as we try passing, it'll wake up."

"Then as soon as it dozes, I'll go for help," she says. "You can distract it while I run."

I look at Dain. He shakes his head. He doesn't trust her to bring help. I think he's wrong. She will tell her clan, but that doesn't mean anyone will believe her. She already lied to them about my being paralyzed by a spider.

So now the princess is trapped by a gryphon? What are you up to, Alianor?

I crawl to Malric. There's blood on his fur, but when I tried to check him earlier, he snapped at me. This time, when he snaps, I snap back. Jacko hops over and chatters, as if telling the warg to be still. Malric grunts and lowers his muzzle to the ground.

I examine him. Some of the blood doesn't have a wound below it. That means it isn't his. The rest are shallow scrapes and cuts.

I feel for broken ribs. He doesn't even flinch when I rub my hands over his chest. He's fine. He really was only faking it with the gryphon.

Alianor crouches beside me and watches intently. When I look over, she says, "His wounds should be cleaned, but I hate to use the water. They'll be fine until morning." She straightens. "I've trained under our healer. That's what I'm supposed to be when I'm grown."

"A healer?"

I must sound surprised, because she smiles. "Couldn't you tell by my amazing bedside manner?" She shrugs. "I like healing. I'm pretty good at it, too. I just want more."

"You want to be a leader."

"Honestly, I'm not even sure. Right now, my main concern is making sure Lanslet doesn't become warlord of our clan. If he does, I don't think we'll *be* a clan much longer. A lot of our clansmen won't follow him. They already think he's incompetent."

"And your father doesn't realize that?"

"He does. He just thinks they're wrong."

I nod. She continues examining Malric.

"Does he seem well enough to walk?" I ask.

"Walk, yes. Fight, no."

I move to my pack and remove my field journal and quill. I write a message. Then I slide it into the slot in Malric's collar.

"He can take that to the castle," I say. "Then he can lead Berinon back. The problem is getting him out of the cavern. I'll need to distract the gryphon so Malric can run past."

"I can handle that," Alianor says. "The best way to raid a camp is to divert attention. I'm an expert at that game."

I hope she's right.

CHAPTER TWENTY-NINE

The gryphon lies curled up, as if sleeping. Its eyes are shut, its chest rising and falling. I'm not sure if it's faking or actually dozing. It's not fully asleep, though. I can tell that by the way its ears twitch at every sound.

So we make some noise. We bustle about the rear cave, talking and bumping into the walls. The gryphon peers our way several times. It soon realizes that these sounds don't mean its prey is emerging, though, and it stops peeking.

As Dain and I talk loudly, Alianor creeps out. She's left her boots in the rear cave with us, and she moves silently, rolling her feet. I watch the gryphon's ears. They don't move. Alianor reaches the back corner of the cavern. Then she looks my way.

I take a deep breath. This is the part of her plan I don't like. The part where she needs to wait in that corner while we help Malric through the very tight hole into the cavern. His entire body fills it, which means we can't see out. Can't see

Alianor. Can't see the gryphon. There's a moment where Malric sticks like a cork in a bottle, and all we can do is push. If the gryphon spots Alianor, we'll be powerless to help her.

Finally, Malric is through. The gryphon hasn't moved. When I motion to Alianor, she races across the cavern floor, her bare feet slapping the rock. The gryphon's eyes fly open. It leaps to its feet, front talons and back claws scraping the rock. Behind the beast, Malric creeps as quietly as he can. Alianor whoops so the gryphon doesn't hear Malric's nails clicking. The beast lunges toward her, and she slides through the opening into the smaller side cave, the one we couldn't all fit into.

The plan is for her to slide into that side cave and leave her feet sticking out. To kick and make a commotion, so the gryphon will try to grab her. I don't like that part either. It's necessary, she said, to make sure the beast doesn't give up too easily and notice Malric sneaking out.

Jacko lets out his alert cry from where he's wriggled up under me to watch. Alianor is safely plunging into the hole, but all the baby jackalope understands is that the gryphon is going after Alianor, and I'm not doing anything about it. Maybe I don't see my companion in danger. So he needs to tell me. As soon as he sounds his alert cry, my hand slaps over his mouth. It's too late. The gryphon is already turning.

I withdraw fast, and I hear Alianor valiantly trying to regain the gryphon's attention, but his head whips the other way, past us and over to . . .

The gryphon spins and lunges at Malric. The warg dodges, and the gryphon's beak snaps the end of his tail. Malric runs for the cavern opening. He makes it through, and he's crouching to jump when the gryphon grabs him around his neck.

I burst into the cavern. Dain shouts in alarm. Jacko squeaks. I don't care. I run across the cavern floor, sword in hand. But I'm already too late. The gryphon throws Malric. The warg hits the cavern wall, and that crunch rings out. That terrible crunch I will never forget—the one I heard when the gryphon pitched my aunt head-first into a rock.

I scream, and I rush at the gryphon. It doesn't even look my way. It's going for Malric, lying motionless on the floor.

I take a running leap and stab with my sword. The blade plunges into the gryphon's haunch. And then I'm hanging there, gripping the hilt, my sword embedded in the beast's thick hide. The gryphon screams, but the short blade is barely halfway in. My feet aren't even touching the ground. I've done nothing but enrage the beast. When I try to yank the sword out, it won't budge.

The gryphon wheels and slams me into the cavern wall. I'm crushed between the beast and the rock. The fur of its haunch presses against my face. I can't breathe. I let go of my sword—I must. I punch and claw at the gryphon. Then it shrieks, and I look up to see something on its back.

It's Jacko, digging in all his claws and his teeth. The beast snarls and shifts, and I fall free. Hands grab me.

"Jacko!" I scream.

The jackalope leaps from somewhere above me and lands on my head. I hear a clang, as if my sword has fallen out of the gryphon, and I should go after it, but arms drag me away. Before I can even see who it is, I'm being shoved into the rear cave.

I twist to see Dain. He pushes Jacko and me inside. I scramble around, and Dain grabs me as if I'm about to run again. Inside the cavern, the gryphon stomps about, shrieking in rage. That's all I see. The gryphon . . . and a blood-smeared wall.

"Malric," I whisper. "Where's—"

Alianor pops her head out from the side cave and calls, "I have Malric. He's alive, just—"

The gryphon wheels and snaps at her. She yanks her head back just in time.

The beast keeps stomping and snarling and raging. It tries again to shove its head into our rear cave. Tries to shove it into Alianor's side one. When it can't do either, it retreats to the middle of the cavern and settles in, one eye on each cave entrance.

"Is Malric okay?" I shout.

"He will be. One of his legs is broken, and I think he has a head injury. He'll recover but . . . he won't be taking that message, Rowan. I'm sorry."

"It was a good plan," I call back. "Thank you for trying."

I mean that. It was a very good plan. But Jannah always said that no matter how good a plan is, you can't control every variable, so you need a backup.

I don't have a backup.

I'm sitting on the rear cave floor, with Jacko on my lap. He's purring, but it sounds forced, as if he's doing it for me.

"We'll figure something out," Dain says.

"Like what? I'm supposed to *kill* this thing. If I don't, I'll never become the royal monster hunter. My mother will lose the kingdom, and Heward will take over. He'll destroy it, and it will be all my fault, unless I kill that . . . that thing." I jab my finger at the cave opening. "That thing that I can't even get *past*. Forget killing. I can't even escape it."

"But you did, right? In the battle where your aunt died? It had you, and you escaped."

"That was different."

"Yes, because it had you in its talons. That was worse."

No, *this* is worse. I knew we shouldn't have come through the canyon. Dain and Alianor came this way for me. So the princess would get her pegasus. Now I've lost her, and I might lose them, too.

Dain, Alianor, Jacko, Malric . . .

They might all die in this cave, and it's my fault.

CHAPTER THIRTY

The sun is starting to drop outside the cave, shadows inside lengthening. We've been sitting in silence. Thinking. Hoping, too—hoping the gryphon will give up. It hasn't. I've injured it, and now it's more determined than ever to wait us out.

I've been adding the jba-fofi page to my field journal in hopes that will distract me, but it hasn't. Finally, I set it aside and call out to Alianor, checking in with her. She's fine. Just resting and tending to Malric.

I look over at Dain. "I'm sorry."

"For what?" he asks.

"Everything. We changed our route for me. The gryphon attacked because of me. Now it's wounded—and angry—because of me. We're all going to die because—"

"Uh, no. Sorry, princess, but I don't plan on dying today."

"It won't be today. It takes three days to die of thirst."

He laughs at that, a sharp guffaw that startles Jacko. The jackalope chatters at him before settling in again.

"Let me rephrase that, princess. I have no intention of dying anytime soon. While I do appreciate your scientific assessment of our situation, I plan to be rescued by magic. Or a witch." He scrunches his nose. "Maybe a wizard."

I force a smile for him.

He walks over and hunkers down at my side. The falling light casts half his face in shadow, but he's close enough for me to see a scar crossing his nose, a thin, pale slash against his brown skin.

"Did you drag me on this adventure, princess?"

"No, but—"

"Did you order me to come?"

"No, but—"

"Did you force me up that tree? Did you push me into the spider's burrow?" He meets my gaze. "You led. I *chose* to follow."

"I changed our route because—"

"No, I changed our route. I suggested this one. I said it was safe." He leans against the wall. "I did a very fine job of getting us into this mess. Don't go hogging all the credit."

I shake my head.

He pulls his knees up, settling in. "You asked how I ended up with Wilmot. Would you like to hear the story?"

Before I can answer, he says, "I know, it's not the time. But we're both going nuts trying to figure out a plan. We need a break. We need a story. Would you like one?"

I nod. "Yes, please."

"Okay, so after the queen stole—" He stops, as if remembering who he's talking to. "After my parents lost their farm, they sold—gave—*asked*—me to work for the village mayor as a rat catcher."

I don't miss the way he quickly changes the verb in that sentence. His parents did not *ask* him. They didn't give him to the mayor for fostering, either. They sold him into indentured servitude.

Indentured servitude means that a person must work for an employer for a certain number of years. The only way to get out sooner is to pay for your freedom, which is nearly impossible when your already low wages are docked for room and board.

When our first king took the ivory throne, he had to respect the traditions of the other clans. Indentured servitude was one of those traditions, but within two generations, Clan Dacre outlawed it.

I can't say that, so I only murmur, "That must have been awful."

"My parents had no choice, princess. Your mother—" He clips off the word. "And this is not the story I intended to tell you. I know your mother isn't an evil queen. You're too kind to have been raised by a terrible parent. I don't know what happened, but it's something for me to take up with her."

I say nothing, and he doesn't seem to expect me to.

"Okay," he continues. "The important part is that I *was* a rat catcher—not how I became one. So when I was eight, we had a hoop snake in the chicken coop. The mayor summoned Wilmot. As soon as I discovered that a legendary monster hunter was coming, I stayed up two nights in a row, hoping to catch the snake myself. I did. Wilmot arrived, and I presented it to him. They thought I did it to earn Wilmot's fee myself. I didn't. My plan was to give Wilmot the hoop snake *and* the reward, and then ask him to buy my service from the mayor so I could become Wilmot's apprentice. I wanted to be a monster hunter."

"And Wilmot was so impressed by you catching the snake that he agreed."

"Uh-uh. He said he had no use for an apprentice. That I should take the reward and put it toward buying my freedom. But the mayor refused to pay me. So I released the hoop snake."

I snicker. "I bet the mayor loved that."

"Oh, I was in trouble. A lot of trouble actually." His eyes cloud over at the memory, but he throws it off. "Anyway, Wilmot caught the hoop snake. When he left, I snuck out and followed. I tracked him all the way home, and he never realized I was there. This, I said, proved that I could be a monster hunter."

"So he took you in."

"Nope. He sent me home. He told me the best and safest path back to the village. He warned me to stick to the trail. Whatever I did, I was not to go north of it. A warakin lived there, one he'd been trying to frighten off. So I left, but I ignored the warning."

"Because you wanted to kill the warakin."

Dain shakes his head. "Even at eight, I knew I couldn't fight a warakin. But after Wilmot captured the hoop snake, I'd seen him sedate it so he could release it in the forest. So I waited until he fell asleep, snuck in, found his hunting pack and stole a needle full of sedative. Then I went off to capture the warakin."

"You drugged it and brought it back, and *then* he made you his apprentice."

"Uh, no. The problem with a sedative is that you need to get close enough to use the needle. The warakin cornered me. By then, I'd lost the needle, and I was armed only with my stick."

"Your stick?" I try not to laugh.

He mock-glowers. "It was a very fine stick. That's what I used against the rats. I'd sharpened a stout branch, and I'd poke at them with it, to drive them off. Warakins don't like being poked with sharp sticks. They really don't."

"I'll remember that," I say, trying not to laugh. "But you survived, obviously. Did you poke it in the eye?"

"No. That's a fine idea, but I didn't think of it. The warakin had me cornered. Just as it lunged for the kill, Wilmot ran in. He saved my life."

"And then he took you on as an apprentice, because you'd passed his test."

"No . . . Have you been listening, princess? I failed. I didn't catch the warakin. Wilmot did take me on after that, though. He said someone had to train me, before I got myself killed."

"Wilmot didn't just *happen* to show up at that moment. Just like he didn't just *happen* to warn you about a warakin north of the path. He wanted to see what you'd do. You accepted the challenge. You were also mature enough to realize you couldn't kill a warakin and clever enough to come up with another way to defeat it. He didn't expect you to succeed.

He just wanted to see what you'd do. See whether you'd make a proper monster hunter."

"Huh." Dain leans back against the cave wall. "I never thought of it that way. You're right. He did show up just in time to save me."

"He let you get scared for your life. That was a lesson. One you need to become a proper monster hunter. So what happened then?"

"Wilmot returned to the mayor and said there'd been a mix-up, that I thought he'd bought my freedom, and that's why I followed him. Then he did buy my freedom . . . and gave it back to me. He said what the mayor did was wrong and illegal. If I stayed with Wilmot, it had to be my decision. That's why I owe him so much. He can be gruff, and he is the most stubborn person I've ever met, but he has always been fair to me. I'm with him by choice. Now I'm caring for him by choice."

I'm quiet for a moment. Then I leap to my feet, startling both Jacko and Dain.

"Princess?" Dain says as Jacko squeaks.

I grab my pack and pull out a small padded case. The bottom corner is wet, and it stinks of chemicals.

"No," I whisper. "Please no."

I pull out a broken bottle. It's cracked at the base, some of its contents leaking. It's more than half full, though. I exhale in relief and set it on its side so it can't leak anymore. Then I remove a needle.

"Sedative?" Dain says.

"Your story gave me an idea. A quarter of a needle made the pegasus groggy. Two full ones should knock out the gryphon."

"You only have one needle."

"I know, but I can refill it."

"Run up to the gryphon, inject it and refill the needle?" He crouches beside me as I rummage through my pack. "Even getting close enough to inject it *once* would be difficult."

I pause. He's right. Even if I get the first dose in, that will alert the beast, like it did the filly. The gryphon will never let me get close enough for a second. I look down at the bottle, the contents shifting from one side to the other.

"It's viscous," I say.

"Viscous . . . ?"

"Thick. Gummy. I can coat my sword with it."

"The sword that's lying out there in the cavern?" He shakes his head. "Getting near the beast isn't the answer. I learned that with the warakin. What we need is a way . . ."

He trails off as his gaze lands on his quiver.

"Yes!" I say. "We'll coat the arrowheads in the sedative. You have four left, right?"

He nods.

That should be enough.

It has to be.

CHAPTER THIRTY-ONE

The arrows are ready. Dain is ready. I've called over to Alianor and told her the plan. There's nothing she needs to do. I just don't want her thinking anything's wrong when the gryphon starts crashing about after he's been sedated.

Dain crouches at the hole. It's waist-high. *My* waist height, not his.

"It's a lousy firing position," he says. "If I had my crossbow, I could lie on the floor."

"You have to make do with what you've got."

"I know, princess. I'm just . . ." He wipes his brow. "I don't know if I can hit the gryphon four times. Not after it starts moving. And when that first arrow hits, it's going to start moving."

"You just need to hit it with three. That'll be enough to take it down. Then I'll run out and jab in the rest with the needle."

"I can do that," he says.

"No, you shoot, I run. You don't get to have all the fun."

I smile when I say it, but my voice quavers, and he doesn't smile back. He kneels and draws back his bow, checking his position. Then he positions himself on just one knee and nods, meaning he's stable enough.

"Three," he says. "I can do three."

"If you don't, that's fine. We'll figure something out. This isn't all your responsibility, Dain."

"Yeah, it kind of is."

He gives me a strained smile. Sweat drips down his forehead. I pass him a spare tunic from my pack and motion for him to wipe the sweat. He does, and he plasters his hair back. Then he takes a deep breath.

"Three shots," he says. "One to spare. If I manage all four, even better."

"Don't get cocky."

Another smile, more genuine now. He adjusts his position. I scoop up Jacko to keep him quiet this time.

When Dain signals that he's ready, I crouch behind him. My heart thumps so loud I can barely breathe. I hug Jacko tight. Dain draws back the string. He fires and nocks the second arrow so fast that he's firing it before the first even hits.

And it does hit. It strikes the gryphon in the haunch. The beast snarls. The second embeds itself beside the first, and Dain's already got the third nocked. The gryphon rises, but it's still right there, a huge wall of feather and fur that Dain cannot possibly miss.

He fires . . . just as the gryphon flies up into the air, the arrow passing under it.

"No," Dain whispers. "No."

— 247 —

"It's okay," I say quickly. "You've got one more. You couldn't have expected that. I didn't even think it had room to launch in here."

Outside, the gryphon shrieks. It flies at our hole, but the sedative makes it clumsy, and it hits the wall instead. The whole cavern shakes.

The gryphon lowers its head to our cave hole. It peers in. Its pupils are dilated from the sedative, but it's not enough.

We need one more arrow strike . . . and the gryphon is right outside the hole.

A perfect, unmissable shot.

Dain draws back the string. The gryphon rams its head into the opening.

I set Jacko down and snatch the needle. I keep my foot in front of the jackalope so he can't upset Dain's shot.

The bowstring stretches taut. The gryphon batters the opening.

I grip the needle. I'll wait for the gryphon to teeter away from the opening. It will. No need to rush—that'd be danger-ous. Let the sedative daze the beast, and then I'll rush out and deliver the final dose.

Dain releases the string . . . and it breaks. The bowstring snaps, the arrow smacking into the wall.

Dain grabs the arrow and lunges at the beast. The gry-phon backs out of reach. Dain barrels through the opening. Running *into* the cavern.

"Dain, no!"

I shove the needle into my pocket and race out. Dain stands there, arrow in hand, the gryphon right in front of him.

He's stopped, seeing how small he is, how puny that arrowhead is. His eyes widen.

The gryphon lunges. Dain dives to the side. The gryphon's beak snaps. It catches Dain's bare foot. He drops the arrow as he falls clear of the beast and rolls across the cavern floor.

Dain vaults to his feet and pulls his sword. The gryphon advances, its talons clicking against the rock.

My sword lies on the other side of the gryphon. I race over, snatch it up and charge the beast. I slash at its back leg. It screeches and wheels away from Dain.

"Hey!" Alianor shouts, out of her cave and waving her arms. "Over here! Easy pickings right this way!"

The gryphon ignores her. It keeps bearing down on me. Dain runs for the arrow he dropped. Before he can reach it, the gryphon spins, its beak slamming into him, sending him flying.

As the beast turns, I see the angry red scabs on the foreleg I injured a week ago. I swing my sword right at the same spot. The blade slices in. The beast lets out a terrible screech of pain and rage. It stumbles into the cave wall. Rocks rain down. One strikes Dain's head as he rises. He falls back down. The gryphon flies at him.

Alianor races toward Dain, shouting at the gryphon, trying to attract its attention. She's waving her dagger, but the beast doesn't seem to care.

I'm behind the gryphon. I run at it, my sword raised. The beast is poised over Dain. I shout, and it glances over its shoulder. Something hits my arm. Something that feels like the crack of a whip. It's the gryphon's tail, lashing my elbow so hard I gasp. White-hot pain slams through my arm, and my hand opens before I can stop it.

My sword clangs to the rock floor below. I scramble to grab it, but the gryphon's massive back paw lands on the blade. Then the beast turns. It spies me without my weapon. It knows I'm the one who hurt its leg. It *knows*.

I am right beside the gryphon. So close that as it turns, its mane brushes me. Those huge amber eyes fix on mine as it screeches in victory.

I want to see a gryphon.

I want to touch its wondrous mane.

I want to hear its terrible screech.

I want to meet it, to stand before it and look up into those amber eyes and say hello.

"Rowan!" Alianor shouts.

Rowan, do something.

That's what she means.

Rowan, save us.

I must save them. I'm the royal monster hunter. They followed me into this. They are my people. I need to keep them safe.

How? I dropped my sword. I rushed out after Dain and left my dagger behind. What can I possibly—?

The needle.

Yes!

As I fumble to pull the needle from my pocket, something darts across the cavern floor. A brown blur leaps onto the gryphon's injured leg. Jacko bites the beast right where I just sliced it.

The gryphon shrieks in agony.

Perfect! I just need to plunge the needle into the beast's flank while it's busy with Jacko. But the needle tip is caught in my pocket, and if I pull too fast, I'll break it.

The beast's head swings toward the jackalope. Its beak opens. I slam my foot into Jacko. I hate that so much, but it's all I can do. Knock Jacko out of the way before that beak crushes him.

The jackalope goes flying . . . and the beak closes on my boot instead.

The gryphon's head whips up, yanking me off my feet. I grab the only thing I can reach—the beast's mane. I wrap my hands in it to give myself leverage as I wrench my leg. My foot doesn't pop free from the gryphon's beak, but I manage to keep my grip on its mane.

The beak tightens on my boot. Pain shoots up my calf. I grit my teeth, look over my shoulder and kick my free foot at the beast's eye. It makes contact, and the gryphon's head snaps back, its beak opening, my foot falling free. Then I'm hanging on its mane. An image of Jannah flashes. My aunt on the manticore. Riding the manticore. Driving her dagger into the back of its neck.

I heave myself up. The gryphon twists, and my leg doesn't make it over the beast's back. When I try again, the gryphon bucks, and that's exactly what I need. I shoot onto it. Nearly shoot *over* it and tumble down the other side. But I keep my grip, and then I'm lying flat on the gryphon's broad back, face-down, my fists wrapped in its mane.

Below, Alianor and Dain shout. The gryphon goes still.

Its head turns from side to side as it looks for me. My hand slides into my pocket. I grip the beast's back with my knees and keep hold of its mane with my other hand as I unhook the needle tip from the fabric it's caught on.

As I pull the needle from my pocket, the gryphon bucks. By sheer luck, my hand clamps down on the needle instead of dropping it. The beast rears. I keep my grip on the needle and ease my hand up to the gryphon's neck. It's twisting now. It knows I'm on its back, and it's trying to figure out what to do about that.

Its wings fly out. One knocks my foot up, and I slam face-first into the beast's neck. I clutch its mane with my left hand, the needle in my right. Below, Dain and Alianor attack the gryphon. So does Jacko, his squeals ringing out. In the corner of my vision, I see Malric staggering toward us, one rear leg dragging.

I squeeze my eyes shut. I must do this. Stop waiting for the right moment. Stop waiting for the *safe* moment. Inject the sedative, and if the beast throws me clear and tramples me afterward, that is what happens. Every moment I hesitate is another moment for someone else to die.

I release the gryphon's mane. I raise both hands, clutching the needle between them. I grip the beast with my knees, as tight as I can. Then I slam the needle into the gryphon's neck. Slam it in. Hit the plunger. Watch the liquid rush in.

The beast rears. I drop the empty needle and grab its mane. I clutch it with both hands and bury my face in it.

The gryphon bucks and twists. I hold on for dear life as the beast thrashes. It stumbles. It trips over its own feet. I close my eyes and feel its heartbeat thudding beneath me. Feel its heartbeat slowing as the sedative slides through its veins.

I just need to hold on. The beast will crash to the cavern floor, and I can climb off safely.

It continues to stagger and lurch.

"Rowan!" Dain shouts.

I keep my eyes closed. I'm fine. Just fine.

"Rowan, jump—!"

The beast lunges. My eyes open. The cavern entrance sails toward me. I see the night sky over the gryphon's head. Hear the crack of its mighty wings. And I realize what it's done. Fled in the only way it knows. Flying out of the cavern. With me still on its back.

CHAPTER THIRTY-TWO

I twist to throw myself off the gryphon, but the cavern doorway is already whipping past. We're outside, soaring into the canyon. Then the beast sheers to one side. Its whole body tilts, and I grab its mane as tightly as I can. It veers again, and I realize it isn't trying to get rid of me. It's trying to stay aloft.

Any moment now, the sedative will do its work, and the gryphon will fall asleep and crash to the canyon floor.

I look around wildly, but there's no way to escape. If I jump from this height, I'll die.

If the beast falls asleep and crashes from this height, we'll both die.

I need to make it fly lower.

No, wait. It's about to fly out of the canyon. As soon as it clears the walls, I'll let go and fall a safe distance. I'll—

The gryphon swoops back into the canyon. Ahead, something white streaks across the sky. I'm trying to get a look at it when the gryphon lurches to one side, and I have to cling to keep from sliding off. Then it veers the other way, as if it's trying to stay level. Another bone-jarring turn, and it heads straight for the wall. At the last second, it manages to swerve away, but one wing scrapes the rock, feathers flying.

The gryphon is going to crash. It will fall asleep and drop like a stone. And I'll fall—

Do not freak out.

I need to make the beast fly lower before it falls. I don't have any weapons, though. My dagger is back in the cave. My sword is gone. I dropped the needle when it was empty.

I kick and punch the gryphon, but it doesn't even seem to feel me. It keeps careening toward the canyon walls. If it doesn't fall asleep in flight, it'll smash into the wall. Either way, we'll both die.

I slam my fist against the spot where the needle went in, hoping it might be tender. I'm pulling back for another blow when that white rematerializes in the night sky. A streak of light, like a falling star. It's coming straight for us. A pale blur . . .

The pegasus filly.

She's flying right at the gryphon. It sees her and gives a garbled shriek, as if it can barely work up the energy for that. At the last second, the filly turns. The gryphon lurches after her. Its wings beat erratically as it begins losing the battle against sleep.

For a moment, the gryphon seems to forget about the pegasus filly altogether, and it hovers in place, wings flapping. I look down. It's a long drop. A very long drop onto a rocky canyon floor. But this might be the only chance I get. I release my hold with one hand.

The filly reappears. She comes from behind, skimming right over us, close enough for me to see her underbelly. She passes in front of the gryphon and dives. The beast goes after her. I see the canyon floor below. The moment the gryphon slows, I'll let go. I just need it to slow—

The gryphon drops. It loses consciousness and plummets toward the ground, and there's nothing I can do but hold on with all my might and—

The beast skids along the canyon floor before collapsing in a heap . . . with me safely on top of it.

CHAPTER THIRTY-THREE

When I tumble off the gryphon's back, I stagger like I'm the one sedated. Every muscle in my body has been clenched so tight I can barely move. The jolt of the landing didn't help. I'm struggling to stand upright when the pegasus filly prances over. She nudges my pockets and then looks at me reproachfully.

I laugh at her expression. "I agree. You deserve a bushelful of apples."

A squeak sounds to my left. Jacko tears along the canyon floor. He launches himself, and I reach to catch him . . . but he lands on the gryphon instead. He climbs up its back, perches on its head and lets out a long, shrill squeal.

"Is that your victory cry?" I say. "Yes, Jacko. You helped bring down the terrible beast."

"But the main credit goes to the crazy princess who wanted a gryphon ride," a voice calls.

I turn to see Alianor, scrabbling over rocks, panting with exertion. Dain follows, staying behind Malric, who drags his back leg.

"So you did it," Alianor says.

"I think we all did it."

"Mmm, pretty sure it was mostly you, princess." Dain hefts my sword. "I brought this, though you won't need it much longer. One final stroke, and you'll earn another sword."

I frown.

"Did you hit your head, princess?" He waves toward the gryphon. "You killed the gryphon. Your aunt's ebony sword is yours. You just need to do the actual killing part." He passes me my sword.

The entire time I was fighting the beast, I thought only of escaping. Never once did I consider fulfilling my quest. But now I have.

"Take the sword," Alianor says.

"But this isn't . . . It wasn't supposed to . . . I didn't *mean* to fight it."

"Which is a good thing," she says. "Because you'd never have defeated it with a sword. You defeated it with ingenuity and bravery."

"Doesn't matter what you intended," Dain says. "You took down the gryphon. You'll be the next royal monster hunter. All that remains is the final blow."

I take the sword and turn to the gryphon, sound asleep on the canyon floor.

"I—I can't," I say.

"What?" Alianor says. "This monster killed your aunt. Lamed your brother. Almost slaughtered all of—"

Dain cuts her off with a raised hand. He steps toward me, lowering his voice. "It's sound asleep. It won't feel a thing. If you need to know where to strike . . ."

"I know where," I say. "But the council was very clear. I must slay the gryphon. If I fail, I forfeit the kingdom."

Dain's brows knit. "You *are* slaying it."

"So *you* say. So *Alianor* says. But if there's any possible way for Heward to claim I wasn't here when it died . . ."

Alianor nods. "Rowan's right. Heward might be Clan Dacre, but his mother is Clan Bellamy. My father says he's a cunning old fox. Even if Rowan had half the queen's army as witnesses, he'd find a way to say she found it already dead. He needs to see it with his own eyes."

Dain looks at the massive, sleeping beast. "How are we going to do that?"

Alianor smiles. "I have an idea."

I spend the rest of the morning sitting with a sedated gryphon. It's a very boring end to my grand adventure, but we can't leave the beast here, and we can't drag it back to the castle. So Malric, Jacko, the filly and I hang out with the unconscious monster. Well, actually, we hang out a hundred paces away, in case it wakes up. I jog over hourly to check its heart rate and breathing. The sedative does its job, and the beast stays asleep.

While I babysit a gryphon, Dain heads home to convince Wilmot to come with us to the castle. It turns out that's done easily enough, given Wilmot's condition. He's forgotten any issues he had with the royal family, and within a few hours Dain returns with Wilmot, plus food, water and all the sedative Wilmot had in storage.

It takes longer for Alianor. She returns to tell her clan what we've done and offer her brother a deal. If Clan Bellamy helps us get the gryphon to the castle—and doesn't claim any credit for bringing down the beast—then I won't tell my mother what they did. This is Alianor's idea. I hate the prospect of letting Lanslet get away with trying to murder me. Yet I was raised to be queen, and while I despise politics, I understand that sometimes we need to make deals we don't like.

In the early evening, Alianor returns with her clan. Lanslet has accepted the bargain. We have our wagon to transport the gryphon, and we have Clan Bellamy to accompany us on the three-day ride.

I'm approaching the castle the same way I did when I brought my aunt's body home. Riding up a dusty side road, my gaze fixed on the distant spires. I want to prod my horse and ride as fast as I can. Get to my brother. My mother. My family. My home.

Instead, I carry on at the speed of the wagon behind me— the one that carries Malric. Alianor sedated the warg so he didn't insist on hobbling alongside us and making his leg worse. Wilmot is in the wagon with Malric, both of them tended by Alianor.

Jacko lies on my horse's neck, straining to see over the mare's head, his nose twitching.

"Almost home," I whisper.

"Someone's coming," Dain says, bringing his horse up beside mine.

I see the cloud of dust first. One rider pulls ahead of two others. The horse is galloping, coming as fast as it can, and when I get a look at the gelding, I smile.

"Rhydd," I say.

I hop off my borrowed mare, startling Jacko, who leaps onto my shoulder. I raise my hand to halt the wagon. Rhydd rides up and swings himself off the gelding. Wooden rods brace his leg, and he struggles to yank a crutch from his saddle. When Dain tries to help, he waves him away.

"Related to the princess, I see," Dain murmurs.

Rhydd doesn't seem to see him. Doesn't even see me. His gaze is fixed on the filly prancing alongside the wagon, her wings fluttering.

"That's . . ." Rhydd says.

"Sunniva," I say. "Her name is Sunniva."

"You—you tamed . . ."

"I need a royal mount, and you know I hate unicorns."

He grins, hobbles over and throws his arms around my neck. I hug him tight. Then I back up and say, "There's something else."

I lead him to the second wagon, pulling up behind the

first. The gryphon lies bound and sedated on it. Rhydd's mouth drops open.

"I know," I say. "I was supposed to be training to defeat a gryphon. But that seemed like so much work. I decided to skip a few steps."

"You *captured* the gryphon?" He looks at the beast. Then he throws back his head and laughs. "Of course you did."

CHAPTER THIRTY-FOUR

After a midday feast, Mom suggests I take a nap, and I cannot resist the allure of my soft bed. Then next thing I know, it's morning, and I leap up in a panic, worrying about those I brought with me, every person and beast that is my responsibility as host.

Of course, Mom has taken care of everyone. I still spend the morning racing around checking on all my "guests," but by early afternoon, I'm alone with Dain. Well, with Dain and Jacko and Malric. Alianor braced the warg's leg because he refuses to rest in my room.

As for Dain, Mom set him and Wilmot up in one of the hunters' cabins. Doctor Fendrel is tending to Wilmot, and Dain has promised me an archery lesson. He hasn't spoken to my mother directly. I know he still believes she's responsible for what happened to his family. That's something we'll need to work out later.

We head to the back pasture, where Sunniva is playing. The filly has stayed, so far. That's her choice. It must always be her choice. She won't go near the stable and has claimed the best pasture instead. Courtois's *private* pasture.

The big unicorn stands on the far side with his back to the filly, doing his best to ignore her. As we approach, she races up to him and feints aside as he wheels.

"Watch that horn!" I shout. "You won't look so good full of holes."

She tears around and runs right at Courtois. He lowers his horn and charges.

I gasp. "Sunni—!"

At the last second, the filly takes to the skies. She soars over Courtois's head. He whinnies and stamps his hooves.

Dain laughs. Courtois hears that and turns to us, shaking his horn in warning. Jacko jumps off my head and lands between us, chattering at Courtois.

I snatch up the jackalope. "Leave the unicorn-taunting to monsters with wings, please."

Jacko bares his teeth at Courtois. Malric plunks down with a heavy sigh. The jackalope hops onto the warg's back and gets comfortable. Malric only sighs again.

Dain sets up the wooden bull's-eye. He's walking back when Rhydd appears, thumping along with his crutch.

"Did I hear something about archery lessons?" Rhydd says.

Dain turns and fumbles a clumsy bow. "Your highness."

"It's Rhydd. And I'm hoping to get in on these lessons."

Dain looks at me, panic lighting behind his eyes. "I, uh, I'm not really qualified to train a king."

"Then it's a good thing I'm not king yet."

He tosses Dain an easy grin, trying to put him at ease. Dain's been avoiding my brother since we arrived. He's comfortable with me, but Rhydd is his future ruler, and Dain doesn't seem to know what to make of him.

Dain gives a slow, careful nod. "Sure, you're welcome to sit in on—"

"Rowan!" a voice calls. We look to see Alianor racing across the pasture.

"What's wrong?" I say.

"It's the gryphon. I performed a more complete examination, and I think . . ." She inhales. "I think we missed something earlier."

She takes off, waving for me to follow, and I race after her.

That evening, we're in the rear courtyard. Everyone's there. My mother. Rhydd. Berinon. Heward. The council. Dain. Alianor and her father and brother.

Malric sits beside me, his yellow eyes fixed on Lanslet.

I hold Jacko in my arms. He'd rather perch on my shoulders, where he can see better, but this is an important meeting. No one's going to take me seriously with a jackalope on my head.

The gryphon is there, too. Bound by chains on all four legs. She's asleep again, sedated. Every time she starts to rouse, we put her under. Heward stays a few paces from the beast. Mom strides past him and bends right in front of the gryphon's head. Then, staying close enough to touch it, she turns to Heward and says, "Your knowledge of history has always been better than mine, cousin. I don't think anyone in Clan Dacre has ever *captured* a gryphon before. Am I correct?"

"Princess Rowan's orders were to kill it," he says.

"Yes, and she could have, but she wanted everyone to be sure she was the one who did it. I understand her concern. It has been a difficult time for us all. Now that's over. She has brought the beast, and she can slay it here, in front of you and the council, so there can be no mistake."

"Of course she can slay it now. It's unconscious. It'll hardly put up a fight."

"The *fight* came when she captured it."

"And we're supposed to take her word that she did that?" Heward says. "Perhaps she found it fevered and unconscious from its earlier injuries."

"It wasn't," Dain says. "I was there. Alianor, too. We can tell you the whole story."

Rhydd grins. "You'd enjoy the tale, Heward. It's a new legend for Clan Dacre. Someday, I may even forgive Rowan for having such an adventure without me."

"That's the problem," Heward says. "She wasn't with you or *anyone* from the castle. Do you really expect me to take the word of two children? A rat catcher turned rogue monster hunter? The daughter of a bandit warlord?"

Everard bristles. Before a fight breaks out, I step forward and say, "Then take the word of the royal princess. I can relate every detail of what happened to us. I can account for every cut and bruise. I can show you the cavern where it happened. I can show the marks in the dirt where the gryphon fell. I brought it down. I had help—plenty of it. But I drove the needle in, and I brought it down, and therefore I defeated it."

"You were charged with killing it."

"Which she will do," my mother says, her voice heavy with exasperation. "That's why we're here."

"I will, if so commanded," I say. "But I'd like to request a stay of execution for the beast. She's pregnant. That may be why she fought so fiercely. That means we have the opportunity not only to study a live gryphon but to raise one from birth."

"Raise . . . raise a . . ." Heward sputters. "Are you mad?"

"A jackalope and a pegasus followed her home," Rhydd says. "If anyone can raise a gryphon, it'd be Rowan."

"I'm not asking to raise it as a pet," I say. "But think of what it could teach us about gryphons. The better we know them, the less of a threat they'll be to us. That's what Jannah wanted. What she always wanted. Maybe we can find a way to drive them back to the mountains or keep them there so we don't need to risk our hunters' lives killing them."

"The princess is correct," one of the council members—Liliath—says. "This is indeed a rare opportunity, one Jannah would have wanted us to take. I see no reason why Rowan should be obligated to kill the gryphon. She has defeated the beast. That is enough."

One of the other council members nods.

Mom looks at them. "All in favor?"

Those two agree. The third starts to, but at a glare from Heward, he holds his tongue.

"I presume you are not in favor, Heward," Mom says. "But that's still an even vote and so mine decides the matter. The motion carries. The beast shall live. That also means Rowan has proven herself worthy of the ebony sword. Is that correct?"

The same two agree. The same two—including Heward—do not. My mother's lips set in a thin line. This is too tight a vote. It will be trouble. But for now it's good enough.

"The motion carries, then," Mom says. "My son will inherit the throne when I retire. In light of my sister's untimely death, Rowan will take the ebony sword immediately."

"No," Heward says.

My mother turns on him. "The council has voted. Rowan has earned her place—"

"As royal monster hunter–*elect*," he says. "She will carry the sword someday, but there are still steps to be completed. Full training, plus the ordeals. Your sister's death is indeed untimely, but Rowan can't skip all the traditional tests."

"She took down a *gryphon*," Rhydd says. "She'll sleepwalk through the ordeals."

"Let's hope so," Heward says. Then he smiles at me.

I see that smile, and I know my ordeals will not be easy. But I'll beat them. For now, our throne is safe. And someday I will be the official royal monster hunter. Getting there will be an adventure . . . and I'm ready for it.

Monsters

a field guide

Warakin

poor eyesight, rely more on smell and hearing

sloping shoulders mean forelegs are slightly longer than rear

stripes for forest camouflage

boar-like tusks formed from elongated canine teeth

tail is feline

paws are canine, with non-retractable nails

THE BALLAD OF PIG AND PUP

An old bard song tells the romantic tale of a feral pig who fell in love with a farmer's dog, and the two ran off into the Dunnian Woods together, where they gave birth to the first warakins. Jannah says this is scientifically impossible, and I must agree, but I still know every stanza of the ballad by heart.

Warg

A warg is a giant wolf, in the same way a cave bear is a giant bear. While there are some behavioral differences, the two animals are physically identical.

ruff is thicker than a common wolf's, more similar to the northern wolves

paws are larger than a common wolf's, but proportionally consistent with northern wolves

ORIGIN

Wargs originated in the colder climate of the northern mountain range. Some believe they are an evolution of the northern wolf, but Jannah thought that the northern wolf may actually be the hybrid offspring of wargs and common wolves.

SOCIAL STRUCTURE

Adults live alone or with a mate. Litters average only two pups, who stay with their parents for an extended period, usually not leaving until 2-3 years of age.

Jba-fofi

Having now seen both an adult
and baby jba-fofi, I must
acknowledge they are not
an extinct species, as
Jannah believed, and I have
begun this page based on
my very limited observations.

JUVENILE STATE

Baby jba-fofi live in trees, which
supports the folklore. They spin
webs of black silk. Each juvenile is
approximately the size of my fist and
has relatively short legs, each no longer
than its body. In my encounter, the juveniles did not
attempt to bite or otherwise harm me.

PREY

The jba-fofi injects venom through
its fangs to temporarily paralyze its prey, which it then
wraps in silk. According to lore, spiders suck their prey
dry. This is not true with ordinary spiders and is unlikely
to be true with the jba-fofi. Instead, it seems from my
limited observations that—like some other spiders—they
chew holes into their prey and vomit their digestive
juices into the holes, sucking the liquefied meat out.
This would result in the mummified corpses I encountered
in the burrow.

Firebird

FEATHERS

The feathers of a firebird are a fiery orange, yellow, and red. When flying at night, it is said to look like a flame streaking across the sky. The most remarkable thing about the feathers is that they continue to glow even when detached from the bird. This means feathers are not bioluminescent (i.e., the firebird is not creating its own chemical reaction). Instead, they appear to refract existing light.

head plumage ("crown") present on both sexes

eyes glow red at night

strong curved beak used in self-defense, especially against humans who try to pluck its feathers

elongated tail feathers ("train") can be raised in a fan, also present on both sexes

FOLKLORE

According to lore, firebirds once possessed a beautiful voice. Anyone who heard their song would follow it, entranced. Then they'd see the firebird, in all its glory, and they'd try to capture it. So the firebird learned to hide its voice and over generations, it changed to the harsh croak the bird has today. Jannah says this makes sense from an evolutionary standpoint—that the firebirds who had the worst voices lived to procreate.

Gryphon

HABITAT

According to lore, gryphons live in massive
eagle-like nests atop mountains. Stories tell of
adventurers discovering these nests filled with the
bones of the prey. However, as Jannah pointed out,
most birds and felines are far too tidy to keep
rotting prey in their sleeping quarters.

Also, a gryphon's hindquarters—and therefore
the reproductive organs—are mammalian, not avian.
Gryphons give birth to live offspring. Therefore
a mountaintop nest would be unnecessary and
impractical. Jannah speculated they live in
mountain caves instead.

PREY

Gryphons are carnivorous and strongly prefer
fresh prey. Unless ill, they will not scavenge. They
use their talons to hold their prey while eating it
alive, like eagles and hawks. They will also smash
their prey on rocks. It is believed gryphons will
cache prey, and travelers have reported seeing
the remains of goats and sheep wedged high in
mountain treetops.

unlike birds, gryphons do not possess a third (nictitating) eyelid

proportionally smaller eyes than an eagle, still possesses excellent eyesight

mane and ears of a lion on avian forequarters

talons are used to hold prey securely during flight and feeding

feline rear paws with non-retracting claws

Pegasus

manes and fetters come in the full range of equine colors (roan, gray, brown, black)

wingtip color usually matches mane color

white body, which is said to help disguise them in daytime flight

bodies are very gracile, with thin bones that break easily

enhanced digestive system means food is digested and expelled quickly to avoid extraneous weight in flight

hooves are hollow, lighter than horse hooves but more easily damaged

SOCIAL STRUCTURE

Like unicorns and horses, pegasi live in herds led by a mare. Both mares and stallions appear to share all duties, and if there is a hierarchy within the herd, it is less apparent than with other wild equines.

HABITAT

Some say pegasi are nomadic. Others contend that they have hidden pastures deep in the mountain ranges. Sightings of pegasi herds are so rare that it has been impossible to test either theory.

Manticore

FOLKLORE

According to legend, the manticore used to have the face of a bat, to match its wings. It also used to be the size of a house cat. But manticores are gluttons and will eat more than they need, and so it began to grow, and it needed larger prey to satisfy its appetite. Eventually the manticore became a man-eater, devouring humans in a single gulp, and its features began to change, as a warning to humans.

While this makes a chilling bedtime story, there is no evidence of smaller or bat-faced manticores. They eat quickly, but do not devour their prey in a single gulp. And while all large predators will eat humans, the manticore is no more likely to than a gryphon or a starving warg.

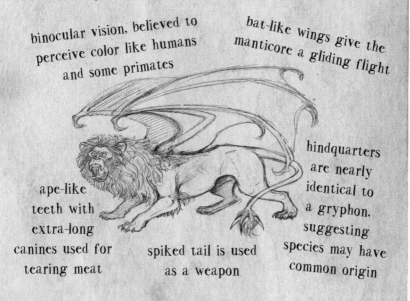

binocular vision, believed to perceive color like humans and some primates

bat-like wings give the manticore a gliding flight

hindquarters are nearly identical to a gryphon, suggesting species may have common origin

ape-like teeth with extra-long canines used for tearing meat

spiked tail is used as a weapon

Jackalope

Jackalopes are carnivorous (predatory) rabbits. Stiff penalties against jackalope fighting and poaching have brought the beast back from near extinction.

antlers are permanent (they don't shed them each year)

antlers are used for self-defense

adult jackalopes grow to twice the size of rabbits

both females and males have antlers

striped fur provides camouflage in long grass & forest

claws extended as weapons; semi-retracted for traction while running

long legs & ears suggest more closely related to hares than rabbits

Dain & Jacko

PERSONAL OBSERVATIONS
Baby jackalopes have prongs instead of antlers.
They're incredibly fierce, attacking beasts 100x
their size (or maybe that's just Jacko). Also,
they make a rumbling sound like a cat's purr.
Note: I don't know if adults do this. I don't dare
cuddle one to find out.

Property of

Rowan